MURDER AND THE GLOVEMAKER'S SON

LESLEY COOKMAN

Published by Accent Press Ltd 2018

Octavo House
West Bute Street
Cardiff
CF10 5LJ

www.accentpress.co.uk

ISBN 9781786155917
eISBN 9781786155900

Printed and bound in Great Britain by Clays Ltd, Elcograf S.p.A.

Acknowledgements

As usual, many thanks to my editor, Greg Rees, Hazel Cushion and all at Accent Press, my family for their support, and, of course, my readers. In fact, so wonderful are my readers that we have set up a Reader Chat Group on Facebook, and I can also acknowledge here the help they have given me. They're very good on ideas. I would also like to give a mention to a charity I support in Turkey - Adrasan Animal Aid. This is in honour of Jeff-dog. They, in turn, support me.

One of the oddest acknowledgements I have to make is to a modern-day touring company called The Lord Chamberlain's Men. While doing research, I discovered I had unwittingly recreated them for this story. They are, of course, named for the original company, and my touring company, The Glover's Men, are most definitely not based on them. I am delighted to have discovered them, and recommend them to my readers wholeheartedly.

And lastly, as always, apologies to the police forces of Great Britain. I know you'd never get any crimes solved if you conducted investigations like this.

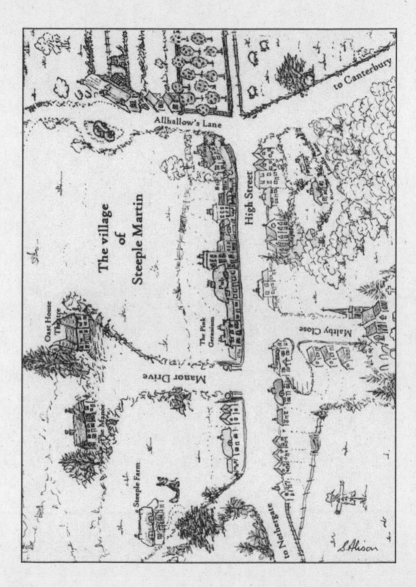

The village
of
Steeple Martin

Allhallow's Lane

High Street

to Canterbury

Manor Drive

Oast House Theatre

The Manor

The Pink Geranium

Maltby Close

Steeple Farm

to Nethergate

S. Alison

Cast list of regular characters

Libby Sarjeant	Former actor, sometime artist, resident of 17, Allhallow's Lane, Steeple Martin. Owner of Sidney the cat.
Fran Wolfe	Formerly Fran Castle. Also former actor, occasional psychic, resident of Coastguard Cottage, Nethergate. Owner of Balzac the cat.
Ben Wilde	Libby's significant other. Owner of The Manor Farm and the Oast House Theatre.
Guy Wolfe	Fran's husband, artist and owner of a shop and gallery in Harbour Street, Nethergate.
Peter Parker	Ben's cousin. Freelance journalist, part-owner of The Pink Geranium restaurant and life partner of Harry Price.
Harry Price	Chef and co-owner of The Pink Geranium and Peter Parker's life partner.
Hetty Wilde	Ben's mother. Lives at The Manor.
DCI Ian Connell	Local policeman and friend. Former suitor of Fran's.
DI Maiden	DCI Connell's former sergeant.

Adam Sarjeant	Libby's younger son. Works with garden designer Mog, mainly at Creekmarsh.
Belinda Sarjeant	Libby's daughter. Lives and works in London.
Dominic Sarjeant	Libby's elder son. Lives and works in London.
Sophie Wolfe	Guy's daughter.
Flo Carpenter	Hetty's oldest friend.
Lenny Fisher	Hetty's brother. Lives with Flo Carpenter.
Jane Baker	Chief Reporter for the *Nethergate Mercury*. Mother to Imogen.
Reverend Patti Pearson	Vicar of St Aldeberge's Church.
Anne Douglas	Librarian, friend of Reverend Patti.
Tim Stevens	Landlord of the village pub.
Dr Nigel Peasegood	Village doctor.

Chapter One

'But,' asked Libby Sarjeant, 'is there any real proof that Shakespeare's company came to Steeple Martin?'

The young man on the other side of the table almost bounced in his chair, and a lank lock of mousy hair fell forward over his eyes. He pushed it away impatiently.

'Yes, there is – I've actually seen it!' He looked at the other people seated round the pub table, his light blue eyes shining. Although that was probably incipient myopia, thought Libby.

Peter Parker, sitting next to Libby, his long legs stretched out before him and his own blond hair more artistically draped across his brow, was frowning disbelievingly. 'And there are no other records anywhere? After all, the various tours were quite well recorded – Maidstone, Hythe, Fordwich, New Romney – but I don't recall any mention anywhere of Steeple Martin.'

His cousin Ben Wilde, Libby's significant other, leant his elbows on the table and bent an amused glance on the young man. 'And where, exactly, Tristan, did you see this proof?'

A faint colour came into the young man's pale cheeks. 'Well, I'm not actually allowed to say yet. You see, it's being investigated by people at the V&A –'

'Like Hamnet's Glove,' said Libby, apparently irrelevantly.

In the sudden silence the three men turned to look at Libby.

'Well, that was investigated by experts at the V&A, too. Being a Shakespearean relic.'

1

Both Ben and the young man frowned.

'I've never heard of it,' said Ben.

'Then your education is sadly lacking,' said Peter with a laugh. 'Does Hamnet not ring a bell, Ben?'

'I know!' The young man's face lit up. 'Hamnet! He was Shakespeare's son who died when he was – what – ten?'

'That's him,' said Peter.

'And you mean to say –' the young man was now breathless '– there's a *glove*? Where? How do I not know about it?'

Libby laughed. 'Don't get excited! Hamnet's real, but his glove isn't. It's part of a plot by Ngaio Marsh.'

'Who?' By now the young man was looking completely bewildered. Peter took pity on him and patted his hand.

'One of the longer-lasting Golden Age detective writers. In fact that particular book was late sixties, wasn't it, Lib?'

She nodded. 'And one of my favourites. But I'm sorry – I interrupted.'

'That's all right – it's rather interesting, especially with our own mystery.' Tristan Scott swallowed the last of his coffee. 'Well – that's it, really. We would love to bring the tour here and include it in the publicity. After all, it's a National Shakespeare production, so very prestigious. And you never know – by the time it comes here we might be able to produce the actual documentary proof.'

'If the V&A let it out of their sight,' said Libby.

'Did you know,' said Peter, after they had waved off their visitor and ordered more drinks from Tim the landlord, 'that there was some debate about whether there actually *was* a glove?'

'When?' Libby was incredulous. 'Don't be daft. I'd have known.'

2

'Why would you?' Ben put down glasses on the table.

'I just would,' said Libby. 'How do you know, Pete?'

'It was in my early days at Reuters. One of the stories I was sent off to research – but nothing came of it.'

Peter had worked for the international news agency for years, until he went freelance, which gave him the freedom to indulge his passion for theatre with Libby and Ben at their Oast Theatre, and to help when necessary at the little restaurant he owned with his partner Harry, the *chef patron*.

'Oh, that's a shame,' said Libby. 'Think what a scoop that would have been! Was Ngaio Marsh still alive then?'

'You should know,' said Ben. 'You're the fan.'

'Yes, she was, thinking about it. Early eighties she died, didn't she?'

'I don't know!' said Ben and Peter together.

'So what do we do about young Tristan's offer?' said Peter. 'Do we let them come?'

'I don't see how we can say no to the National Shakespeare,' said Libby. 'And he might be right. They might be allowed to use the document, whatever it is, in the publicity – and think what a coup that would be!'

'It's a pity,' said Libby some seven months later, 'that they aren't bringing the *Dream* here. That would have guaranteed an audience.'

Ben looked at her sideways and swung the car into its parking space opposite number seventeen Allhallow's Lane.

'It wouldn't play as well on the booth stage,' said Ben. 'I'm still wondering whether it will fit on ours.'

The National Shakespeare tour, by a company to be known as The Glover's Men - as a nod to The Chamberlain's Men and The King's Men - had already begun, with performances at Dover and Maidstone, from

3

where Ben and Libby had just returned. They were performing on a traditional Elizabethan booth stage, based on illustrations from the time, on which the travelling companies would have played.

'Oh, well, *Twelfth Night*'s nearly as good,' said Libby. 'Very funny, after all. And if they get the right Olivia...'

'Why Olivia?' Ben climbed out of the car. 'Surely, Malvolio and the two knights provide the comedy?'

'But Olivia can steal the show. There was that wonderful all-male production...'

'But this isn't. And surely part of the humour in that production came from the very fact that it *was* all-male.'

'Not at all!' Libby looked shocked. 'You haven't seen it, have you? We'll find it on DVD.'

Ben opened the front door and Sidney the silver tabby shot out.

'Do we have to?' asked Ben. 'I think I'm going to be Shakespeared out over the next few weeks.'

'I might get it for myself then,' said Libby. 'I'm finding it all fascinating. I thought I knew quite a lot about Shakespeare, but I didn't. There's so much out there about him, the plays, his identity...'

'Oh, yes.' Ben waved a whisky bottle at her. 'Whether or not they were written by him?'

Libby nodded. 'And who was he really? There seems to be such a difference between the Stratford man and the London one. In Stratford he was mean and ill-educated, in London, generous and articulate.'

Ben handed her a whisky glass. 'Sounds as though you're in the anti camp.'

Libby shook her head. 'Oh, no. Shakespeare wrote those plays. A lot of the other authors who were suggested, like Kit Marlowe and the Earl of Oxford, were dead before many of them were written.'

'And what about artefacts?' Ben settled into his corner

4

of the sofa. 'Like the letter. Have there been a lot of fakes?'

'Oh, yes, loads over the years. I believe there've been several *Love's Labours Won* discovered. But from what young Tristan says this letter's been authenticated by the highest in the land. I'm just hoping that his team keep on top of all the journalists who are bound to descend on us. Poor Beth's got to put them up in the hall again,' said Libby.

Bethany Cole was the local vicar and technically in charge of the church hall, which had been pressed into use as an incident room for the police in the past, as well as rehearsal rooms for the now defunct ukulele club. Now it was to be the temporary headquarters of National Shakespeare's press team, where a full press conference was set to take place in two days' time before the opening of *Twelfth Night* two days after that.

'Well, thank goodness it's not our problem,' said Ben. 'We can just sit back and watch.'

By Tuesday evening, several of the cast had arrived to check into the Manor, Ben's family home and now an occasional bed and breakfast - mainly for visiting theatricals, as Peter put it. Ben's mother Hetty had her own ground floor quarters and was helped when necessary by a flotilla of village ladies. Libby worried about her, but Hetty assured her it kept her amused, and gave her something to talk about in the meetings of the "old biddies" as she called them, held in Carpenter's Hall most weeks.

The management team had arrived earlier on Tuesday and set up the church hall ready for the press conference. They had booked the few rooms in the pub, although Tristan had booked Steeple Farm, the house rented out by the Wilde family as a holiday let. This, he told them importantly, was because the current owner of the

5

Shakespearean document would be with him.

'Although,' said Ben, as he and Libby walked towards the pub that evening, 'I can't see why.'

'Why what?' asked Libby. 'Why he's staying at Steeple Farm or why he's coming down?'

'Either. Last time we spoke to Tristan he wasn't any too hopeful, was he?'

'He must have been persuaded. After all, it's brilliant publicity for The Glover's Men.'

'Yes, but that's already been done. All the advance publicity has been out for months.'

'Along with the doubts,' said Libby. 'Several of the broadsheets have been fairly scathing.'

'Ah, well, perhaps the genuine letter will put a stop to all that,' said Ben, holding open the front door of the pub.

Tristan had been in touch with Ben and Libby personally as well as through official theatre channels since they first met, but they still knew little about both the owner of the letter, and the letter itself. Tristan's explanation was shrouded in mystery and owed not a little to a *Boys' Own* adventure story.

'Did he say anything when you met him earlier?' Libby asked. Ben had opened Steeple Farm House ready for Tristan and his guest in the afternoon.

'Nothing. Really nothing – he didn't even mention it. Except he hoped to see us here tonight.' Ben looked round the bar. 'But he's not here.'

'Where was he eating?'

'No idea. He had all the info on places to eat, but he didn't say a word. Perhaps he was going into Canterbury?'

Tim, the landlord, appeared behind the bar.

'You here to meet the bigwigs?' he asked, reaching for two pint glasses.

'Only one of them,' said Libby. 'Have you seen any of

6

them?'

'The cast,' said Tim. 'They all ate here earlier. Scatty lot, if you ask me. Worse than those musicians last year.'

'You've had actors here before,' said Libby. 'You had some during panto.'

'But not so many,' said Tim, leaning on the bar and handing over glasses. 'Most of your actors were local, so only came in here for drinks. But this lot are proper classical actors, aren't they?'

'Certainly are,' said Ben.

'Worse than the panto lot, I reckon.' Tim turned away to serve another customer and Libby and Ben went to find a seat.

It was another twenty minutes before Tristan slipped into the bar looking faintly furtive. Ben stood up.

'Tristan! There you are. What will you have?'

'Um – thanks.' Tristan came over to their table and sank down in a chair. 'Brandy, please.'

Ben's eyebrows shot up, but he nodded and signalled to Tim. Libby eyed the newcomer curiously.

'Tristan? Is anything wrong?'

Tristan pushed back the errant hair and cleared his throat. 'No, no...' He glanced sideways at Tim, who was approaching the table with a brandy balloon. 'Nothing...'

Tim placed the glass on the table and Ben sat down again. Silence fell, Tim shrugged and went back to the bar.

'Come on, Tristan – what's the problem?' asked Libby. 'Something's the matter. What is it?'

Tristan continued to stare into his brandy.

'The letter,' he said at length. 'I had a phone call.'

'Yes? Who from?' prompted Ben.

'An old bloke who worked for the V&A.'

'And?' said an exasperated Libby after a moment.

'He said he was one of the experts who tried to

7

authenticate the letter originally.'

'Only they couldn't? What about the experts who were trying to do it this time?'

'They couldn't either,' said Tristan hopelessly.

'Why?' Libby frowned.

'It's disappeared.'

Chapter Two

'Disappeared?'

Tristan nodded miserably.

'How could it disappear from the V&A?' said Ben. 'Their security would be tighter than the Bank of England's.'

Tristan heaved a huge sigh. 'I'd better tell you from the beginning.' He shifted in his chair and twirled his brandy glass between his fingers. 'A couple of months ago I got the first phone call.'

'This was from the old expert?' said Libby.

Tristan nodded. 'And he said he'd read about the letter and the Glover's Men tour and he was rather worried.'

'Worried?'

'Because he said he and the other experts had come to the conclusion that it was a fake.'

'A fake?' Libby looked aghast.

Tristan nodded again. 'And at that point, the original owner took it back and presumably, hid it away. And it wasn't until his nephew inherited that anyone knew anything about it.'

'So the nephew decided to exploit it? And sent it back to the V&A?' said Ben.

'Yes. And told us about it.' He took a sip of brandy. 'And then went quiet. And then I heard from this old boy. He said he couldn't live with himself if he didn't put the record straight, and couldn't we back out of the arrangement quietly. I didn't see how, but I promised to keep as quiet as I could. I don't think he was satisfied, but I was too scared to just go and blow the whole marketing plan sky high.'

'What happened next?' asked Libby.

'I told the owner. I mean the nephew of the original owner. He was furious, and demanded that I didn't tell anyone else. I said I hadn't.'

'When was this?' asked Ben.

'About a month ago. It was awful. The tour was about to start, all the publicity was in place, the big push down here...' He seemed to pull himself together. 'Anyway, I talked to the V&A people, just to see if he'd been in touch, and they told me he'd withdrawn the letter.' He shook his head. 'They said they couldn't possibly authenticate as they hadn't finished their tests, but privately, one of them said to me he was very doubtful that it was genuine.'

'So what does the owner say?' asked Libby.

'That's just it. He's disappeared too.'

Ben and Libby stared at Tristan in horrified silence. He looked up at them.

'So will you come over to the hall with me? I've got to confront the team.'

Libby shook her head. 'I don't see what good we'll do. If you haven't told them anything about the news from the V&A, they aren't going to be happy about having it sprung on them whether we're there or not.'

'They aren't likely to try and cancel the production, are they?' Ben scowled at Tristan.

'I don't see how they could,' said Tristan, 'even if they wanted to. The company are thoroughly enjoying themselves.'

'As far as I can see,' said Libby, 'the only effect on us would be to lose audiences – although I can't see why – but I suppose some people might be coming just for the, I don't know, the sensationalist aspect.'

'As long,' Ben warned darkly, 'as we don't get

accused of fraud.'

'Fraud?' echoed Tristan.

'Misrepresentation,' clarified Ben.

'Oh no!' Tristan put his head in his hands.

'No point in second-guessing,' said Libby briskly. 'Just go and tell them and get it over with. You never know, they might decide to make capital out of it. You know – "Disappearance of document and owner – mystery surrounds Shakespeare tour." Might work.'

Tristan looked up gloomily and nodded. With a sigh, he stood up. 'All right, I'll go – if you're sure you won't come with me.'

Ben and Libby remained seated.

'Right.' He swallowed the remainder of his brandy and smiled weakly.

'Go on, then,' said Libby. 'We'll be here for a little while if you've got time to come and tell us what happened.'

Tristan nodded again and left.

'I wonder what they'll do?' said Ben, his eyes following Tristan out of the door.

'I wouldn't be surprised if they do what I said. Turn it to their advantage.' Libby shrugged. 'Look how unlikely some of the stories in the media are these days.'

Ben sighed. 'Oh, well, no use worrying, I suppose. It really isn't anything to do with us.'

'Hmm,' said Libby.

Tristan didn't make another appearance, nor did any of the acting company, so Libby and Ben went back to Sidney the cat, still wondering what was about to happen.

The following morning, Ben went off to supervise his new micro-brewery, which was nearing completion, while Libby settled down to phone Fran Wolfe, her best friend, to keep her up to speed with the situation. Fran, a former actor like Libby herself, lived a few miles away in

Nethergate on the coast, with her husband, artist and gallery owner Guy. Libby, having rediscovered herself as an artist, produced occasional paintings for Guy, which he sold in the gallery shop, and occasionally turned into postcards, although the market for these was falling off now. Who wanted a postcard, when you could take a photograph on your phone and send it instantly to all your friends wherever they might be in the world.

'Well, I can't see that it'll harm you much,' said Fran, having been apprised of the situation. 'It might taint National Shakespeare and The Glover's Men with a touch of scandal, but that could be good for business.'

'That's what I said last night,' said Libby, 'but as we haven't heard from young Tristan since then, things are a bit up in the air. Ben went and opened up for the company this morning, and the director and technicians turned up, so we assume everything's just going ahead.'

Libby's mobile beeped.

'Hang on – I've got another call – oh!' Libby stared at the screen in surprise. 'I'll have to go, Fran. That was a text from Ben saying Ali at the shop is trying to ring me. What on earth for?'

'How do I know?' Fran sounded amused. 'Go on, find out and let me know.'

Libby rang off and immediately the phone began ringing.

'Libby, it's Ali here.'

'Yes, Ali – Ben told me -'

'I've got a man here and I don't know what to do with him.'

'Eh?'

'He wanted to know about the theatre people and where they were. I didn't think I should send him to the theatre -'

'No, no – don't do that. I'll come now. Thank you,

12

Ali.'

Ali and Ahmed owned the eight-til-late shop in the high street, which also, to the relief of many of the older villagers, contained the post office. When Libby arrived, Ahmed was behind the shop counter, his wife was behind the post office counter, and Ali was fluttering nervously round an elderly man seated on a chair in the corner. He darted up to Libby, his face wreathed in smiles of relief.

'Libby, this gentleman -' he began. Libby patted his shoulder.

'Don't worry, Ali. I'm here now.' She went up to the man, who stood up and smiled hesitantly. 'Hello, I'm Libby Sarjeant, part-owner of the theatre here.' Not strictly true, but near enough.

More relief on the face of the visitor. 'Ah! You can help me then. I came in here to the post office to try and find a young man called Tristan Scott, who I believe is here?'

'Yes.' Libby turned to Ali. 'OK, Ali, thank you, you've been very helpful. We'll leave you in peace, now.'

Libby led the visitor along the high street to the pub.

'Would you like a drink?' she asked. 'Or coffee?'

'Coffee would be very nice,' said her guest. She installed him at the table in the corner and went up to a frankly inquisitive Tim.

'New fancy man, ducks?'

'No, and don't be cheeky. Two coffees, please. And no, I didn't ask if he wanted a new-fangled posh sort.'

'Now,' she said, sitting down at the table. 'May I ask what this is about?'

The man looked slightly affronted. 'It's personal.'

'Oh.' Libby, no whit abashed, sat back in her chair. 'Nothing to do with Shakespeare, then.'

Now he looked cornered. Libby smiled.

'Would I be right in saying you've been in touch with

13

Tristan recently because you were worried about something?'

He beamed. 'Oh, you know! How did you guess it was me?'

'Frankly,' said Libby with a frown, 'I don't know! But I did and I was right. You're worried that the letter is a fake?'

'I'm certain of it.'

'Well, you needn't have worried, because it was withdrawn.' Libby looked round the bar and leant forward. 'And both it and the owner have vanished!'

'What?' The man's face registered horror. 'What's happened to him?'

'He's just gone,' said Libby, surprised. 'I expect he thought it was a good idea to disappear if he was attempting to – er – perpetrate a fraud.'

The man shook his head. 'That's what I was afraid of. I couldn't have borne it if it was actually hailed as genuine when I knew it wasn't.'

Tim called from the bar and Libby excused herself to go and collect the coffees.

'You know we've got a free room, if he needs to stay?' muttered Tim, peering inquisitively over Libby's shoulder.

'Oh? Someone gone missing?'

'One of the bosses. Checked out this morning and dashed back to London. Know what it was about?'

Libby could take a good guess, but shook her head. She carried the cups back to the table.

'Apparently,' she said, 'one of the team from National Shakespeare has gone back to London, post-haste. Damage limitation, I would think.'

'Do you think I should offer to go and see them?' Her guest sounded nervous.

'I'll ask Tristan, if you like,' said Libby. 'And if you

14

fancy staying down here – perhaps to see the production – the landlord says he's now got a room free. And could I ask your name? I need it to tell Tristan who's here.'

'I'm sorry.' He held out his hand. 'Gilbert Harrison. I'm very pleased to meet you.'

'And I you.' Libby smiled at him. 'And now I'll call Tristan, if you'll excuse me.'

Tristan's phone went straight to voicemail, so Libby left a message.

'Now,' she said. 'Would you like something to eat? It is lunchtime.'

'Perhaps a sandwich?' suggested Gilbert. His small white moustache whiffled, suggesting its owner was slightly hungrier than he tried to appear.

'Yes, Tim does a very good sandwich,' said Libby. When they'd ordered, she asked, 'So what made you suspect this letter wasn't genuine?'

'There are very few letters in Shakespeare's own hand,' said Gilbert, 'and it seemed highly unlikely that he would have written this one when all the details of the tour would have been organised by someone else.'

'Of course,' said Libby. 'The whole subject of the Shakespeare industry has always fascinated me. What people think they can get away with. It was a book that set me off.'

Gilbert smiled, his face dissolving into a thousand tiny lines. 'I bet I know which one!'

'You do?'

'Would it have been by a writer called Ngaio Marsh?'

'You do know!' said Libby delightedly. 'Very few people do.'

'Of course not – she's hardly fashionable today. You know there was a story about whether there actually had been a glove?'

'Yes, my friend Peter used to work for Reuters, and he

15

said he was sent to research the story but nothing came of it.'

'Sadly, no.' Gilbert sighed. 'And what a story it would have been. So tell me how you're connected with this production.'

Libby was halfway through telling him the story of the Oast Theatre and her own involvement when their sandwiches arrived.

'So your – partner? One doesn't say boyfriend these days, does one?' Gilbert whiffled his moustache again.

'No, partner has to do.' Libby bit into her ham sandwich. 'Mmm, lovely.'

'So he lives at The Manor, and the oast house was part of their estate?'

'No, his mother still lives there, but Ben lives with me in my cottage. We're both on the board of the Oast Theatre, along with Ben's cousin Peter – the journalist I told you about.'

'Excellent!' Gilbert sounded excited. 'And do you know how long the family has lived there?'

'I'm afraid I don't.' Libby was puzzled. 'Nineteenth century, I think.'

'Only,' said Gilbert, putting down his sandwich, 'in Tristan's letter it stated that the company stayed at the Manor of Quinton St Martin. And while we think the letter is fake, we do know that part was true. And that Manor was your Ben's Manor!'

Chapter Three

Libby almost choked on her sandwich. Gilbert patted her on the back.

'There – I'm sorry. Is it really such a surprise?'

'Well, yes.' Libby cleared her throat. 'I didn't realise it was that old, to be honest. And it isn't that big. I never knew it was called Quinton St Martin, either. Was that the whole village?'

Gilbert nodded. 'It was. That was one reason we – the V&A, that is – thought the letter was a fake. There was just a chance Shakespeare might have got it wrong – think of all the alternative spellings of his own name, for instance – but it was a comparatively well-known place, and house, come to that.'

'Really? Why?'

Gilbert smiled, a little smugly, Libby thought. 'One of my specialities is the Elizabethans. And Quinton was almost as famous as Mortlake.'

'Mortlake?' Libby frowned. 'Isn't there a brewery there?'

'Ah, but who *lived* at Mortlake?'

'I've no idea,' said Libby, beginning to feel a little irritated.

'John Dee,' said Gilbert triumphantly.

'John -' gasped Libby. 'The magician?'

'Magician, mathematician, astrologer and advisor to Queen Elizabeth.'

'So who lived at Quinton? Another magician?'

'That was something they didn't call themselves, but yes. And again, an advisor to the Queen – *Quinton* is a reference to "Queen". His name was Titus Watt, and like Dee, a contender for the inspiration for Prospero.'

'Wow!' Libby sat back and stared. 'So whoever constructed that fake letter knew his stuff. There's an automatic Shakespeare connection for a start. What was the village called before the "Quinton" was tacked on?'

'Because the records are so sketchy and often difficult to read, we think possibly St Martin, or just Martin, but it's difficult to be certain.' Gilbert took a sip of coffee. 'And of course, there's another connection to Shakespeare, too.'

'Blimey! Is there?'

Gilbert put his head on one side like an elderly budgie. 'How much do you know about Elizabeth's spies?'

'Um, Cecil? Walsingham?'

'And very possibly Dee and Watt.' Gilbert sat back, the smug expression on his face once more. 'And, very probably – Shakespeare, too. Remember the missing years?'

'No!' Libby's eyes were wide. 'There's enough there for the company to trade on despite the fake letter, isn't there?'

'I don't know much about these matters,' said Gilbert, picking up his coffee cup, 'but anything connected to the great man always stirs up interest.'

'Hmm.' Libby was thoughtful. 'How much is actually known about this Titus Watt? He's never popped onto our radar at all.'

'He wasn't documented as well as Dee, sadly, but there's enough to prove that he lived here, which is why the person who created that fake letter chose to address it to him. I should imagine there will be something in your county archives.'

'Ah! Another job for our Andrew,' said Libby.

'Sorry – Andrew?'

'Andrew Wylie – he's a retired historian. Well, professor of history. Called an emeritus professor for some reason.'

Gilbert's face lit up. 'I know Andrew Wylie! Known him for years. Do you know him well?'

'Quite well – he lives not far away in Nethergate, and often does odd little jobs for us like searching the archives.'

'Jobs?' Gilbert frowned.

'Too long to explain now,' said Libby hastily. 'But I'll give him a ring and let him know you're here. Meanwhile, do you think I could go and tell the Shakespeare people about this Titus Watt?'

'Of course, if you think it will help. But what is being done about the man who tried to convince you all about the fake?'

'I don't actually know,' said Libby. 'He withdrew it from the V&A and then both he and it disappeared. Deliberately, I daresay.'

'Of course. I don't know how he dared.' Gilbert shook his head. 'After all, his – uncle, was it? – had already withdrawn it from us once. Why did he think he would do any better?'

'New techniques, perhaps?' suggested Libby.

'Surely not! They would be more likely to show up any trickery. You should see some of the things they can do now to authenticate both documents and paintings. Quite remarkable.'

'Right,' said Libby. 'I'll give Andrew a quick ring and let him know you're here, then I'll give you his number and you can ring him.'

'Give him mine,' said Gilbert, drawing a phone from his pocket.

Luckily, Andrew Wylie was in, and intrigued by Libby's message, promised to ring Gilbert immediately.

19

'He'll explain everything,' said Libby. 'He's right beside me now, but I've got to dash off, if you'll excuse me.'

'Off you go then,' said Andrew. 'No doubt we'll be in touch shortly.'

Leaving Gilbert to enjoy his chat with an old friend, Libby left the pub to make her way across the road and down Maltby Close to the village hall, where she knocked and entered, finding a small group of serious-looking people clustered round a long table at one end.

'Libby!' Tristan stood up and came towards her. 'We've just been finalising policy.'

'And what have you decided?' asked Libby, glancing warily at the others, now all watching intently.

'Oh, spin,' said Tristan uncomfortably. 'Not much else we can do, is there?'

'Well, I've just had a little bit of information that just might help. It might have to be verified, but that's in hand.'

'What?'

'Can I explain to everyone, please? Then I won't have to say it twice.'

Tristan led her to the table and introduced her to the committee of disconsolate people around it. It didn't take long to tell them of Gilbert's disclosures and when she'd finished, although it was too much to say they were enthusiastic, the mood had obviously lightened.

'And you say this Titus Watt has to be verified?' asked one.

'By both the retired V&A expert and a historian who I've worked with before. He's going to trawl the county archives.' Libby crossed her fingers behind her back, hoping Andrew was going to do just that.

'Is he real?' asked another.

Libby's eyebrows rose. 'Of course he's real. And I'm

sure,' she crossed her fingers again, 'you know that there was suspicion during his lifetime that Shakespeare himself was a spy.'

There was a shocked mutter of protest. Libby frowned. They really hadn't known? They were supposed to be experts.

The oldest of the company tapped on the table with a pen. 'We need to formulate a plan,' he said, 'and issue a statement.'

'Haven't you told anyone yet?' said Libby, shocked. 'But we open -'

'Yes, yes, I know,' came back the testy reply. 'If you'll excuse us, Mrs Sarjeant -'

They all turned towards him, and most drew pad, paper or tablet towards them. At his obvious dismissal, Libby tightened her lips, swung round on her heel and marched out of the hall.

'Libby – wait!' Tristan called breathlessly, as he ran to catch up. 'I'm sorry. That was rude of them.'

Libby stopped and faced him. 'I'll say it was! I've a good mind to tell the real story. I've got contacts in the media.' She omitted the fact that those contacts were only local TV and newspapers.

Tristan paled. 'No – please don't do that. I'm in enough trouble as it is.'

'You are? Why?'

'I'm the one who persuaded them to put on the tour, on the back of the letter.'

'I thought they were going to do it anyway?'

'It was being discussed, but when I came to them with the story of the letter and we found an actual theatre in Steeple Martin – well, that was it! I'm only a small part of the PR department. I don't carry much weight, and if anything else goes wrong, I'm for the high jump.'

'Well, all right,' said Libby grudgingly, knowing she

wouldn't have done anything of the sort, 'but you can go in there and tell them I'm surprised and disappointed at their attitude, and, unless it improves, I can easily shut down this week's performance on the basis that it was booked under false pretences.'

Tristan stared at her in horror. 'Oh, Libby!'

'Look, Tristan. I'm as shocked at the whole turn of events as you are, but at least I've tried to ameliorate the effect. I have no need to, and the terms of our contract with National Shakespeare allow me to cancel the production. Which would bring even more disapprobation down on your collective heads. Just tell them.'

She turned on her heel and continued her march back down Maltby Close. She was going to have to admit to herself that whether National Shakespeare wanted to go further in revealing Steeple Martin's links with Elizabethan spies, she was extremely keen to find out – not only about Titus Watt being a rival, or colleague, of John Dee, but about what he did and his ownership of the Manor. And if it really was the Manor of Quinton St Martin.

She looked into the pub, but the lounge bar was empty.

'Gone up to his room,' said Tim over the bar. 'Said a friend was coming to collect him.'

'Oh, right. I'll just give him a quick ring.' But before she could, Gilbert appeared in the doorway, beaming.

'Libby! I can call you Libby, can't I?'

'Of course. Is Andrew coming to pick you up?'

'Yes, he is, and taking me back to his flat for dinner. He says we can do a good deal of research online.' Gilbert looked excited. 'I must say I haven't bothered much since I retired, but this might have whetted my appetite.'

Libby grinned. 'Good for you. So a disaster might have a silver lining?'

'Maybe. What did the Shakespeare people say?'

'They're discussing exactly what to do,' said Libby. 'I'll let you know as soon as I can.'

Outside the pub, Libby hesitated. Go home, or go up to the Manor and impart the news? The Manor won.

As Libby pushed open the heavy oak door, she was met with a restrained welcome by Jeff-dog, Hetty's latest acquisition, a rescued border collie. As Libby herself had rescued him, Jeff-dog and Libby had a special relationship, although he remained firmly Hetty's dog. Libby bent down to rub his ears.

'Come on, boy. Where's Hetty?'

Jeff-dog turned and trotted towards Hetty's own sitting room, pushing the door open with his nose. Hetty, in the big armchair in front of her gas fire, looked up.

'Gal,' she said in some surprise. 'Want tea?'

'Not just now, Hetty.' Libby perched on the footstool. 'I've got news.'

Hetty's eyebrows rose. 'Told Ben?'

'Not yet. Shall I get him? It concerns the house.'

'Go on then.' She stood up. 'Even if you don't want tea, I do. In the kitchen when you're ready.' She and Jeff-dog went off towards the kitchen and Libby went back out the front door towards the new micro-brewery, situated in the old barn behind the house. Ben, heavy apron over his jeans and shirt, was lovingly polishing one of the huge tanks.

'Sorry to interrupt,' she said. Ben turned and grinned.

'That's all right – happy to be interrupted. To what do I owe the pleasure?' He took off the apron and walked towards her.

'I've got some news.' Libby frowned. 'I think it's quite exciting, but it's... well, just let's say I don't know what you and Hetty will think.'

'Hetty and me?' Ben let them out of the barn and turned to lock the door. 'What's it got to do with us?'

23

'Let's go into the kitchen so I can tell you both together.' Libby led the way into the big room where Hetty was filling the brown teapot from the old fashioned kettle.

'You see,' she said, sitting down at the table, 'it's to do with the house. This house. It belonged to someone famous.'

Chapter Four

Hetty and Ben both frowned.

'Famous? Not since our family have owned it,' said Ben.

'Well, no, obviously. And when was that? That it came into the family?'

'Last century,' said Hetty.

Ben grinned at his mother. 'Century before last, Mum. You haven't caught up yet.' He turned back to Libby. 'Around 1850, as far as I remember. I'll look it up. It'll be in our records. So it must have been before that?'

'Well before,' said Libby a little smugly. 'Sixteenth century.' And she repeated the story Gilbert had told her.

'Why have we never heard about this?' asked Ben when she'd finished.

'Don't ask me,' said Libby. 'Did your nineteenth-century ancestors never look into the history of the house?'

'Can't have done, can they?' He gazed round the kitchen. 'It's obviously been considerably altered since then. Do you think we ought to get one of those archaeological architects in?'

'The building people? If you can afford it, perhaps. They might find something hidden away, mightn't they? Think of what we found at Dark House that time.'

'And what was his name? Edward? And then there was Lewis's place.'

'Creekmarsh, yes. Well, Andrew's taken this Gilbert back to his flat for dinner and research, and they'll go and trawl the county archives tomorrow if they can't find

25

anything online. You see, it would add tremendously to the publicity for the play. Might make up for losing the letter.'

'Which,' Ben mused, 'when you think of it, was directly responsible for this discovery.'

'That's true,' said Libby. 'Hetty? What do you think? You haven't said anything yet.'

Hetty looked amused. 'Don't need to, gal. You two can say it all. Not my – what d'you call it – ancestral home, is it? Just my home.'

Ben looked uncomfortable. 'Sorry, Mum.'

'No need to be sorry, son.' Hetty patted his hand. 'You done more to keep the house going than I ever could. Your dad was proud of you.'

Ben ducked his head and looked more uncomfortable than ever. Libby rescued him.

'Anyway, perhaps we could ask Andrew to come and look round here? And perhaps this Gilbert, too? If you both think it would be all right?'

'Andrew, yes,' said Ben. 'Mum and I don't know this Gilbert. And what about Edward? He's down here somewhere, isn't it he?'

'Gilbert's speciality is the Elizabethan period, and he knows a lot about Shakespeare and John Dee. And about Mortlake, Dee's old house, so he'd know what to look for.'

'I don't know.' Ben looked at his mother. 'What do you think, Mum?'

Hetty shrugged. 'Your business, duck. As long as they don't go poking around my things in my rooms.'

'They might want to look at the walls, Mum.'

'Walls are all right. Go on, gal, you ask 'em.'

Libby looked at Ben, who nodded reluctantly.

'Why don't you want them to come?'

'It's not that...' Ben stood up and moved restlessly

26

round the table. 'It just seems as though we'd be getting into something too big for us.'

Hetty and Libby watched him in silence.

'It might take over. You know what the Shakespeare industry is like. There could be a frenzy.'

Libby nodded slowly. 'But we're not talking about Shakespeare, here, we're talking about a sixteenth-century wizard, astronomer and spy. Well, possible spy.'

'And the minute someone who's heard the tales of Shakespeare *also* possibly being a spy hears this, it'll all kick off.' Ben sighed. 'Could we keep a lid on it?'

'Not if The Glover's Men want to use it as publicity.'

'But what exactly *do* they want to use?'

'I'm not sure,' hedged Libby. 'We'd better wait and see what they say.'

They sat in silence for a few minutes until Libby's mobile rang and made them all jump..

'It's Andrew, Libby,' said an excited voice. 'And yes, it was Titus Watt's house. No mention of Shakespeare ever going there, but there's quite definite documentation of Watt, and a veiled mention of something to do with the Queen. Not easy to decipher at the moment, though.'

'Right.' Libby glanced at Ben. 'So what are you going to do?'

'I thought you could pass on the message to your Shakespeare friends in case it'll help. That's what you wanted, isn't it?'

'Yes, as long as you've properly authenticated it.'

'Oh, it's quite definite. But, as I say, no Shakespearean references.'

'OK, thanks, Andrew. I'll pass it on. Oh, and would you like to pop in to the Manor for tea when you bring Gilbert back?'

'He's staying for dinner,' said Andrew. 'Won't it be too late when we get back?'

27

'Oh, yes.' Libby thought for a second. 'Well, how about Ben and I meet you in the pub when you drop him off? It won't take a minute. Is he enjoying himself?'

'We both are,' said Andrew, the grin sounding in his voice. 'See you later.'

Libby relayed the conversation to Ben and Hetty. Hetty looked satisfied, Ben slightly worried. Libby sighed and stood up.

'Come on, Ben, let's go and get something for dinner. We can talk about it. Besides, I've got to let National Shakespeare know.'

'Why not tell that Tristan lad?' said Hetty. 'His job.'

'Oh.' Libby was surprised. 'Yes – good idea. Thanks for the tea, Hetty. We'll keep you posted.'

Ben went back to the micro-brewery to lock up while Libby went on ahead. Just as she came out on to the high street, Tristan appeared from Maltby Close and waved. Libby stopped.

'Did you tell them?' she asked as he crossed the road towards her.

'Yes.' He turned a little pink. 'They blustered a bit, and then apologised. They asked if you would let them know if this wizard person was definite, and decided they *could* use an aspect for publicity.'

'Good – well, as it has been confirmed, yes, they can. But do *not* allow them to link Shakespeare to the house. There's no evidence whatsoever that he visited, and there wasn't a theatre here then, anyway. I think I'd like to see the PR piece before it goes out if you don't mind.'

Tristan looked dubious. 'I don't know...'

Libby adopted her best schoolmarm tones. 'It wasn't a request. If the slightest hint of anything – *unfortunate* – appears, I shall cancel the production.'

Tristan nodded unhappily.

Ben joined them at that moment and looked

quizzically at the younger man.

'I've told him what he can and can't do,' said Libby briskly, 'and asked for approval on whatever they put out. Or else,' she added to Tristan, who grinned weakly.

'They'll turn the whole theft and disappearance to their advantage,' said Libby as they continued home.

'Strictly speaking, it isn't theft,' said Ben. 'The chap who removed it is the rightful owner.'

'I wonder,' said Libby thoughtfully.

'Oh, come on,' said Ben. 'The V&A would have checked the provenance that far. But it does make you wonder who did it. Was it the uncle? Who had it first?'

'I don't know, and frankly, I'm a bit sick of it, now. Let's get some dinner.'

Between them they concocted a meal, which they ate in front of the news, then Libby called Fran to keep her up to date.

'And you're going to see Andrew and this Gilbert later?'

'Yes. Why?'

'Well, we missed our usual Wednesday night in the pub yesterday, didn't we? I thought perhaps Guy and I could come up and meet you in the pub.'

'Good idea!' said Libby, and called out to Ben, who stuck his head round the kitchen door and put his thumb up. 'Yes, that's OK. We'll wander down about eightish. See you then?'

Libby and Ben had just arrived when the pub door opened and Fran, tall and dark-haired, compared to short and roundish Libby, came in followed by her husband. Like Ben's, Guy's hair was going grey, but oddly his neat goatee beard wasn't. Libby always thought he looked like a slightly mischievous satyr.

When Ben had provided them all with drinks, Fran started to ask questions.

'When was the original enquiry made about the letter?'

'To the V&A, you mean?'

'Yes. By the first owner. An uncle, was it?'

Libby frowned. 'I think so, yes, but when it was I have no idea. Why?'

'I mean, was it recent? If so, I can't see why the nephew would have tried again.'

'Good heavens, I don't know! But yes, I suppose you're right. Come to think of it, Gilbert is now retired, and he was actually working on it the first time round, so it must be a few years ago, at least.'

'Mmm.' Fran nodded. 'I just wondered what prompted the nephew to try again.'

'Money,' suggested Guy. 'He thought he might be able to sell it?'

'But he didn't offer to sell it to National Shakespeare. He was loaning it to them,' said Ben.

'To raise its profile,' said Libby. 'Must be. He knew they would make capital out of it, which they were – look at the interest it's generated, and how worried they are now.'

'Which is why he's disappeared, taking the artefact with him. Which means he knew it was a fake,' finished Fran.

'I just hope they will manage to turn it to their advantage,' said Libby. 'They're rather a grim lot on the committee. Tristan's the only halfway human one. I don't know if they'll use this other information about the house.'

'Yes, explain that,' said Guy. 'I didn't really follow it when Fran told me.'

Libby explained about the house and Titus Watt. 'And we're hoping Gilbert and Andrew will have managed to verify those facts when they come back here tonight.'

'Quinton St Martin, eh?' mused Guy, pursing his lips

30

and stroking his beard. 'That rings a bell.'

'It does?' The other three looked at him in surprise.

'I've seen it somewhere. I can't remember in what context, though.'

'Well, with any luck, Andrew will tell us everything we want to know,' said Libby, 'although I think Gilbert probably knows as much, if not more, about the Elizabethan world of sorcery, or whatever it was.'

'Astronomy, mathematics, alchemy and something called Hermetic Philosophy,' said Fran. 'I looked it up. It's something about one true doctrine, but I didn't really understand it.'

'Was John Dee a practitioner?'

Fran nodded.

'I don't see what that has to do with Shakespeare, though,' said Guy.

'There was a suggestion that he was a spy, too, like John Dee,' said Libby. 'I don't know much about it, but if you start looking into Elizabeth's spies he comes up quite a bit.'

'Didn't she have the first proper spy network?' asked Guy.

'I don't know about that,' said Libby, 'but it was certainly a sophisticated one. Francis Walsingham and so on.'

'And this Titus was one, too,' said Ben. 'Interesting. So there might be hints somewhere in the Manor – unless it's been completely ripped about since that time.'

'It makes you wonder,' said Fran, 'if this fake letter didn't have something to do with the Manor, too. It was supposed to mention Steeple Martin, wasn't it?'

'But it shouldn't have done,' said Libby. 'It would have been Quinton St Martin back then, or at least just St Martin. If that was the case, I'm not surprised it was thrown out. It would have been obvious.'

'I don't think it would have been that obvious,' said Fran. 'But it obviously connected with the village, or National Shakespeare wouldn't have been so keen to bring the company here.'

'Yes, that's what Tristan said in the first place. They were pleased to find a theatre here.'

Behind them, the door swung open and Gilbert trotted in, beaming. Behind him, Andrew Wylie, equally trim and dapper, grinned round at the company.

'Well, well, well!' he said. 'All together again, I see!'

Ben stood up. 'What can I get you gentlemen to drink?'

'I'd say champagne except that Andrew has to drive back home again,' said Gilbert. 'But I feel like it!'

'Is that good?' asked Libby cautiously.

'I'll say it's good,' said Andrew. 'Proof positive that Shakespeare came to Quinton St Martin!'

Chapter Five

'What?' Libby's mouth dropped open.

'Yes!' Gilbert was rubbing his hands together and practically dancing on the spot. 'You see -'

'Wait until Ben gets back with the drinks,' said Libby. 'Then you won't have to tell it twice.'

When they were settled at the table and Libby had introduced them all to each other, Andrew began.

'As you know, I've looked into several things for you over the last few years, but I don't think anything was quite as interesting as this. I had heard of Quinton St Martin, of course I had, any historian worth his salt would know of notable houses and buildings in this area. But I don't think anything of particular interest about it had come up. Until I spoke to Gilbert today. And he told me about Titus Watt – who, of course, I had heard of.'

'Not sure there's any of course about it,' said Libby. 'We hadn't.'

'Well, no, maybe not – but you had all heard of John Dee, hadn't you?'

Heads nodded all round the table.

'And Elizabeth the First's spy network?'

More head-nodding.

'There you are then. Titus Watt was a pupil of Dr Dee, and the house, Quinton St Martin, belonged to his father, Henry Watt. He came back to live here at some time during the 1570s on his father's death. He was, as far as we could find out today, part of the circle which included Dudley and Walsingham. And there is actually documentary proof that Shakespeare's company stayed

33

here during the tour of 1597. In the household accounts there is a record of "Mr Shakespeare's Company." Spelt "Shaks-pere". It looks as though they may have played outside on the forecourt. Of course it would have been an open courtyard then, without the high street beyond, or even the oast house. That wasn't built then − neither were the barns.'

Libby and Fran were wide-eyed and Guy looked amused. Ben was frowning.

'This is all certain?' he said.

'Oh, yes,' said Gilbert. 'We were able to check several sources, not just the county archives. Andrew has many resources at home. And tomorrow we'll go to the archives in Maidstone and have a look at the physical documents.'

'So the letter could have been genuine?' said Fran.

'It could, but we're pretty sure it wasn't,' said Andrew. 'There were various indications, including the spelling of Shakespeare. As I said, it is shown in the letter as Shaks-pere, hyphenated. Now while this was a variant spelling it wasn't used during this period of his life. And while the event it refers to did take place, it was supposed to be private correspondence, which is unlikely.'

'But clever,' said Gilbert. 'Because the visit here isn't well-documented until you go hunting for it.'

'So,' said Ben slowly, 'whoever forged it had access to some of the material you discovered. So someone known to my family?'

'Possibly.' Andrew looked at him curiously. 'What are you thinking?'

Ben sighed. 'I'm just wondering how the original owner got hold of it, and if we knew him. My parents, anyway.'

'We don't know how old he was, do we?' said Libby. 'Or how old the nephew is.'

'You could ask whatsisname,' said Fran. 'From

34

National Shakespeare.'

'Tristan Scott,' said Gilbert. 'That's an idea.'

'I think I assumed he was fairly young,' said Libby. 'Forties, maybe.'

'It depends what you call young,' said Fran. 'Most people wouldn't call forties young.'

'I don't even know the name,' said Libby. 'Tristan was very cagey about the whole thing. Worse now, of course.'

'The name,' said Gilbert, fishing in a waistcoat pocket. 'I've got that here – the original owner's name, anyway.' He rummaged through what looked like bus and train tickets until he came up with a small blue piece of paper. 'Here we are. Nathan Vine. The nephew was – let me think. He wasn't a Vine, so I assume he was a sister's son. Oh, it'll come to me. And Tristan's sure to know anyway.'

'If he decides to tell us,' said Libby.

'Why shouldn't he?' asked Gilbert.

'Oh, I don't know,' said Libby. 'Just because the whole thing has been so hedged about with secrecy. I shall, frankly, be glad when they've all gone.'

Everyone stared at her in surprise.

'But it's Shakespeare!' said Andrew. 'You love Shakespeare.'

Libby sighed. 'I know. But not Shakespeare surrounded by mystery. I'd just like to see Twelfth Night played on our stage, and then wave them all off after the run.'

'But you got involved,' said Ben.

'You always do,' said Fran accusingly.

'Didn't have much choice,' said Libby. 'I was worried about the reputation of the theatre.'

'Do you think that would have been harmed?' asked Guy. 'After all, it wasn't your production or company, was it? You were only the venue.'

'And when people remember it, it will be, "Oh, that show that was cancelled at The Oast." Hmm.' Libby took a sip of lager.

'She's right,' said Ben.

'Well, are we doing anything to help?' asked Fran. 'I'm confused now.'

'The whole reason I got in touch with young Tristan,' said Gilbert, slapping his hands palm downward on the table, 'was because I was worried about the reputation of National Shakespeare. The provenance of the fake letter would have been put under the spotlight the minute it was revealed and their reputation would have been shot to pieces. So yes, I agree with Libby, and I think she didn't have a choice.'

'And by clearing up as much as possible and uncovering a genuine link to him, we're protecting both the company and the theatre,' said Andrew.

Ben smiled at Libby and patted her hand. 'There. Happier now?'

'Sort of.' Libby grinned round at her friends. 'How many times have I done this? Said I don't want to be involved and that I never will be again?'

'There could be a problem, though,' said Ben, looking thoughtful. 'As I said to Libby earlier, if National Shakespeare decide to publicise the link with Shakespeare and Titus Watt, will we get a horde of people wanting to go over the Manor?'

'Surely they could make it very clear in the publicity that it's not open to the public?' said Guy.

'They could try,' said Gilbert doubtfully, 'but you know what marketing departments are like. I've dealt with them before. They might want to push that angle.'

'Well, they can't,' said Ben. 'Besides, there isn't anything to see. The interior is entirely Edwardian and Victorian.'

'There's the panelling in the small sitting room,' said Libby.

'I doubt if that's earlier than eighteenth century,' said Andrew, who'd seen it. 'But would you let Gilbert and me come and have a look after we've been to the archives? Just for interest's sake?'

'Yes, of course,' said Ben. 'Hetty would like to see you again.'

After Libby had left a message for Tristan asking the name of Nathan Vine's nephew, the conversation became general, until Andrew regretfully got up to go.

'I'll collect you just after ten, Gilbert, and don't forget you're going to come and stay with me from tomorrow onwards.'

'Yes,' said Gilbert, when Andrew had gone, 'I decided to spend a few days down here. I can see the play and have a look at some of the other places Andrew's investigated over the years.'

'We know some of them,' said Fran.

'I know, he told me.' Gilbert beamed at them. 'The civil wars story was particularly fascinating.'

Libby wasn't altogether surprised when Tristan didn't return her call, but decided the following morning to go in search of him. She tried Steeple Farm first, but there was no reply at either the front or back doors, so she went on to the Manor. Some of the actors were lounging around the large sitting room, which Libby viewed today with a slightly more critical eye, and the remainder of the company appeared to be in the theatre. There was no sign of Tristan nor the rest of his committee, so Libby moved on to the church hall, where, at last, she tracked him down.

'Should have come here first,' Tristan said morosely. 'Where else would I be?'

'Haven't they come up with a strategy yet, for

37

goodness' sake?'

'They think Titus Watt isn't sufficiently interesting to compensate for a genuine letter from Shakespeare.'

'Bloody ridiculous! You know we can now prove that Shakespeare was actually here?'

'You can?' Tristan's face changed.

'Yes. It's in the archives at Maidstone. Gilbert and Andrew are collecting evidence today. And did you get my text last night?'

'Er – yes.' Tristan looked furtive.

'And why didn't you tell me?'

'I – um – I don't know.'

'Well, tell me now. Nathan Vine was the uncle, who was the nephew?'

'Duncan Lucas,' muttered Tristan.

'There, that wasn't too hard, was it?'

He sighed. 'Oh, well, I suppose you'll find out eventually.' He stared into spaced for a moment.

'Find out WHAT?' Libby almost yelled after what seemed an interminable wait.

'The police got on to me .' He took a deep breath. 'He's dead.'

Libby just gaped. '*Dead*?' she whispered eventually. 'Do – they – know?'

Tristan nodded miserably. 'Had to tell them. We're going to be questioned.'

'Questioned?' She frowned. 'It wasn't a natural death, then?'

'No. They wouldn't tell me anything else, though.'

Libby guided him to a chair. 'How did they get on to you?'

'I called him again and they answered.'

'Mobile or landline?'

Tristan looked surprised. 'Mobile. Why?'

'Doesn't matter. What did they say?'

38

'When did I last see him or speak to him, what was our business together. That sort of thing.'

'I hope you were honest with them.'

Tristan bridled. 'Of course I was.'

'You told them about the letter?'

'Yes.' Tristan wouldn't meet her eyes.

'You didn't!'

'I did.' He made a face. 'Just not all of it.'

'Well, you'll have to,' said Libby. 'Either Gilbert or I will, anyway. Why didn't you want to tell them?'

'I didn't want to be associated with it. If it was murder.'

'Of course it was murder!' Libby was scornful. 'So you don't know where he was found? Or how? We don't know which force is investigating?'

'Good God — no!' Tristan looked horrified. 'Why would I? And what does it matter?'

'If he was somewhere nearby, we'll be more involved. Where was his landline number?'

'I don't know!' Tristan was now bewildered. 'It began with 02, I'm pretty sure.'

'London, then. Well, let's hope it happened up there.'

'I wish it had, too, Mrs Sarjeant,' said a familiar voice behind her and she turned sharply.

'Oh, bloody hell, Ian. It had to be you!'

39

Chapter Six

DCI Ian Connell regarded Libby sourly. 'Why am I not surprised?'

'I don't know,' said Libby nervously. 'Why aren't you?'

'Even without the location, the mere mention of theatre and murder in the same breath would be enough to indicate your involvement.'

Tristan was now staring at Libby wide eyed.

'Oh – er, Ian. This is Tristan Scott from National Shakespeare. Is it him you want to see? Tristan, this is Detective Chief Inspector Connell.'

'Mr Scott.' Ian inclined his head but did not offer a hand, then turned back to Libby. 'How far are you involved in this business?'

'You know perfectly well we've let the theatre to National Shakespeare as part of their tour. You're coming to see it yourself.'

'And what about Duncan Lucas?'

'That's Tristan's part of the story.' Libby nodded to Tristan, stepped back and pulled herself up a chair.

'Mr Scott?' Ian turned back to Tristan.

'Well...' Tristan looked from Ian to Libby and finally to the uniformed officer standing stoically behind Ian.

'Tell you what, Ian,' said Libby reasonably, 'why don't you tell us what you know and what you want from us? Then we'll know where we're going.'

'That's irregular. Mr Scott rang the mobile phone of a recently discovered murder victim. It was quite natural for us to wish to question him.'

'Then you know the identity of the victim and the cause of death?'

'Libby!' Ian used his warning voice. 'Mr Scott, please tell me all you know about Duncan Lucas.'

Hesitantly, Tristan began the story of the fake letter. Occasionally, Ian interrupted when Tristan's narrative became too muddled to be understandable, and Libby would step in to clarify. Eventually Libby took over most of the explanation.

'And this Gilbert – Harrison? The expert?' Ian asked when she wound down.

'Yes. He and Andrew are at the archives this morning.'

'That's Professor Wylie? And they're looking for -?'

'Well, they found the evidence online, but they need to see the original documents at the archive.'

Ian ignored her and turned back to Tristan. 'Can you tell me when you were approached by Lucas? And how?'

'Last year,' said Tristan. 'We were in discussion about this tour – which is a booth stage tour -'

'A what?'

'A booth stage. We take this replica stage, like a sort of marquee, around and play in it wherever it's erected.'

Ian looked at Libby. 'I understood the production was going to be on your normal stage?'

'It is. The booth will be erected on it.' Libby grinned at him.

Ian grunted and nodded at Tristan.

'And I received an email from Lucas. Well, I say me, actually it was sent to the marketing department and I was a junior so opened all the unknown emails. Anyway, when I told the company, they said go and investigate but it sounds like a hoax. So I did.'

'And?'

'He convinced me. He said it was undergoing tests at the V&A and that was good enough, so I went back to the company.' He shrugged. 'I've told you the rest.'

'And Harrison? When did he get in touch?'

'Not long ago,' said Tristan. 'And by that time Lucas had disappeared, taking the letter with him.'

'Which argues that he knew it was fake,' said Libby.

'And Lucas apparently inherited it from his uncle? What was his name?'

Tristan shook his head.

'Nathan Vine. He was the first person to submit the letter to the V&A,' said Libby. 'That's why Gilbert Harrison was worried. I told you that.'

'There was a lot of information in that first explanation,' said Ian with a lift of the eyebrow. 'So Lucas wasn't the forger.'

'No – couldn't have been,' said Tristan.

'But the uncle could,' said Libby.

'Did he know Ben's family?' asked Ian.

Libby and Tristan both sat back in shock.

'Oh, hang on,' said Libby slowly. 'That's what Ben said. He wondered how the original owner had got hold of it, or the faker knew about the archive material. He wondered if his parents had known him.'

'And has he asked his mother?'

'I don't know.'

'Right.' Ian got to his feet. 'I'll have to ask to see all correspondence you had with Lucas, Mr Scott, and we'll have to talk to the rest of the company.'

Tristan looked horrified again. 'But they never met him!'

'I shall still want to talk to them,' said Ian. 'Libby, you can go now, but I'd like to talk to Ben and possibly Hetty later. And Harrison and Wylie when they get back.'

The uniformed officer and Tristan were both looking at Ian and Libby curiously. Libby grinned at them.

'We're old friends,' she explained. 'Family and all.'

'Indeed,' said Ian dryly. 'See you later, Libby.'

Libby nodded to Tristan and left the hall. As soon as she was out of earshot, she pulled out her mobile.

'Ben – we need a council of war,' she said.

'Why? What's happened now?'

'I'll tell you when I see you. I'll come up to the Manor. Is Hetty there?'

'If she hasn't taken Jeff-dog out, yes.'

'OK. See you in a bit.'

Walking down Maltby Close, she dialled Andrew's number. He answered quickly.

'Libby? What's up? We're just about to come back home.'

'Can you come back here instead?' asked Libby. 'The police are here, and they want to speak to you.'

'The *police*? What on earth for?'

'It's a bit complicated,' hedged Libby, 'but I said I'd tell you. Ben and I will be up at the Manor with Hetty. Can you come there?'

'Yes, of course. Gilbert would like to see the Manor, anyway. We'll be about half an hour, I should think.'

When she arrived at the Manor, she found Ben and Hetty in the kitchen. Jeff-dog stood up and very politely came to greet her.

'I've had quite a morning,' she said, subsiding into a chair.

'Tea?' asked Hetty gruffly.

'Yes, please. Andrew and Gilbert will be here soon, and they might prefer coffee...'

'I'm quite sure Mum can run to both,' said Ben. 'Come on. Tell us. You're obviously rattled.'

Libby took a deep breath and accepted a mug from Hetty. 'Well, the first thing that happened was I found Tristan at the hall and he told me that the errant nephew was dead.'

'Dead?' echoed Ben and Hetty together.

'Yes. The police had been on to him, but he didn't know where from or anything else. He hadn't been very forthcoming, as far as I could tell, but it didn't matter, because almost straight away, the police arrived. Well, I say the police -'

'But what you really mean is Ian,' said Ben. 'Bloody hell.'

'Ian?' said Hetty, frowning. 'Why?'

'I would guess that the murder must have taken place in the vicinity,' said Ben. 'Am I right?'

'I don't know. All he really did was ask Tristan questions.' She grimaced. 'Most of which I answered. That boy is *so* dumb.'

'Classic clever clogs with head in the clouds.' Ben nodded. 'Saw a lot of them at university.'

'Anyway, he wants to see Andrew and Gilbert. He's thinking along the same lines you were.'

'I was?' Ben frowned. 'What do you mean?'

'You said yesterday you wondered if the original owner knew Hetty and Greg.'

Ben and Libby looked at Hetty in silence. She merely looked puzzled.

'If you did,' Libby attempted to explain, 'he might have known enough to look into the archives -'

'We haven't got any,' Hetty interrupted.

'At the archives centre, Libby means,' said Ben.

'Yes. And found out that Shakespeare actually *did* come here.'

'Eh?' Hetty was startled. 'Well, how would he know that if we didn't?'

'I don't know, but it makes a sort of sense, doesn't it?' said Ben.

Hetty just shook her head.

'That'll be either Ian or Andrew,' said Libby, standing

at a sharp knock on the door. 'I'll go.'

In fact, Ian was at the door and Andrew and Gilbert were just getting out of Andrew's car.

'Timing,' said Libby. 'Come in. We're in the kitchen.'

Gilbert's eyes were everywhere as she led them down the passage. In the kitchen, he gazed spellbound at the rafters, mouth open. Libby called him to attention and introduced him to Hetty and Ian.

'This is quite informal and not standard procedure,' began Ian, 'but as you'll see, Professor Harrison, these people are friends and somehow seem to impinge on every other case that comes my way, so it's become second, reprehensible, nature to have a chat in the kitchen.'

'I think it's delightful!' Gilbert beamed round at them all. 'I feel quite privileged.'

'Thank you,' said Ian with a wry smile. 'Now, Professor Wylie – what information did you pick up at the archives centre?'

'Well, quite a bit.' Andrew looked smug as he pulled a fat folder of documents out of a briefcase. 'These are all photocopies, obviously.' He spread them out on the big pine table.

'Mostly household accounts?' said Libby, craning her neck to read upside down.

'Mostly. And a couple of other things. But this is what you're interested in.'

He pushed a copy of a crabbed document towards them in a plastic wallet. It was, indeed an account regarding "Mr Shakespeare's Company", although it wasn't quite clear to Libby if they had been put up at Quinton St Martin or merely allowed to perform there.

'You said you checked some other sources, too?' said Libby.

'Yes. There are no civic documents for the village, as

it barely existed then, but there is a note in the church record of a "reward" being given to the company. That's how they were paid, by reward. There are fuller accounts of Dover, of course, and Faversham, although they're slightly dodgy. The route could have brought them through here. Anyway, it's definitely substantiated.' He looked round the table with a satisfied smile.

'And you knew nothing of this, Hetty?' Ian asked. She smiled at him.

'Not a thing, love.'

'What about Dad?' asked Ben.

'He wasn't interested, son. He left all that to his cousin, Russell.'

'Cousin?'

The company was suddenly on the alert. Hetty looked surprised. 'What did I say?'

'Cousin? A cousin of Dad's? Did I know him?' Ben was sitting forward on his chair now.

'I expect you met him. Came here quite a lot when you were a kid. Never much of a one for kids, Russell. Never took much notice of his own son. Didn't bring him here.'

'Was his father Grandfather's brother?'

'Yes. Richard Wilde. Your granddad's younger brother. That's why your dad got the house.'

'And did Russell resent it?' asked Libby shrewdly.

'Always more interested than your dad was. Took away all the old books and papers.'

'*What*?' The outraged cry came from Gilbert, Andrew and Ben.

Hetty shrugged. 'That's why I said, we haven't got any old archives.'

Ben groaned and put his head in his hands.

'Is Russell still alive, Hetty?' Ian asked, obviously amused at the distress of the others.

'No. Got a letter about it. From his son.'

46

Libby looked at Ian. 'Are you thinking what I'm thinking?'

'That the son might be Lucas?'

'And Russell the enigmatic Nathan Vine?'

Hetty looked at Ben. 'What are they talking about?'

'A theory, Mum. Don't worry.' Ben turned to Ian. 'Now, will you tell us what's been going on?'

Chapter Seven

'A call came in early this morning from a small guesthouse in Canterbury. They'd found a guest dead in his bedroom.'

'Duncan Lucas?' asked Libby.

Ian nodded. 'The officers attending found some publicity material about the Glover's Men tour, and when his phone was checked, found missed calls from Tristan Scott. Then, of course, he called and an officer answered.'

'Was he – murdered?' asked Gilbert.

'It certainly looks like it. Of course, we have to hedge our bets until after the post-mortem. Now Libby and Tristan have· explained the whole story we have something to work on. Hetty – would you have any old contacts for Russell Wilde?'

Hetty looked at Ben. 'Dad's old address book?'

'I'll fetch it.' Ben left the room.

'Does all this hang on the fake letter?' asked Andrew.

'It's an angle we have to consider,' said Ian. 'What do you and Gilbert know about it?'

'I was only really involved when Nathan Vine brought it to us at the V&A, and we wouldn't verify its accuracy,' said Gilbert. 'I only heard about the newest attempt when I saw some publicity about the Glover's Men tour, which was when I got hold of Tristan Scott to tell him what we'd found out. Then I got hold of the young chap who had been dealing with it at the V&A this time round. He agreed with me. Then when I arrived here yesterday, Libby told me about the nephew – Lucas - and his disappearance, Andrew and I decided to look into what

48

provenance we could find for a visit by Shakespeare to Steeple Martin.'

'And you said Scott told you, Libby, that Lucas had withdrawn the letter.'

'And then that he had disappeared, yes,' said Libby. 'That was when National Shakespeare got their knickers in a twist because they'd promoted it – the letter, I mean. And what we hoped was if we could find proof that Shakespeare's company had really come here, they could use that, instead. And the fact that this house, or Quinton St Martin, had been owned by Titus Watt... well, we thought that would help.'

Ian looked at her in silence for a moment. 'I don't know how you manage it,' he said eventually.

'What?' Libby coloured a little and lifted her chin.

'Getting involved,' said Ben, coming back into the room. 'To be fair, Ian, it wasn't Libby's fault at all. National Shakespeare got hold of the Oast Theatre Trust about bringing this tour here, so the fault, if there is one, is mine and Peter's as much as Libby's, for saying yes.' He handed a battered-looking leather-bound address book to Hetty. 'Have a look.'

Hetty handed it to Ian. 'You look,' she said.

Ian took it with a smile. He and Hetty got on well, and when he came to stay at the Manor she treated him like a son. 'Only more so,' Ben had been known to say, 'because he hasn't got a woman to look after him. Old-fashioned, my mum.'

He flicked through the address book. 'There's one here for Russell Wilde, but I can't see one for his son. Do you remember his name, Hetty?'

She shook her head.

'Might as well look for Nathan and Duncan, then -' said Ian. And stopped dead.

'What?' said everybody.

'Vine. Nathan Vine. He's in here.'

Gasps and mutterings of astonishment erupted round the table.

'Now, why?' Ian was frowning.

Hetty was looking as puzzled as everyone else. 'Never heard of 'im.'

'Neither have I,' said Ben. 'Or rather not before today.'

'How could we get hold of Russell's son, Hetty? Are there any other relations?' Ian asked.

'I'll go through the address book,' said Ben. 'And could I ask Pete as well? I know he's from Mum's side of the family, but he might remember someone.'

'Ask Flo,' said Hetty. 'Memory like an elephant.'

Gilbert, by this time, was looking thoroughly confused.

'Friend of the family,' Libby explained. 'We're an almost incestuous lot. Peter is Ben's cousin, married to Harry who is owner and chef at The Pink Geranium in the village.'

'M-married?' stammered Gilbert.

'Yes.' Libby raised her eyebrows at him. 'I hope I'm not going to be disappointed in you, Gilbert.'

Colour flooded into his amiable face.

'I do have a suggestion, Professor Harrison,' said Ian, retrieving the situation. 'You say you got in touch with the expert who had been evaluating the letter recently?'

'Michael Allen.' Gilbert nodded.

'Could you ask him if he'd be willing to answer a few questions?'

'I'll give you his personal number if you like.'

'No, I'd rather you asked him first.'

'Now?' Gilbert looked worried.

'As soon as you feel able,' said Ian politely, although Libby felt sure it was through gritted teeth.

50

'Do you want us any more, Inspector?' asked Andrew, standing up.

'If you'd be kind enough to send me copies of these documents,' said Ian.

'I'll do them now,' said Ben. 'Or I could scan them in and then send you the link?'

Ian and Ben went off together to the office taking the documents with them. Gilbert sighed.

'It sounds exciting, getting involved with investigations, but it's quite disturbing really, isn't it?'

'Yes, that's what people don't understand,' said Libby. 'Are you going to get in touch with this Michael person?'

'Michael Allen.' Gilbert sighed again and pulled his mobile out of his pocket. 'I suppose I'd better. I hope I can find his number.'

'Go into the sitting room,' said Libby. 'That'll be more private.'

'I'll take you,' said Andrew, and Hetty and Libby were left alone in the kitchen.

'I don't like this, gal,' said Hetty, pouring more tea into her mug.

'I don't suppose the Manor will have to be involved,' said Libby. 'I think it's just...' She searched for a word.

'Bloody annoying,' supplied Hetty, and Libby laughed.

'How are you getting on with the actors?'

'Hardly see 'em. Don't even have breakfast, they don't. Make 'emselves a drink in their rooms and off they go. Not like those panto types. Or even those dancers.' Hetty smiled reminiscently. 'Nice boys, they were.'

'Most of them,' said Libby darkly.

Andrew and Gilbert came back into the kitchen.

'Michael wants to come down.' Gilbert stared worriedly at Libby. 'What do we do?'

'Do? Nothing! He's welcome to come down.' She

51

turned to Hetty. 'Have we got any rooms left here?'

'Couple. I was saving one for Ian in case he wants to stay...'

Libby grinned. 'I'll tell him. Well, that leaves one for this Michael. Are there any at the pub, do you know?'

'There's my room,' said Gilbert, 'now I've left.'

'Well, then. I'm sure Ian would be glad to see him.'

'I'll ring him back,' said Gilbert. 'He was talking about tomorrow.'

'Tomorrow? My Bel's coming tomorrow. Is he coming by train?'

. Ian and Ben came back into the room and Libby told them about Michael Allen's plan.

'By all means,' said Ian. 'Why don't you ask him if he'd like to travel with Bel? She could show him the way.'

'Er, yes.' Gilbert went out of the room again, frowning at his phone.

'And Ian, Hetty's saved a room for you if you wanted to stay here over the investigation.'

Ian smiled at Hetty. 'Thank you, Hetty, I might take you up on that.'

Hetty grunted something that might have been an acknowledgement.

Gilbert came back, holding his phone out to Libby.

'Michael wants a word.'

Raising her eyebrows Libby took the phone.

'Hello?'

'Hello, Mrs Sarjeant. Michael Allen.' Voice sounds all right, thought Libby. 'Professor Harrison says your daughter may be travelling down tomorrow. I shall be driving, and would be glad to offer her a lift, if she would be comfortable with that?'

'Well, yes,' said Libby, wondering how, in fact, Bel would take this. 'I don't know...'

'Perhaps you could give her my number and she could phone me first? I quite understand if she would rather not.'

Libby took down the number and handed the phone back to Gilbert.

'Well, he's coming tomorrow. Not sure why.'

'He's probably fascinated by the link with Shakespeare and Titus Watt,' said Andrew. 'I am myself, and it isn't my speciality.'

'I'd better get back,' said Ian. 'I've got the rest of the tour committee to interview. Where did you say Tristan Scott was staying? Is he here?'

'No, at Steeple Farm. In fact,' said Libby, as a thought struck her, 'originally he was bringing the owner with him, which was why he booked it.'

'Come on, let's leave Hetty to herself,' said Ben. 'And I'm sure Andrew and Gilbert want to get off.'

Gilbert looked relieved, but Andrew seemed as though he would have preferred to stay. Eventually, Ben and Libby were able to leave Hetty on her own in her little private sitting room, and shut the big oak front door behind them.

'You'd better ring Bel,' said Ben, as they walked down the drive. 'And I'll ring Tristan.'

Bel was not averse to saving a train fare, and inclined to think an expert from the V&A was respectable enough as a chauffeur. Libby gave her Michael's number and put her phone back in her pocket.

'Will he want to stay with Tristan?' said Ben. 'Or shall we give him the option of Hetty's rather than foisting him on Wonder Boy?'

Libby grinned. 'Good idea. Bel will ring us when she's made arrangements. I only hope she isn't indiscreet...'

Chapter Eight

What did this man think of it, wondered Belinda Sarjeant as they drove slowly up the short drive towards the Manor. The mullioned windows, the heavy oak door, the tall chimneys. She looked at him out of the corners of her eyes. He was intent on the building in front of them, and as he pulled up in front of it, he just sat and looked.

'Well?' said Bel.

He turned to her, blue eyes crinkling. 'Fabulous. Doesn't look as though anything's been done to it.'

'Oh, it has!' Bel laughed. 'Ben and Mum fitted bathroom pods in most of the bedrooms for a start. Very tastefully done, of course. Come in and meet everyone.'

Michael Allen slid out of his car, unfolded his tall, lean body and stretched. Bel looked hastily away. She'd had a lot of trouble keeping her eyes to herself during the drive down. They would keep straying to the muscled thighs in the pale chinos, the brown V of neck above the deep blue open shirt, and the short, thick hair...

'Come along then,' she said, climbing out of the car and reaching into the back to collect her bag. 'Bring your bag.'

She led the way into the house and turned left into the kitchen, where she found Hetty standing at the Aga, and Ben and her mother sitting at the long table with, surprisingly, Professor Andrew Wylie and another man.

'Hello,' she said. 'This is Michael.'

Everyone stood up, and Libby shot a knowing look at her daughter.

Michael shook hands all round, appearing to be a very

laid back, amiable young man.

'I've heard of you, of course,' said Andrew.

'And we've corresponded,' said Gilbert.

'Shall I show you to your room?' asked Ben.

'Or would you like tea or coffee first?' added Libby.

Michael grinned. 'As I guess you're all dying to talk to me, I'd love coffee.'

Hetty put the cafetière on the table and Libby fetched mugs while everyone seated themselves.

'Lovely kitchen,' said Michael.

'Isn't it?' enthused Gilbert. 'You don't get many as untouched as this.'

'So,' said Michael. 'Can you all explain the situation?'

Everyone looked at everyone else, and eventually, Gilbert took it on himself to be spokesperson. He spoke about the initial approach by Nathan Vine to the V&A, then the follow-up approach by Duncan Lucas, who then approached National Shakespeare. At this point, Libby and Ben between them took up the story, finishing up with the discovery of Lucas's body.

'And now the police want to ask me a few questions?' said Michael, when they'd finished. 'Do you know what questions?'

'How much contact you had with Lucas, I expect, and what information he gave you,' said Libby. 'That's what I want to know, too.'

'Right. When am I likely to meet this policeman?'

'Any time now, I expect,' said Ben. 'I believe you might be sharing accommodation.'

'What?' Michael looked startled.

'If he's on a case here, or in this area, he often stays here,' said Libby. 'DCI Connell is a friend of the family.'

'Yes, Mum, where *does* Ian live?' asked Bel.

'The other side of Kent,' said Libby glibly, unwilling to admit in front of a stranger, that Ian had refused to disclose this information for as long as they'd known him.

'So how well did you know. Lucas?' asked Gilbert, obviously impatient with these domestic details.

'Not well at all. He approached us by letter at first, quoting his uncle's failed attempt to get the document verified.' Michael took a thoughtful sip of coffee. 'One of my predecessors had recently retired, in fact the one who had been dealing with it, and we got in touch with him first. He said he hadn't been able to testify to its veracity, but that we might have more tools in our arsenal these days, so why didn't we give it a go.'

'So you did?' said Ben.

'We invited him in to show us the document.'

'And he came?' said Andrew.

'No, that was the first odd thing. He didn't. He said he would send us the document Special Delivery. Even when I tried to insist we dealt with him personally, he refused, so in the end we accepted. And sure enough, it arrived. It wasn't just me, of course, I was there as a specialist in Shakespearean artefacts and history, but the other experts were the more technical kind – paper and ink and so on.'

'The bits I could never cope with,' said Gilbert.

'You weren't the predecessor Michael got in touch with, then?' said Libby.

'No. The man Michael got in touch with had been the team leader on the project. He did consult me, though.'

'So what happened next, Michael?' asked Andrew.

'We began looking into it, but as time went on, we all became more and more convinced it was a fake. Then we saw the pre-publicity for the Shakespeare tour.'

'And decided you ought to tell him not to go ahead.'

'Exactly.'

'And then – what?'

'He withdrew the document. We were worried that he was going to go ahead anyway.'

'I don't suppose, by some random piece of luck, he actually went to collect it himself?' said Libby.

'No.' Michael smiled. 'He requested its return by the same courier company.'

'Return address?' said Gilbert hopefully.

'No. No address supplied. I understand everything is conducted from their offices.'

'Bum,' said Libby.

Gilbert and Bel looked faintly shocked. Everyone else laughed.

'There was better luck with Vine, though, wasn't there, Gilbert?' said Michael. 'You saw him in person.'

'Yes, we all met him. Rather a nice old boy,' said Gilbert with unconscious irony. 'I'm pretty sure – we all were – that he knew nothing about the fact that the document was fake. We rather thought someone had palmed it off on him.'

'There was no evidence of that, though?'

'Actually,' said Ben and Libby together.

'You go on,' said Ben.

'Well, we've just found his address in Ben's father's old address book,' said Libby. 'So we have to believe that they were in touch. Ben's mum doesn't remember him, though, do you, Hetty?'

Hetty shook her head.

'And your family didn't know about the history of the house?' Michael was leaning forward now, eyes intent on Ben.

'Hetty and I certainly didn't,' said Ben. 'But anything Dad thought wouldn't interest Mum he didn't bother to tell her about. And I went off to university and never really came home until the last few years, when I took over the running of the estate, such as it is, these days.'

'But what about that cousin – Russell, was it?' asked Andrew.

'What's that about?' asked Michael.

Ben sighed. 'We just wondered if Russell turned out to be Nathan, and his son to be Lucas. But then we found Nathan's address as well as Russell's so it doesn't look very likely.'

'No.' Michael sat back in his chair. 'It's also very confusing.'

'We also heard that Russell was more interested in the history of the house than Ben's Dad, and took away all the papers relating to it,' said Libby.

'I didn't even know there were any,' said Ben.

'I did, but I didn't take any notice,' said Hetty.

'So there are none left?'

'Only what we found at the county archives,' said Gilbert. 'And whatever you found out in your researches.'

'Which were much the same as yours,' said Michael. 'Well. There isn't much I can do, is there?'

'Ian wanted to ask you questions, don't forget,' said Libby. 'Did he say what time he was coming, Hetty?'

'Supposed to be going to see it tonight, ain't he?'

'Yes, we all are,' said Libby. 'Can we get Michael in, do you think, Ben?'

'Not sure. We're stuffed to the rafters as it is.'

'I'm on the bar, aren't I?' said Libby. 'He can have my seat, and I'll nip up into the Lighting Box. That is, if you'd like to see the performance, Michael?'

'I would, very much, but it's putting you to a lot of trouble.'

'No, it isn't. And it's a free seat, so don't try and give us any money.' Libby grinned at the young man, who was looking rather embarrassed.

'They haven't said anything in the press about the situation, have they?' said Gilbert suddenly.

'Not that I've heard,' said Ben.

'Nor me, and I've kept an eye out for it,' said Michael,

waving his phone in the air.

'Well, I expect there will be questions from the press tonight,' said Ben. 'We seem to have shedloads of journalists coming. All keen to see a genuine sixteenth-century production.'

The three historians grimaced.

Bel took Michael up to his room, Hetty retired to her sitting room and Gilbert and Andrew went back to the pub, where they booked an early dinner. Ben and Libby wandered over to the theatre, where they found Tristan Scott and Ian Connell in the bar area. Tristan looking most uncomfortable.

'Ben, Libby.' Ian stood up. 'Has Dr Allen arrived yet?'

'Doctor?' Libby raised her eyebrows.

'I looked him up,' said Ian. 'Very eminent.' He turned to Tristan. 'That's all for now, Mr Scott. Just do not let any of this go any further than it already has. No press!'

Tristan skulked off into the auditorium.

'The press will be here in force tonight,' said Ben. 'They're bound to ask. What will the company say?'

'That's up to them to figure out,' said Ian. 'Any news?'

'One thing,' said Libby. 'Gilbert – Professor Harrison – actually met Nathan Vine, the original owner of the fake.'

'Why didn't he say so?'

Ben shrugged. 'No idea. Perhaps he didn't think it was important.'

'I'll speak to him tonight.'

'Well, I'm doing the bar,' said Libby, 'so I've got to be here early, so we'd better go and forage for a bit of supper. Michael's waiting for you over the way, don't forget.'

'So what do we know now?' Libby asked Ben, as they walked down the Manor Drive. 'Nathan knew, or at least was in touch with your dad.'

'And he had the fake.'

'And your dad's cousin Russell had taken all the old household documents away. So it was odds on that he knew all about the Lord Chamberlain's Men coming to Quinton St Martin. So, again, odds on that Russell and Nathan knew each other.'

'How do you make that out?' Ben frowned.

'Well, it's not exactly a well-known story, is it? Or a well-known house, come to that. It's only really known by historians, and then only certain historians. And Nathan wasn't a historian.'

'We don't know that,' said Ben. 'He could have been.'

'Then why did he need verification from the V&A?'

'As you said – only certain historians. Perhaps he was an expert on – I don't know – nineteenth-century Greece or something.'

'Well, for whatever reason, Nathan had been in touch with your Dad, perhaps to verify the document? Or the history of it, anyway.'

'Maybe,' conceded Ben. 'But then he upped and died.'

'Leaving the document to his nephew Duncan Lucas. Who then has another go at verifying the fake. Does he realise it *is* a fake before he sends it away?'

'Look at his secrecy about it all. The courier service, no address – I would say he definitely *did* know.'

'That's true. But we don't think Nathan *did* know?'

'I suppose we'd know more if we knew what he talked to Dad about – assuming that he did.'

'I still think,' said Libby, 'that we ought to find your cousin, or second cousin, or whatever he is, Russell's son. Hetty said she'd had a letter to tell her when Russell died. Why didn't she keep it?'

'Why should she?' asked Ben reasonably. 'We weren't close as a family. Russell had got the papers years before and apart, as Mum said, from him visiting when I was a boy, which I don't remember, we didn't keep in touch.'

'I suppose so. But now we need to know about Duncan Lucas. And if he really was Nathan's nephew, or was he this mysterious son of Russell? And how did he die?'

Chapter Nine

Amidst the roar of applause, cheers and whistles, Libby slipped down the spiral staircase into the foyer, to find Peter already behind the bar.

'Thought you might need a hand, dear heart,' he said. 'With all those ravening journalists and avid critics. How did it go?'

'Great. I enjoyed it, anyway. Twins, as usual, were the weakest, poor things, and Orsino wasn't quite the handsome hero, but Olivia and the comedy trio were terrific.'

'And Feste? Hal's always wanted to have a go at Feste.'

'Much clownier than usual.' Libby checked the ice in the bucket and straightened the drip towels. 'Where are they all? Still taking bows?'

The auditorium doors suddenly burst open and the young director, unfortunately named Hereward, shot through, red of face and excited of manner.

'Went well,' said Libby.

'Fabulous,' gasped Hereward. 'I need a drink!'

'I should think you'll be bought quite a lot, don't you? What do you want?' asked Peter.

'Gin and tonic, please, although we'll all have fizz a bit later, courtesy of management.'

'And where are management?' asked Libby.

Hereward frowned. 'Not many of them here. Do you think it's all that fuss about the Shakespeare letter?'

'Possible,' said Libby carelessly. 'Oh, look, here they come!'

The next twenty minutes were busy, to say the least. The foyer was packed, and Peter and Libby were kept too busy to have time to chat, even when Ben ushered Gilbert, Andrew, Michael and Bel to their reserved table.

'Where's Ian?' Libby whispered to Ben as he collected the tray of drinks for his party.

'No idea. What about Tristan?' said Ben.

Libby shook her head and shrugged.

Eventually, the rush subsided, and the foyer cleared enough for Libby to see Tristan surrounded by what looked like a crowd of journalists. He looked flustered and uncomfortable. Of Ian, there was still no sign.

'What time are we closing?' asked Peter.

'Soon,' said Libby. 'I think Hetty's allowing them to use the big sitting room at the Manor for their celebration, so we haven't got to stay open. I might go and chivvy people along. Especially Tristan – he looks as if he needs rescuing.'

'Go on, then. Bring me as many glasses as you can.'

Ben was loading glasses from his party on to a tray. 'Time to go?'

'Yes. Will you all go to the Manor, or will Gilbert and Andrew go back to Nethergate?'

'I think they want to go straight back. I don't know about Michael. He and Bel seem rather friendly.'

'I wondered about that earlier,' said Libby with a grin. 'If they go back to the Manor, they don't have to go into the big sitting room with the cast – they can go into the kitchen.'

'So could we, come to that. What about Ian?'

'Still haven't seen him,' said Libby. 'He did watch the performance, didn't he?'

'Yes, but he disappeared at the end. Didn't you see him leave?'

'No, but if he managed to get out as soon as the bow

was taken, he could have been gone before I got down the staircase.'

'I wonder why, though?' said Ben and picked up his tray.

Libby went across to Tristan and squeezed through the journalists to his side.

'We're just about to close, Mr Scott.'

He looked at her in surprise. 'Eh?'

Libby smiled at the faces around her. 'Sorry, ladies and gentlemen. I must ask you to leave now.'

There was a disgruntled muttering and a few protests, but Libby was adamant, to Tristan's obvious relief.

'What about the rest of them?' he asked as Libby shut the door on the last journalist.

'The company? They're all going to the Manor, aren't they? Hetty's given them the big sitting room to use. Hereward says there'll be fizz. But no one from Management appears to be here, except you. Do you know why?'

'I think they're trying to distance themselves from the whole thing.' Tristan looked uncomfortable once more. 'I think they thought that was the best way to minimise the damage.'

'And what were the journalists asking?'

'Why wasn't the Shakespeare document on display, was this the actual venue - ridiculous! - of the first performance – all sorts of things. I tried to laugh it all off.'

Libby looked dubious. 'Didn't look like it.'

Tristan sighed. 'I didn't say I was successful.'

'What did they say about the production?'

'Not much – they honestly didn't seem interested. There wasn't a theatre critic among them.'

'Really?' Libby opened her eyes wide.

'There were a couple of "arts commentators", but the rest were just journos.' Tristan sighed again. 'None of it seems worth it, somehow.'

'Well, at least you brought it here to us,' said Libby. 'We're grateful for that, at least. And the audience enjoyed it.'

Tristan nodded. 'OK. I'll just go backstage and see if they're ready to go.'

Ben was getting ready to usher Gilbert and Andrew out of the door.

'And we'll go, too,' said Bel. 'We can sit in the kitchen, Ben says. Are you coming?'

'Yes, just for a little while,' said Libby. 'I was hoping Ian would put in an appearance, but he's disappeared again.'

At last the theatre was empty except for Ben and Libby themselves, who did the usual rounds of doors and lights before leaving with sighs of relief.

'Quick nightcap over the way?' said Ben. 'Then I assume we leave the young folk on their own?'

'I can hardly insist Bel comes home with us, can I?' said Libby. 'She's not sixteen any more. Thank goodness,' she added after a pause.

'I wonder what happened to that musician she was seeing last year?' mused Ben. 'I quite liked him.'

'I don't think that was a particularly happy period in her life,' said Libby. 'I just hope this won't be tainted, too. If there is a "this" of course.'

In the kitchen, it certainly looked as though a 'this' was in progress. Both protagonists were leaning forward, elbows on the table, in earnest conversation. Bel even blushed slightly when her mother walked in.

'Did you want coffee?' she asked. 'I made a pot.'

'Hard stuff for us, Bel,' said Ben. 'Either of you want a proper drink?'

'Whisky, please,' said Libby.

'Could I have a white wine, please?' asked Bel.

'Michael?'

'I suppose there isn't a beer?' he said hesitantly.

Ben smiled broadly. 'Certainly is. A choice of local bottled ales. Come and see.' He led Michael away to inspect his collection.

'All right, love?' asked Libby.

'Um, yes, thanks, Ma,' Bel looked down at the table. 'He seems nice, don't you think?'

'Oh, yes. Very fanciable.'

'Mum!' Bel protested, blushing even harder.

Libby laughed. 'Well, he is. Ben wanted to know what happened to that musician you were seeing last year?'

'Oh, that was only a – I don't know – a passing thing. Because of the circumstances, you know?'

Libby refrained from pointing out that this could be, too.

Ben and Michael returned with all the drinks, just as the door opened to admit Ian.

'I wondered if I'd find you here,' he said, when Ben had supplied him with a whisky. 'Not with the main party?'

'No, certainly not. Tristan is. He's the only member of the management team that is,' said Libby.

'That could be because one of them's just been arrested,' said Ian.

'What?' His four listeners spoke together.

'Well, not actually *arrested*. Helping police with their enquiries is the usual phrase.' Ian took a sip of whisky.

'Not for Duncan Lucas?' said Ben incredulously.

'Yes, incredibly.' Ian smiled round, amused at their astonishment. 'I suppose I'd better tell the tale, hadn't I?'

Libby turned to Michael. 'Ian occasionally tells us details of the case if we're involved. And I suppose we are this time. But you're not to breathe a word to anyone else, or we'll make you leave the room.'

Michael crossed his chest with a long finger. 'I swear,' he said solemnly.

'As you would expect,' Ian went on, 'Lucas's flat was searched earlier today. What they were looking for was correspondence with or regarding his supposed uncle Nathan Vine. They found nothing, although there's more to go into more thoroughly. What they did find was correspondence with someone called Gideon Law, who turns out to be on the management team of National Shakespeare, particularly responsible for the money side of things.'

'No!' gasped Libby.

'So what had he done?' asked Ben. 'Did he go to Lucas to ask him about the document? Bypassing Tristan and the V&A?'

'Apparently not. The correspondence the CSI's found -'

'CSI?' asked Michael.

'Crime Scene Investigators – although these weren't, actually, because Lucas wasn't found in his own home. The officers, let's say, then found correspondence dating back to well before Lucas contacted Tristan Scott. Before, in fact, he submitted it once again to the V&A.'

'Golly,' said Libby.

'Wow!' said Ben.

'Huh?' said Bel.

Ian turned to Michael. 'Did you have any contact with this man Law?'

Michael shook his head. 'No. Only with Tristan Scott, and very little of that. It was mainly Lucas himself – except, as I told you, I never met him.'

Ian sighed. 'Well, thank you for coming down to talk to us, Doctor. We could have come to you, but it was very kind of you.'

'Doctor?' said Bel.

'Of history,' said Michael with a grin. 'Took years!' He turned to Ian. 'Actually, if Mrs Wilde will have me, I'd quite like to stay on down here for a few days.' He looked at Libby. 'Do you think that would be all right?'

'I'm sure it would,' said Libby. 'We'll be glad to have you around.' She ignored Bel's now familiar blush. 'So now can you tell us a bit more about Lucas's death, Ian?'

'There's not a lot to tell. I told you earlier where he was found, in a small guesthouse in Canterbury. We know nothing about why he was there, and the only reason we came to National Shakespeare was the tour flyer and Tristan Scott's missed calls.'

'But how was he killed?' asked Libby.

'The ubiquitous blunt force trauma, and before you ask, sometime the evening before, we think. Or the doctor does. No PM as yet.'

'Why not?' asked Ben.

'The coroner hasn't ordered one yet,' said Ian. 'He will.'

'And no witnesses?' said Michael. 'I don't mean someone standing there watching the whole thing...'

'No, sadly. None of the guesthouse staff saw anything.'

'So you think it was this Gideon Law?'

'Not necessarily. But he's certainly got some questions to answer.'

Chapter Ten

'I wonder,' said Libby to Ben, as they walked back down the drive towards the high street, 'who made contact with whom.'

'Eh?' said Ben.

'Gideon Law and Duncan Lucas.'

'It only makes sense if it was Lucas who contacted Law,' said Ben. 'Law wouldn't have known anything about the letter.'

'Unless Nathan Vine had been in touch with National Shakespeare,' said Libby.

'Isn't it a fairly new organisation? When did Vine die?'

'Oh, some years back, I assume. We don't actually know, do we? So no, perhaps discount that idea. So Lucas gets in touch with Law first. Why Law? What did he know about him?'

'Perhaps it was just a shot in the dark? You know, "Would this rare document be of any interest to your organisation?" sort of thing.'

'Could be,' agreed Libby. 'And then what?'

'He suggests the tour, and having been told what's in this rare document, suggests Steeple Martin as a venue. Then Lucas comes out in the open and that's when Tristan comes into the picture.'

'It's plausible,' said Libby, 'but what's in it for Gideon Law? What's he getting out of it?'

'I don't know, unless he's just got the good of National Shakespeare in mind. And in that case, why would he kill Lucas?'

'Lucas had withdrawn the letter.' She sighed. 'Getting us nowhere. Ian's not likely to tell us any more details, and the play hasn't been shut down, so I suppose it's time to back out.'

'Oh, yes?' Ben grinned at her in the darkness. 'That'll be the day!'

Sunday morning and after a leisurely breakfast, Libby called Fran to update her.

'Well, that all sounds exciting,' said Fran when she'd finished. 'And what was the production like?'

'Lovely. They'd erected this little marquee-thing on stage, which was their version of an Elizabethan booth stage, and it was played only with original instruments – just like they do at the Globe. You'll enjoy it.'

'I will, but I'm a bit worried about Guy!'

'It will appeal to his artistic sensibilities,' said Libby. 'So what do you think about our murder?'

'Nothing,' said Fran firmly, 'and I don't think you should, either. Much better to concentrate on what young Michael can find out about Titus Watt and the house back then.'

'Yes, but what about Ben's uncle and cousin?'

'What about them?'

'Well, they seem to me to be the only people who knew anything about the house and the fact that Shakespeare could have been here. Which means they were the only people who could have supplied the information to the forger.'

Fran sighed. 'All right. Try and find out about them, then, but leave the murder alone.'

'All right, killjoy. If I don't see you before, I'll see you on Tuesday.'

'Fran thinks we should concentrate on finding out about your relatives,' misquoted Libby when she ran Ben to earth in the garden. Ben regarded her suspiciously.

'She actually said that, did she?'

'Yes. After all...'

'After all what?'

'They were the only people who could have supplied the forger with enough info.' She looked at him out of the corner of her eye.

Ben laughed. 'And therefore, mixed up in the murder.'

'Oh, no!' Libby looked horrified. 'I didn't mean that at all!'

'It's OK, Lib.' Ben got up from the deckchair beneath the cherry tree and came to put an arm round her. 'Actually, it's a good idea. I ought to try and find some of the relatives, however estranged they are – or were. Especially after Russell's son wrote to tell us he died.'

'Did Hetty answer the letter, do you know?'

'I expect so. She was brought up in the age of always sending condolence cards and thank you letters at birthdays and Christmas.'

'But she hasn't kept the address.' Libby sighed. 'Well, there's always Google.'

'And genealogy sites,' agreed Ben. 'I'll have a go. Tell you what, after lunch I'll go into the office and do some searches on the computer.'

Sundays were lunch with Hetty days. Hetty did a roast, and whoever was available was welcome to join in. If he wasn't needed to help Harry in The Pink Geranium, Peter came sometimes, as did his younger brother James if he was visiting, Fran and Guy if they were visiting, Libby and Ben, and any of Libby's offspring who happened to be free. Ian was sometimes included, although Libby didn't expect him to be there today with a fresh murder on his hands.

'Michael will be there, I expect,' said Libby. 'And I assume Bel came home last night?'

Ben grinned. 'Yes, dear. *And* he walked her home.

Very old-fashioned gent.'

'How do you know?'

'I heard them outside.'

'Anyway, you always used to insist on seeing me home before you moved in,' said Libby. 'And Hal and Pete did, too. Honestly, you'd think I couldn't look after myself.'

'And who's been bashed over the head almost outside her own door before now? And nearly run down in the high street?'

'Oh, all right. I'll go and wake her up. She'll need a couple of hours to get ready if Michael's going to be there.'

'Ooh, miaow!'

Sidney's ears twitched.

At one o'clock, Libby, Ben and Bel were back at the Manor. They found Michael already in the kitchen putting cutlery on the table. He grinned at them.

'She wouldn't let me do anything else.'

'You're lucky,' said Ben. 'She's only just started letting us wash the pots and pans up after Sunday lunch.'

'Get the wine, son,' said Hetty, not turning from the Aga. 'And you get the plates, gal.'

Ben dutifully went to fetch some of Hetty's fine selection of wines, her taste inherited from Ben's father, while Libby took plates from the dresser and put them in the warming oven.

'That Ian coming?' asked Hetty.

'Shouldn't think so,' said Libby. 'Not with a murder investigation going on. Did you see him this morning?'

'No. He stayed though.'

'He can have only had a couple of hours sleep,' said Michael. 'He hadn't come in before I went up to bed.'

'Maybe he arrived while you were walking Bel home,' said Libby innocently and watched gleefully as both Bel *and* Michael blushed.

Hetty turned round and gave her a warning look. Libby shut up.

'I've been thinking about Russell and his son, Mum,' said Ben, coming in with bottles. 'If we could find out where the son lives, we might be able to trace those papers you said Russell took away when I was young.'

Hetty shrugged.

'Was it before or after Greg died that you heard about Russell, Hetty?' said Libby.

'After. Otherwise he'd have written to the son.'

'Right.'

'You don't remember anything about the letter, or where he came from?' said Ben.

'Durham – Dublin? Something beginning with D.'

Hetty and Ben exchanged frowns.

'Excuse me for butting in,' said Michael, 'but couldn't you look up the details online?'

'I'm going to, right after lunch,' said Ben, 'but we don't know the son's name.'

'If you'd like me to, I could have a go,' Michael offered diffidently.

'He's a historian,' said Bel.

Libby looked at Ben. 'That is what he came down for, really, isn't it? The whole Titus Watt thing?'

'Good idea,' said Ben. 'We've got Russell's address – and Nathan Vine's, come to that, so maybe we could find something there.'

'Great!' said Michael. 'Birth dates?'

'No, sorry. I suppose Russell would be round about 80? Mum?'

'Older than your dad,' she said. 'Dunno, really.'

'Well, we'll have a look after lunch,' said Ben. 'Shall I pour wine, Mum?'

Lunch finished, Michael and Ben disappeared into the

office, and Libby packed Hetty off to her sitting room while she and Bel loaded the dishwasher and tackled the roasting tins.

'What do you think they'll find, Mum?' Bel asked.

'I'm hoping they'll find Russell's son, just to see if he knows anything about the stuff his dad took.'

'Is that all?'

Libby frowned. 'Well, I suppose I'd really like to know if Russell was the original forger, or knew the original forger.'

'Or if his son was,' said Bel. 'And if he was, he's not going to admit it, is he?'

'No,' sighed Libby.

'Also, Mum, we don't know that the whole fake letter thing is anything to do with this Lucas person's murder, do we?'

Libby looked startled. 'No, I suppose we don't. I've just assumed...'

'You do that rather a lot,' said Bel, with a wry smile.

'I know,' said Libby, now looking sheepish. 'Jumping to conclusions again.'

After an hour, Libby went to the office to ask after progress. 'I wanted to know whether to make a pot of tea here, or wait until we got home.'

'We normally go to Peter and Harry's on our way home,' said Ben. 'Have we stopped drinking?'

'Well, it's a bit different this afternoon, isn't it?' said Libby. 'So, how are you getting on?'

'Interesting,' said Michael, looking up from the computer screen, 'but I do keep veering off in other directions.'

Ben rolled up his eyes and grinned at Libby.

'Actually we've found out a few things,' said Ben. 'You put the kettle on and we'll come in and tell you.'

Libby made tea in the big brown teapot, and Bel took a

74

cup in to Hetty. Ben and Michael appeared looking pleased with themselves and with a sheaf of notes.

'Right,' said Ben. 'We've found Russell's son, Richard, obviously named after his grandfather, and we looked at the records of Nathan Vine's address as found in Dad's address book. Pity we can't look at the details, but they still aren't released to the public for 100 years. Still, we googled it and there are no records of it being sold, and we can't look at the Land Registry, so Nathan must have died when he was living there.'

'Unless he moved before then,' said Libby. 'He might have rented.'

'And Lucas came to us in spring last year, so it must have taken him a little while to make up his mind to do that,' said Michael. 'If, of course, he really was Vine's nephew.'

'What about this Richard Wilde,' asked Libby. 'Where's he?'

'On social media,' said Ben, 'so no address. We looked up Russell first, and he turned out to have been a bit of an amateur historian and even had a few things published. So Richard was fairly easy to track through social media, even though it's quite a common name.'

'Have you sent him a message?'

'Yes, but you know what it's like, he might not see it as we don't officially know each other.'

'Anything else we can try?' asked Libby.

'I'm going to try for Nathan Vine's death certificate, working backwards from 2014,' said Michael, 'and Ben's ordered one of Russell Wilde's books – pamphlets, rather. It appears to deal with Tudor houses and households.'

'Wow!' said Bel. 'That's exactly what you're looking for, isn't it? If there were papers here and Russell took them away...'

'That would be the basis of his research! Yes,' said

Libby. 'Well done, you two.'

'Hetty's given me permission to go all over the house with a metaphorical toothcomb,' said Michael. 'Do you know it well, Bel?'

'Not as well as Mum and Ben,' said Bel. 'Why?'

'I thought you might be my guide.' The startlingly blue eyes crinkled at the corners again.

'Oh... well, I suppose...' Bel looked at Ben, who nodded, grinning. 'When were you thinking?'

'Tomorrow, unless you're going back to London?'

'No, I'm staying for a few days,' said Bel. 'Catch up with Mum and my brother Adam. We could start this evening, if you like?'

'Good idea.' The eyes crinkled even more.

'In that case,' said Ben, standing up, 'we'll be off. Got your key, Bel?'

'Oh,' said Libby, also standing. 'Yes... see you later, Bel. Don't bother Hetty.'

'Mum, I'm not a child anymore.' Bel smiled pityingly at her mother.

'No, dear,' said Libby, with a glare.

They said goodbye to Hetty and told her of Michael and Bel's plans, then left to walk down the drive. Ben called Peter to ask if they were too late for their customary Sunday afternoon drink.

'Seemed surprised I should have asked,' said Ben as he ended the call.

'So get us up to date, loves,' said Harry, still in his chef's whites, sprawled on the sofa. 'How's the Boy Wonder?'

'Have you seen him?' asked Libby, from the depths of her usual chintz covered armchair.

Peter handed her a whisky. 'I told him last night. Desperate to see him, aren't you, dear heart?' He grinned across at his partner.

76

'Actually Bel and he seem rather taken with each other,' said Libby. 'They're making a tour of the Manor together as we speak.'

'Ooh, I say! Romance among the toffs,' said Harry.

'We're not toffs,' said Libby, slightly affronted.

'Not you, you dear old trout. Master Benjamin's lofty ancestors.'

'What about Ian's murder?' asked Peter. 'Is it connected to the fake document?'

'It's possible,' said Ben. 'And the problem is, it then could be connected to those self same lofty ancestors.'

Chapter Eleven

'Well, not ancestors, exactly, but my cousins. Second cousins, or something,' Ben corrected himself.

'I say!' Harry swung his legs off the pouffe and sat straight upright. 'That's a turn up, old thing.'

'Not the first time there's been scandal in the family, though, is it?' said Ben darkly.

Everyone looked uncomfortable for a minute. Then Libby said, 'But there's no actual evidence that this murder had anything to do with the fake letter. All Ian had to go on was the flyer in the victim's pocket, and Tristan's number in his phone. And then, of course, Tristan phoned while the police were there.'

'And that was purely circumstantial because he was down here in Kent, with the flyer, and Tristan's number was the last one in his call log,' said Ben.

'So he could have been a villain murdered by another villain?' said Peter.

'Yes,' said Libby.

'Don't sound so disappointed, sweetie,' said Harry, leaning over to pat her hand. 'There'll be another nice murder along any minute.'

'Shut up, Hal,' said Peter and Ben together.

Later in the evening, as Libby was dozing in front of the television, Ben tapped her on the shoulder.

'I've had a reply from Richard. Want to see?'

Libby sat up and reached for the phone.

"Hi, Ben," read the message. "Great to hear from you. Heard from your mother after I informed her of Dad's death, but we don't appear to have had much contact between the two families, although Dad was very keen on the history of the Manor."

Libby turned to Ben. 'There! Proof!'

'Of what, though?' said Ben. 'Read on.'

"Do you still live there? This is a bit of a cheek, but I don't suppose I could visit if you do? I've always longed to see it, having heard so much about it from Dad. I look forward to hearing from you." And there followed an email address.

'Blimey!' said Libby. 'The answer to our prayers.'

'Only about the history of the Manor, and the possibility of Titus Watt being involved with Shakespeare,' said Ben. 'Nothing to do with the murder.'

'Oh, bother the murder!' said Libby. 'I'm interested in the Manor and Shakespeare, now!'

'I'll invite him, then, shall I? He can stay at the Manor, and I'll ask him if he's got any of the documents his father took all those years ago.'

An answer to the email came back almost immediately, agreeing to come to the Manor tomorrow, if possible, and yes, he would love to stay and see the Shakespearean production.

'Hadn't you better tell Hetty?' said Libby, after Ben read out the email.

'It's too late now. We'll tell her in the morning and go and help sort out a room for him.'

'Oh, it's "we" is it? And suppose all the rooms are full? I can't remember how many cast members are in there, and Michael's there now, too.'

'There's always Steeple Farm. Tristan's the only one up there.'

'Really? We can't wish Tristan on a total stranger.'

'Pub, then. Gilbert's checked out to stay with Andrew.'

'Right,' said Libby. 'We'll talk to Hetty first in the

morning, then Tim at the pub. And Ian's at the Manor, too – don't forget that.'

'I won't, but Ian's got a permanent room now. Hetty treats him like one of the family. I'm sure she doesn't charge him. I've seen nothing coming through the books.'

Libby grinned. 'That's because you abandoned her to come and live with me. She's got someone she can mother.'

'With all of us dancing attendance on her? Obeying the summons every Sunday? Come off it,' said Ben scornfully. 'And I've just thought – the Hoppers's Huts. No one's in those, are they? He could be completely private there.'

'We'll give him the option,' said Libby. 'And now, please, I'd like my nightcap and then I'm going to bed.'

First thing Monday morning Richard Wilde emailed to say he would arrive in the early afternoon, bringing with him any of his father's research material that he could find. Ben arranged to meet him at the Manor, before calling Hetty to see if there was a room for him there. However, it appeared that Hetty was full, so Ben and Libby walked up to the top of Allhallow's Lane and across the field to inspect the Hoppers's Huts.

'Oh, well, they're all right, aren't they?' said Libby. 'I'll give it a bit of a dust and hoover and make up the bed and we're sorted. Which one?'

'The end one – it's bigger,' said Ben. 'And I'll do the dusting and hoovering. You go up to the Manor and get the bedding and towels.'

The huts had their own little service area at the end, where cleaning materials were kept, along with spare toilet rolls and soap.

'Mind you,' said Libby, eyeing it thoughtfully, 'most people bring their own these days.'

By lunchtime, the hut was ready. Bel hadn't been seen,

and Michael was clambering about in the Manor's roof. Hetty told them Ian had been in last night and out again this morning very early. The team at the church hall appeared to have dispersed, leaving Tristan as sole representative of "management". This didn't worry the cast and crew, who were happier without people looking over their shoulders all the time, but left Tristan cold. He turned up at the Manor, ready to moan about everything and anything, and was given short shrift by both Hetty and Libby.

'Look, it isn't anyone's fault about the letter being fake, nor about Lucas's murder,' said Libby. 'And the press are leaving you alone, now, aren't they?'

'Yes, but there was going to be such a media explosion. We would have been front page news everywhere,' whined Tristan. 'Now all we've got is snide little comments about "The Fake" in the Sunday gutter press and a few reviews in the cultural press.'

'They're good reviews, aren't they?'

'Well, yes.' Tristan heaved a great sigh.

'Well, just be glad that it's not worse. The company could have been implicated in the murder itself,' said Libby, aware that Ian had been trying to prove just that.

'Oh, God!' said Tristan in horror-struck tones. 'Don't let that happen, please.'

'Well, DCI Connell did come here straight away because your number was in Lucas's phone, and you just happened to phone the crime scene,' said Libby wickedly.

'That's enough, gal.'

Hetty's gruff interjection stopped Libby in her tracks. She grinned across at her mother-in-law-elect. 'Sorry, Hetty, Tristan. Look, we've got a visitor coming this afternoon – a member of Ben and Hetty's family. Do you think you could organise a comp for him for tonight?'

Tristan brightened. 'Does he know anything about the

Shakespeare visit?'

'He might do,' said Libby cautiously.

'I'll go and see to it right away.' He bounced up from the kitchen table and disappeared towards the theatre.

Michael and Bel suddenly erupted into the kitchen looking vaguely sooty and Hetty hurriedly moved a large pot of soup out of the way.

'What *have* you been doing?' asked Libby.

'In these old houses smoke leaks through the bricks,' said Michael cheerfully. 'Your attics are covered!'

Hetty looked stricken.

'Not your fault, Hetty,' said Bel. 'Those attics are never used, are they? It's just really where all the beams are holding the roof up.'

'And did it tell you anything?' asked Libby.

'I've taken some samples for dendro-dating,' said Michael, 'but what I really need is those documents.'

'Well, you might just be in luck,' said Libby and explained about Richard Wilde. 'In fact, he should be here soon. Ben's just gone over to check on his precious brewery, and then we'll form a welcoming committee.'

'Get that soot off,' said Hetty, 'and you can have some soup.'

By three o'clock, Ben, Libby, a reluctant Hetty, a spruced-up Bel and Michael and a brightly alert Jeff-dog all waited in the kitchen for the arrival.

'There's a car,' said Libby, as Jeff-dog pricked up his ears. Ben went to the front door, turned and nodded. Outside, a rather large, shambling man with greying fair hair was climbing out of an old sports car that seemed much too small for him. He beamed across the roof at the party in the doorway.

'Hello! I'm Richard,' he called. 'Hang on a minute.' He appeared to have a struggle with the car door and when it finally shut, gave it a valedictory pat and ambled towards them holding out a huge paw.

Introductions were quickly made, and then, with Hetty excusing herself, the rest of them made for the kitchen and tea offered.

'Where have you come from?' asked Bel, who had taken an instant shine to her new almost-by-marriage relative.

'Norfolk. Practically web-footed.' He smiled at her.

'The Broads?' asked Libby. 'I've always wanted to go there.'

'You must come and visit,' said Richard, 'and let me return the hospitality. 'Not that I'm actually on the Broads, exactly, just close by. Rather isolated, I'm afraid.'

'Is that where your father lived?' asked Ben. 'I barely remember him at all, I'm afraid.'

'No, no. He wasn't far from here. I grew up in London. He never spoke about your side of the family to me. I didn't know you existed until much later when I'd left home and he suddenly sent me this little booklet he'd written, and told me about the papers from the house. Then he told me all about it, and didn't seem to be able to leave it alone. I once asked if we could visit, but he wasn't exactly forthcoming.'

'Was that the one on Tudor houses and households?' said Ben. 'I ordered a copy over the internet.'

'Oh, I wish you hadn't,' said Richard earnestly. 'I've got about a thousand packed away in the garage.'

'What do you do up there in the Broads?' asked Libby, retrieving the brown teapot and pouring tea.

'I moved up there when I went to teach at UEA.'

Yes, thought Libby, you look like a lecturer. Leather elbow patches and all.

'What field?' asked Michael.

'Environmental Sciences.' Richard pulled a face. 'Sounds boring, doesn't it?'

'Oh, no,' said Bel. 'That's fascinating.'

Michael, who was turning out to be very good at sensing atmospheres, said, 'Actually, if you really have got a spare copy of that booklet I'd appreciate one. I've come down to have a look at the house and see what it can tell me, too. I'm from the V&A.'

'Really?' Richard sat up like a pointer dog.

'I'd better explain,' Ben cut in, 'the situation's slightly more complicated than simply wanting to see the papers.'

'Oh?' Richard was looking more and more interested.

Between them, Libby, Ben and Michael told the whole story, with occasional interjections from Belinda. They said nothing about previously thinking Duncan Lucas might be the son of Russell, nor of the suspicion that he may have been the original forger. When they finished, Libby sat back in her chair and waited for a response.

'So,' Richard said slowly, his eyes on the table, 'you're wondering if my father was the person who arranged to have the fake made?'

There was a collective indrawn breath around the table.

'You must see that it was a reasonable idea,' said Ben. 'But once we heard from you, it seemed highly unlikely.'

Richard beamed round at them all. 'I'm glad about that. Obviously, I can't be sure, and he wouldn't have told me if he had, but I can't see what he would have gained from it.'

'Did he know Nathan Vine?' asked Libby. 'Only his name is in Ben's dad's address book, too. Hetty didn't know him.'

'I have no idea,' said Richard. 'Once I left to go to university I never went home again – not until Dad was dying. I can ask my mother. She's still living in the family home.'

'Where's that?' asked Bel.

84

'It was in Dad's address book,' said Ben, 'Barnes.'

'Quite near Mortlake, then,' said Libby. Richard sent her a quick look.

'Yes, why?'

'Coincidence, I suppose. Mortlake was where John Dee lived, wasn't it?'

Richard frowned. 'I think so, but -'

'It's hardly relevant, Lib,' said Ben, and turning to Richard, 'just that Titus Watt, who lived here, was, like Dee, a supposed wizard and apothecary – and spy.'

'Ah.' Richard's face cleared. 'Like Shakespeare.'

Chapter Twelve

Michael broke the resulting silence. 'So your father also knew that.'

'Yes, of course.' Richard looked surprised.

'That wouldn't have been in the household documents,' said Michael.

'No, but he didn't only rely on the documents. Once he'd got really interested, he wanted to verify several facts, so he tracked down various experts. And one of them was a Shakespeare expert, obviously.'

'Who was it?' Michael was leaning forward now. 'We did the same obviously.'

'Oh, I can't remember.' He stood up. 'I've got all the stuff in the car. I'll just pop out and get it.'

When he'd left, the others all looked at each other in some bemusement.

'It's all very well,' said Ben, 'but where does it leave us?'

'How do you mean?' asked Libby.

'It all sounds a bit academic,' said Ben. 'I can't believe respectable experts would be involved in forged letters.'

'Don't be so sure,' said Michael. 'They're the very people who might. Sometimes just to prove a point they've made.'

'But this was hardly that,' said Libby with a frown. 'If you know what I mean. This was...' she broke off. 'Actually, I don't know what it was.'

Richard came back into the room carrying a briefcase. 'Here we are,' he said, emptying it on to the table. 'A lot of the original documents and a copy of his pamphlet. I expect he acknowledges his expert in the front of that.'

Michael was quicker than anyone else and grabbed the booklet. 'Acknowledgements – yes. Oh!' He looked up. 'It's Dr Harrap.'

'Who?' came the chorus.

'He's Reader in Shakespeare, among other things, at Brett University. At least, he used to be. We've used him ourselves.'

'Would he have been consulted in the case of our fake?' asked Libby.

'I don't think our team did, but we could ask Gilbert,' said Michael. 'I can't think we wouldn't have used him over a Shakespeare relic. That was one of his particular fields of expertise.'

'Why didn't you consult him then?' asked Ben.

'We already had the previous team's views, and he's now retired. At least, as much as any academic retires. You've seen yourselves how much work both your friend Andrew and Gilbert still do. And if you're an expert in anything, you'll still be called in.'

'Can we still get in touch with him?' asked Richard.

'I think so, but would it be wise?'

'Wise? What do you mean?'

Michael frowned. 'Well, it's part of a police investigation now, isn't it?'

'It might be, but that hasn't been proved,' said Ben. 'The murder might have nothing whatsoever to do with this. We don't know who Duncan Lucas was, nor if he really had anything to do with Nathan Vine.'

'We need to track him - Nathan Vine - down next,' said Libby.

'How? He's dead,' said Bel.

'Find out who he really was. We've got his old address, haven't we? From Ben's Dad's address book.'

'I wonder why?' said Ben. 'Dad wouldn't have been

interested in anything like this. He'd already handed everything over to Richard's father.'

'Have you looked him up?' asked Richard.

'Er – no.' Ben looked at Libby. 'Have we?'

'No.' Libby sounded surprised. 'Can't think why.'

Michael put his phone on the table and began searching.

'Where did he live?' asked Richard.

'I'll get the book,' said Ben.

Libby's phone rang. She excused herself and stood up.

'Lib, it's me,' said Fran.

'Oh, hi. I've got lots to tell you, but I can't right now. We're deep in conference.'

'About the case?'

'The case?' repeated Libby, amused. 'The one Ian's investigating, you mean?'

'Yes.'

'Well, no. We're looking into the fake.'

'Isn't it the same thing?' said Fran, sounding surprised.

'Not as far as we know.'

'Oh.' Silence.

'Come on,' said Libby, suspiciously. 'What have you come up with?'

'No – nothing. It doesn't matter.'

'Oh, yes it does,' said Libby, even more suspicious. 'Out with it.'

'The first person to go to the V&A – what was his name?'

'Nathan Vine. Michael's Googling him as we speak.'

'Did you look up his address?'

'Yes – Ben's gone to get it. It's in his Dad's address book, along with his cousin Russell's.'

'Well, do you see where it is?'

Libby looked across at Ben, who had re-entered the kitchen with a look of astonishment on his face.

'He lived here!' he said. 'In Steeple Martin.'

'Golly,' said Libby. Then, into the phone, 'How did you know?'

'I don't know. I just did.' Libby could almost hear Fran shrugging. 'He had something to do with finding the documents belonging to the house.'

'How...?' Libby began incredulously, and gave up. 'Look, I've got to go now, but I'll ring you later. I'm not behind the bar tonight, so I can put my feet up. Speak later.'

'Where in Steeple Martin?' she interrupted Ben as she came back to the table.

'Steeple Lane. Where your friend Una lives, just beyond Steeple Farm. It used to be part of the estate.'

There were various exclamations of surprise from everyone.

'That could explain a lot,' said Michael.

'How?' asked Libby.

'Perhaps Nathan, like Richard's father, was interested in the history of the house, and once Russell had taken all the documents, got in touch and – I don't know – helped him with research?'

'In the course of which he turned up the letter!' said Libby triumphantly.

'Or got enough information to pass to a forger,' said Richard.

'We need to find out from Gilbert what Vine said when he took the document to them,' said Ben.

'Have a look through this lot,' said Richard, waving a hand at the pile of papers on the table, 'and see if there's a clue in there.'

'If you and Ben don't mind,' said Michael rather diffidently, 'I'd like to look through them with Gilbert.'

'Excellent idea,' said Ben. 'After all, you both know what you're looking for, and you've both seen the original fake. Can you call a fake an original?'

'I agree,' said Richard. 'And although I'm used to research, it's not my field. What about Dr Harrap?'

'Let's ask Gilbert first,' said Ben. 'Libby?'

'You want me to ring him? And ask him what?'

'If he'd like to come and look through this lot with Michael, and if he knows Dr Harrap.'

Libby got up once again and went outside to call Gilbert. When she'd explained as well as she could, and received his enthusiastic response, she returned to give the good news.

'He and Andrew will both come over in the morning, and yes, he knows Dr Harrap, and once he knows what questions to ask, will be happy to get in touch on our behalf.'

'There, that's settled,' said Ben. 'And now, Richard, we'd better show you your rural accommodation. How long did you come prepared to stay?'

'I'd hoped for a couple of days. I didn't intend to ask you to put me up, though. I thought I'd find a pub...'

'We can ask at the pub,' said Libby, 'but they have been full up this week because of the play. We thought you might like to stay in one of our huts.'

'Huts?' Richard looked faintly shocked.

Ben grinned. 'Come on, we'll show you.'

He led Richard out, and Libby turned to Bel and Michael. 'Are you around for dinner?'

'We thought we'd eat at the pub, if you don't mind,' said Bel. 'Harry's closed on Mondays, isn't he?'

'He is, but I'd book, if I were you. It's a bit busy this week.'

'Er – we have,' said Bel, looking guilty.

Libby smiled. 'Jolly good. See you when I see you then.'

She said goodbye to Hetty and followed Ben and

90

Richard to the Hoppers's Huts where Richard was professing himself delighted.

'Will you come to dinner this evening?' asked Libby.

'Oh, I don't want to put you to any trouble – what about the pub? Or a restaurant?'

'The pub's going to be busy, and Michael and Bel have booked dinner there. Our only restaurant is closed on Mondays, I'm afraid.'

'Bel and Michael?' said Ben. 'Thought I recognised the signs...'

Richard looked from one to the other. 'Ah. I might be intruding, then?'

'Might be better to leave them on their own,' said Libby. 'So, dinner?'

'Yes, please.'

'If you wanted to see the play, we'd better make it early,' said Ben.

'If you can get a ticket,' said Libby.

But Ben got a ticket, and after a hastily constructed stir-fry, took Richard up to the theatre. Libby stretched out on the sofa with phone and remote to hand and prepared to enjoy a relaxing evening.

The phone rang.

'OK, Fran. Pin your ears back.'

When she'd finished, there was a short silence. 'Well, say something.'

'I was just thinking. You're sure about this Richard?'

'What do you mean? Are we sure he's not a fake, too?'

'I suppose so. Or at least hasn't got a hidden agenda.'

'Have you had another moment?'

'No. I was just being naturally suspicious.'

Libby sighed. 'You're worse than me.'

'No, I'm not. I'm just being realistic. Ben found him on social media – it could have been a false profile. Easiest thing in the world to fake.'

'Stop it! For a start, why? Simple curiosity? What would he have to gain? Besides, he brought all the stuff with him.'

'The documents. Are they genuine? Wouldn't they have to have been kept in a controlled atmosphere or something? Remember the muniment room you saw before, and how fragile all those documents were?'

'Hmm.' Libby thought for a moment. 'Those were a lot earlier, though, about 800 years earlier.'

'Well, I'd check, if I were you,' said Fran.

'Gilbert and Michael are going to go through the documents tomorrow, I told you. They can tell us if they're fakes, too, can't they?'

'Yes, and what about those two? Both of them wiggled their way into the investigation, didn't they? No one asked them.'

'Michael was asked. Gilbert asked him. Oh...' Libby scowled.. 'Ian's met them both. He'll have checked up on them, won't he?'

'I don't know, do I?' Fran's tone was sharp.

'What's the matter with you? You're in a crap mood.'

'I'm not.' Now she sounded sulky.

'I know what it is!' Libby was triumphant. 'You're feeling left out!'

There was a pause, then Fran laughed. 'You're probably right, I am!'

'You're coming over tomorrow to see the play, aren't you? Why don't you make a day of it? Eat early at Hal's?'

Fran sighed. 'I can't – or rather, Guy can't.'

'You could come on your own and he could follow.'

'That means two cars and neither of us can have a drink.'

'Very true. How about if I come down and pick you up? We can have lunch at Mavis's or The Sloop and then come back here.'

'OK – if you're sure you don't mind?'

'Course I don't. Besides, I've got a picture to deliver to Guy, so it's a justifiable trip.'

'Except,' said Fran, 'that you could have given it to him tomorrow night.'

Libby brushed this aside. 'Doesn't matter. What time?'

The result of this conversation was that Tuesday morning saw Libby driving to Nethergate through bright sunshine.

'Just the day for a visit to the seaside,' she said to Fran when she arrived, gazing approvingly at the sparkling sea and the families on the beach. 'Do you need any more updating?'

'Is there anything happening?'

'No. Richard apparently enjoyed *Twelfth Night*, and Ben saw him ensconced in his Hoppers's Hut. We're leaving all the academics to get on with it today. It's all beyond me.'

'There's still been a murder,' said Fran.

'I know, but it's not *really* anything to do with us, is it?' Libby looked at her friend sideways. 'Is it?'

'You were the first one to say it was our business,' said Fran. 'Or rather, your business. And it looks very much as if Ben's family got involved somewhere along the line.'

'So do you think his uncle Russell had something to do with the forgery?'

'Maybe.' Fran sat on the window seat, chin resting on knees. 'He passed over all the house documents, apparently. He could have known about the suggestion that Mr Shakespeare came to Steeple Martin, or whatever it was called then.'

'But, surely, Nathan Vine's far more likely? If it was Russell Wilde, he would have tried to sell it, wouldn't he?' Libby frowned out at the blameless sea.

'Heavens, I don't know.' Fran put her legs down and shook out her skirt impatiently. 'And another thing we don't know – was Duncan really related to Nathan?'

'Oh, Gawd!' said Libby. 'It's too complicated! And all the fault of that glovemaker's son.'

Chapter Thirteen

The Blue Anchor stood on the harbour wall next to The Sloop. The owner, Mavis, appeared to serve Fran and Libby herself, and deposited a battered tin ashtray next to Libby, a sure sign of favouritism her rather surly manner belied.

When they'd ordered their sandwiches, Fran sat back in her chair and frowned. 'As I said last night, I suppose we are certain that Gilbert and Michael are kosher?'

Libby was startled. 'Of course they are! I said, Ian will have checked up on them.'

'Has anybody looked at their identification? After all, Gilbert turned up out of the blue, and he was the one who got in touch with Michael, wasn't he?'

'Andrew knew him!'

'No, Gilbert said he knew Andrew. All these people turning up out of the blue. And over something as potentially valuable as a Shakespeare artefact.' Fran looked at her friend. 'Nobody's checked them, have they?'

Libby was silent for a moment.

'But what have they got to gain?' she asked at last. 'They're certifying the letter as fake. If they were saying it was genuine, I could see the point, but not this way round.'

Fran shook her head. 'I don't know. I just wondered. Would Andrew be able to verify either of them?'

'Look, Andrew invited Gilbert to stay with him, didn't he? He must have known him,' protested Libby. 'And Gilbert said he's known Andrew for years. They've been doing research together – Andrew would have spotted a ringer straightaway.'

'That's true.' Fran nodded agreement.

'I think you're looking for excuses to poke about,' said Libby, smiling up at the current girl posing as a waitress who delivered their sandwiches on a somewhat shaky tray.

'Maybe,' said Fran with a sigh. 'You were right when you said I felt left out. Oh, the ignominy!'

'Nah,' said Libby. 'We've both got so used to investigating, whether anyone wants us to or not, it's a habit. It's like when we were both still working. You got so used to being part of a cast you felt bereft when it stopped, and you used to be desperate for the next one.'

'True. That's one reason why I did such a lot of radio towards the end – there was a lot of it about at that time. Not now, though.'

'So many alternative forms of entertainment,' said Libby, opening her sandwich and staring suspiciously at a piece of lettuce. 'Perhaps we ought to go into games. There must be openings for voiceovers in those computer games.'

'Computer-generated, I expect,' said Fran gloomily. 'Thank goodness we do still have live theatre.'

They were silent for a few minutes eating their sandwiches.

'What's going on with Bel and this Michael?' Fran asked eventually.

'Bel's smitten. He seems to be, too, but he's very good-looking and charming, and I would think he has women falling over themselves back in London, so I'm hoping she doesn't get in too deep. Good thighs, too,' Libby added pensively.

Fran choked on the last of her sandwich. 'Oh, Libby!' she said finally, wiping her eyes.

'What?' said Libby indignantly. 'I mean due to propinquity, of course. Getting in too deep, that is, not the thighs.'

'The young get in too deep far too quickly these days, if you ask me,' said Fran.

'I'm sorry to say I agree,' said Libby reluctantly. 'Not that I'd want to go back to the old days, and I have no objection on moral grounds but the more intimate a relationship gets the harder it is to leave it. Even after a weekend.' She sighed. 'Not that it will make any difference, of course. And, by the way, what's going on, if anything, with Ad and Sophie?'

Adam, Libby's youngest son, and Sophie, Fran's step-daughter, had been in an on/off relationship ever since Libby and Fran met. Adam lived in the flat over The Pink Geranium, where Fran herself had lived briefly, and Sophie lived in the flat above Guy's gallery and shop, where Guy had lived before moving in to Coastguard Cottage with Fran.

'I don't think anything is at the moment,' said Fran. 'Doesn't Adam talk to you about it?'

'Of course not!' said Libby. 'He goes all feet-shuffly if I so much as mention anything to do with *guurls*.'

'Here's Bert and *The Sparkler*.' Fran nodded to the little tourist boat sidling up to the jetty almost next to them. 'Nearly peak season for them.'

Bert's trippers disembarked, followed by Bert himself and his "boy", this year, his grandson Little Eric.

'Mornin', ladies.' Bert fetched up beside their table.

'Hello, Bert,' chorused the ladies.

'Good season, so far, Bert?' asked Libby.

'Not bad, not bad. No murders goin' on, then?'

Fran smiled. 'Not right at the moment, no.'

'Ah,' said Bert. 'Won't be long, then.' He touched his cap and rolled away to his own table, to wait for his mate

George to bring *The Sparkler's* stable mate, *The Dazzler*, alongside.

'Now, what did he mean by that?' asked Libby.

'That it won't be long until we find another murder,' said Fran, with a smile. 'And he's right, isn't he?'

'What, because we've already got one?'

'Well, yes, but he didn't know that. He meant we always seem to be involved in a murder investigation, so, if we weren't right at this minute, we would be soon.'

'Oh,' said Libby. 'What a reputation we've got.'

'Haven't we just,' said Fran. 'But we don't do it deliberately, do we? This one just turned up.'

'And,' said Libby, cheering up, 'we actually know hardly anything about it.'

'But that's what we're trying to find out, isn't it?' said Fran. 'Why this Duncan Lucas was killed, who he was and what did he know about Ben's house.'

'And who killed him,' finished Libby. 'Come on, let's go back to Steeple Martin and find out if anyone has any news.'

'I must see to the Blot first,' said Fran, standing up.

'The what?' Libby looked up puzzled.

'Oh, you haven't met the Blot, have you?' said Fran. 'Come along then.'

Back at Coastguard Cottage, Fran opened the kitchen door and peered in. Libby, even more puzzled, peered over her shoulder. With a yelp, she swung round as something landed on her back. Something with very sharp claws.

Grinning, Fran somewhat painfully detached what appeared to be a ball of black wool from Libby.

'What is that?' gasped Libby.

'It's a black kitten. It looks like a blot of ink, so that's what Sophie called it.'

'Is it hers?' Libby reached out and tentatively touched

98

the tiny black nose which peeped out beneath two very blue eyes.

'Yes. But he comes here so he can go outside. He's too small to escape over the wall yet, so he's quite safe in the yard.'

'What does Balzac think?' Fran's black and white longhair was nowhere to be seen.

'Asleep on our bed,' said Fran. 'The Blot can get annoying to a mature cat.'

'I bet,' said Libby, who was now stroking the Blot's head, which was vibrating to the sound of a rich purr. 'He is rather gorgeous, though. How did she get him?'

'A friend's cat had kittens and they all went except the Blot. It's true that black cats don't get chosen. Odd, though.'

'Synonymous with witches and the Devil, do you think?'

Fran shrugged. 'I'll just take him back to the flat and make sure his food bowl's full.'

'And check the litter tray, I should,' said Libby. 'I'll retrieve the car and pick you up there.'

'Kids'll be breaking up soon.' They were driving back towards Steeple Martin between fields of ripening cereal crops and smaller ones full of sheep. 'That means Nethergate will fill up.'

'It also means you've got to get your finger out if you're going to do the summer show at The Alexandria,' said Fran. 'Have you asked Susannah yet?'

'No,' said Libby, with a sigh. 'In fact, I'm wondering if we ought not to give it a miss this year. It was all right for a nostalgia trip when we first did it, but it's a bit tired now.'

'Talk to management at the Alexandria about it,' said Fran. 'It is a huge commitment for everybody, especially Susannah and any other musicians she ropes in.'

'I will,' said Libby, 'and I'd better do it sharpish, or they'll be relying on us, and then they'll have to find something else to fill the gap.'

'But first, we want to find out about Duncan Lucas,' Fran reminded her. 'Although I'm wondering why we need to.' She cocked an eyebrow at Libby.

'To find out who killed him, of course!' said Libby.

'But the police are doing that.'

Libby looked shocked. 'When did that ever stop us? Besides, Ian always asks.'

'No, he doesn't. He asks us as witnesses if we're involved, like last time at the Beer Festival.'

'Or when I discovered that body at the farm.' Libby shuddered. 'I'm surprised I ever managed to eat that turkey.'

Instead of going back to Number 17 Allhallow's Lane, Libby drove straight to the Manor, where she and Fran found Michael, Andrew and Gilbert bent over the table in the formal dining room, which was now covered in old documents. They ran Ben, Richard and Bel to earth in the kitchen.

'Hetty's gone to hide in her sitting room,' said Ben. 'We escaped.'

'Is it very boring?' Libby asked Bel.

'It is to me,' her daughter replied frankly. 'Honestly, Mum, those three in there are getting positively orgasmic!'

'Bel!' said Ben.

Richard laughed. 'I know what she means. I've often seen it in academics. Nothing else moves them in quite the same way. If they think they've discovered something unusual...'

'But have they?' asked Ben. 'They were gabbling on about something or other over lunch, but I couldn't understand half of it.'

Libby filled the big kettle and slid it on to the Aga. 'And what about Duncan Lucas? Have you heard any more about him?'

'No.' Ben looked surprised. 'Well, no one would ask us, would they? We never came into contact with him.'

'What about The Glover's Men? Have they been bothering them?' asked Fran.

Ben shook his head. 'Apparently, the management team have packed up and gone back to London, except for Tristan, who's been left here more or less as damage limitation.'

'Can't have done them any harm, though,' said Libby. 'A murder always attracts attention.'

'But a fake claim to a Shakespeare letter definitely attracts the wrong sort,' said Fran. 'They really don't want to start playing that up.'

The kettle began hissing steam just as the kitchen door burst open.

'Look what we've found!' said Andrew.

'What?' said five voices together.

'A receipt from Nathan Vine,' said Andrew. 'For "various documents".'

'Does it say what?' Ben went over to peer at the piece of paper.

'No,' said Michael, coming in behind Andrew with Gilbert in tow. 'But at least it shows where Vine *claimed* to have got his fake from.'

'So,' Richard was frowning, 'whatever was interesting was given – or sold – to Vine. You won't find anything among what's left, will you?'

'As we've already found one or two gems,' said Gilbert, 'I think we might. There's nothing to say Vine got much.'

'And the existing documentation held at the archives proves that Shakespeare's Players did come here, despite there being no formal record of that along with Dover and Fordwich,' said Andrew.

'Right,' said Richard. 'But this could mean...' He looked across at Ben. 'It could mean that my father caused the fake to be made.'

Chapter Fourteen

The rest of the company looked at each other uneasily.

'Er – did you ever have reason to think your father might act – well, illegally?' asked Ben. 'I didn't know him well enough.'

'I would never have thought so.' Richard was looking distinctly uncomfortable. 'He was rather a...*stiff* sort of person, if you know what I mean.'

'Victorian Dad?' suggested Libby.

'You know,' said Fran, 'I'm only just coming in on this, but it strikes me that someone who took over the family archives because he was interested and Ben's father wasn't, isn't likely to try faking the evidence.'

Everyone turned and looked at her. Richard seemed to register her presence for the first time.

'I hope you're right,' he said slowly. 'It's a good point.'

Gilbert was looking dubious.

'What's up?' said Libby. 'You don't agree?'

'I can't really pass any valid judgement.' Gilbert whiffled his neat moustache. 'But...'

'But you don't agree.' Andrew put his head on one side. 'I think I agree with you, but I'd like to hear your reasons.'

Richard was looking more uncomfortable than ever. 'So would I.'

'Let's all sit down,' said Ben, indicating chairs. 'Did you make that tea, Lib?'

Libby jumped up. 'No, I was interrupted, wasn't I? I'll do it now.'

'Right,' said Ben. 'Gilbert, tell us what you think.'

'The lady's – Fran, isn't it? – point was that Mr Wilde's father would not have done any – er – what would you say?'

'Jiggery-pokery?' suggested Libby.

'Quite.' Gilbert's mouth twitched. 'If he had such respect for the family archives. However, there are two points, here.' He settled more comfortably on his chair. 'First, he did actually pass on *something* to Nathan Vine, whatever it was, which doesn't argue much respect, and second, and almost more important, to my mind, they weren't – aren't – *family* archives at all!'

Everyone looked slightly shell-shocked at this remarkable statement.

'He's right!' burst out Libby, to the imminent danger of the large brown teapot, which crashed unceremoniously onto the table. 'They aren't! They're *Manor* archives – nothing to do with the Wilde family!'

'Exactly.' Gilbert bestowed a proud pat on Libby's arm. 'Well done.'

'Of course!' There were mutterings round the table.

'It's the Manor's history that's up for grabs, as it were,' said Richard. 'Not yours and mine, Ben. That's a relief.'

'Yes,' said Ben, frowning, 'but something illegal's still been done, and it looks as if it's ended in murder.'

'Oh, God,' groaned Richard. 'I was trying not to think of that.'

'Do we know anything about Nathan Vine?' asked Fran. 'Gilbert?'

'I don't.' Gilbert shook his head. 'He was in touch, obviously, about the letter in the first place, but when we said we thought – although we hadn't yet proved conclusively – that it was a fake, he withdrew it. I never heard from him again, until this Duncan Lucas, claiming to be his nephew, submitted it, this time to Michael and his colleagues.'

Libby was pouring tea. 'And none of us have heard anything from Ian? From the police?'

Fran smiled. 'Well, Lib?'

'Well what?' said Libby nervously.

'Oh, here they go again,' sighed Ben.

Richard, Gilbert and Michael looked puzzled. Andrew laughed.

'I think an investigation has started,' he said. 'There'll be a high-level meeting in the pub or The Pink Geranium, you'll see.'

The three other men looked even more puzzled, Libby was red-faced, Ben resigned and Fran serene.

'Libby and Fran investigate things,' he explained. 'Murders, usually.'

'You're detectives?' gasped Michael.

'No, no!' Libby's voice came out as a croak. 'We're just...'

'Nosy,' supplied Fran.

This broke the tension and everyone laughed.

The door opened again and Bel's enquiring face peered in.

'What's going on?'

A gabble of voices told her and Libby tried to look disinterested.

'Oh, is that all,' said Bel. 'That's a normal state of affairs round here. It's why I spend most of my time in London.' She gave her mother a friendly grin.

'And you were very useful in our last case,' said Fran.

'Oh, shush,' said Bel, with a surreptitious look at Michael.

'Yes, well,' said Libby, rushing in to cover the moment. 'I'd better go home and see about dinner. Coming, Fran?'

Fran swallowed half her tea and stood up, looking surprised.

'I won't just yet,' said Ben, frowning. 'What's so urgent?'

'Nothing!' Libby tried a bright smile. 'I just thought... Come on, Fran.'

'What was all that about?' said Fran following her friend's precipitate departure.

'It was all highly embarrassing,' said Libby. 'And I didn't want anything said about the last case. Bel isn't going out with that bloke any more, and she's not going to want to talk about it in front of Michael, is she?'

'True,' said Fran. 'And he is rather gorgeous, isn't it? A real classical face.'

'Classical?'

'Well, it is. Straight brows, straight nose, lovely eyes, what they call a chiselled mouth, I think...'

'Oh, don't,' said Libby. 'That makes him sound too perfect. He needs a couple of defects, surely?'

'Perhaps we just can't see them!' said Fran wickedly.

'He seems all right, actually,' said Libby. 'He doesn't appear to be up himself or anything.'

'You have such a lovely way with words, Libby,' sighed Fran.

They had just turned into the high street when a figure popped out in front of them.

'Well, if it isn't my former tenant,' said Harry. 'Hello, my dears.'

'Hello, Harry,' said Fran. 'Can you fit us in tonight?'

'But I -' began Libby.

'I know you were, but this saves you cooking, doesn't it?'

'Yes, ducks, I can fit you in. Four? Or do all the other adjuncts want to come too?'

'If by that you mean all our visiting academics, I have

no idea. I hope not,' said Libby. 'Or if they do, they can come on their own. My life's been far too taken over with all this business so far.'

'They've all seen the play, I take it?' said Harry.

'Fran and Guy are going tonight, so early dinner, please, Hal dear,' said Libby. 'Is that all right?'

'Anything for the old trout,' said Harry, giving them each a peck on the cheek. 'Off you go, dearies. Back here for six thirty, all right?'

'Right, now.' Fran tucked her arm through Libby's. 'Why are you getting nervous about poking your nose into this murder?'

'I'm not,' said Libby. 'I said, it's embarrassing to talk about in front of... those people.'

'Because they're academics? We've dealt with them before, and Andrew's a friend. And remember Edward Hall? He actually said he wanted to be part of Libby's Loonies.'

Libby smiled reminiscently. 'He was nice, wasn't he? Ben brought his name up the other day, when we were talking about the Manor. He knew a lot about buildings.'

'But his period was more the civil wars, wasn't it? Although I suppose there's a crossover there. Where did he go after all? Did he get his professorship in Kent?'

'Andrew would know,' said Libby. 'We'll ask him.'

'And you'll stop being touchy about everything?'

Libby grinned and dug an elbow into her friend's side. 'I will.'

Ben returned from the Manor and Guy arrived from Nethergate at roughly the same time, just in time to have a pre-prandial drink before leaving for The Pink Geranium, which was almost empty when they arrived.

'Fills up after the show,' said Harry, lounging over to take their orders.

'Will we be going to the pub after the show?' asked

Fran.

'I hope so,' said Libby. 'I want to know what you think of it.'

'And I want to know what's going on with this murder,' said Guy. 'I can't believe you've got yourselves mixed up in another one.'

'We haven't, really,' said Libby. 'It's nothing to do with us, or at least, it wasn't.' She looked at Ben. 'You explain.'

Ben explained the circumstances as well as he could. Harry came up and listened in.

'Sounds like you need that lovely Edward bloke,' he said. 'He was good on houses, if I remember rightly.'

'We were talking about him earlier,' said Fran. 'I agree it would be worth getting in touch with him.'

'But that's to find out if Ben's uncle actually forged the Shakespeare letter,' said Libby. 'Not who did the murder.'

'We think the letter led to the murder,' said Fran. 'And anyway, we wouldn't think Ben's uncle did the forgery himself, would we?'

'I don't know. You girls!' said Harry, and disappeared kitchenwards.

After dinner, Ben and Libby walked up to the theatre with Fran and Guy, and arranged to meet them in the pub later, before going back to the Manor to find out what the visitors had accomplished.

'Andrew and Gilbert have gone back to Andrew's,' said Michael, meeting them in the hall. 'Bel and I are just going down to the pub for dinner.'

'Right,' said Libby. 'No further progress, then? We were thinking of getting in touch with another old friend of ours, Edward Hall. He helped us out a few years ago when we were looking into a seventeenth-century house. Andrew knows him. Incestuous lot, you academics.'

Michael laughed. 'Only in our own fields. But yes, you're right. Can't say I know him, though. Where's he based?'

'That's it – I can't remember. He was in Leicester, but he moved.'

'I'm going to look him up,' said Ben. 'Easier on the computer than on the phone, so I'll go in the study.'

Bel appeared in a flurry of floaty dress, and she and Michael vanished. Ben went to the study and Libby knocked quietly on Hetty's sitting room door.

'Kitchen,' a voice called out, so Libby made her way down the corridor.

'Have they been disrupting you terribly?' she asked, sitting down at the table.

'No, gal. I keep out of their way. Plenty of house for them to poke around in without disturbing me. Tea?'

'No, thanks, Het.' Libby clasped her hands beneath her chin. 'What do you make of all this?'

Hetty shrugged. 'Beyond me. Greg wasn't much interested in what had gone on in the past, so I never knew none of it, see. Never knew that Russell, either, I told you. Not much anyway.'

'What about Richard?'

'Never knew him, either. Seems all right.'

'Do you remember Edward, Het? When we were looking into Dark House?'

Hetty nodded. 'Black bloke? Liked him.'

'We're thinking of asking him about this problem. Ben's trying to find him on the computer.'

Hetty quirked an eyebrow.

'I know. It's a mad world, isn't it? Computers and phones and – and – well, everything.' Libby shook her head and laughed. 'I'll go and see how Ben's getting on.'

Just as she stood up, Ben came in.

'Found him!' He waved a piece of paper triumphantly.

'He's on the Medway campus, so not far away. I've emailed.'

'Excellent,' said Libby. 'Your mum liked him.'

'I remember.' Ben smiled at his mother. 'You're all right, then? Don't need anything?'

Hetty gave him what could have been called an old-fashioned look. Libby laughed.

'When did she ever need anything?'

'True.' Ben went and gave his mother a hug. 'We'll see you tomorrow, Mum. Don't let those men bother you.'

'Where are we going now?' asked Libby, as they left the Manor. 'It's a bit early to go to the pub.'

'Let's go and see if they need a hand at the theatre,' said Ben.

Libby grinned at him. 'You're feeling like a spare part this week, aren't you?'

Ben shook his head. 'I'm not used to having nothing to do. Usually visiting productions need technical help – this one doesn't. I don't even have to lock up every night.'

Peter was behind the bar working out how many interval orders he had to do. Libby went to help while Ben went up to the lighting box.

'I expect I'll be in the way,' he said gloomily, 'but still...'

'He really doesn't like not being in charge,' said Peter, watching his cousin go up the spiral staircase.

'It's his baby,' said Libby. 'Technically, he and his mum own it, he did the conversion and now we run it between us. No wonder he's protective.'

Peter nodded. 'Thinks more of this than he does of you.' He gave her a dig in the ribs. 'Get a move on with those glasses.'

Libby had a brief word with Fran during the interval, but the bar was too busy for more than that.

'People still don't get the idea of ordering interval

110

drinks, do they?' she remarked to Peter as they passed each other carrying glasses.

'What did Fran think?' asked Peter, when the audience had returned to the auditorium, and they were collecting glasses.

'Very good,' said Libby. 'Don't know about Guy, though. I think he's always been a bit suspicious of our joint theatrical careers.'

'But you're not in this. Or even anything to do with it.' Peter threw a tea towel over the beer pumps and began loading the glasswasher.

'No, I know. But I think he's always worried that Fran will be tempted back to the stage if she has too much contact with the theatre.'

'Fran was very well aware of her lack of work by the time she came here,' said Peter. 'There's nothing to go back to.'

'There's us. And she still does the summer show. Oh, by the way -' She shot him a nervous look. 'I'm thinking of knocking that on the head.'

Peter said nothing, but raised his eyebrows.

Libby went on to enumerate her reasons until she ran out of steam. Peter grinned.

'I'm not surprised,' he said. 'And I agree. Let's tell 'em all next week.'

'Have a meeting, you mean? I thought just an email.'

'Personal touch,' said Peter. 'Hurry up with those glasses. And you'd better escape before the end of the play, or you'll get caught in the after-show rush.'

In the pub, Libby and Ben found not only Bel and Michael, but Gilbert, Andrew and Richard.

'Bother.' Libby turned to Tim at the bar. 'Nowhere to bloody hide.'

Tim grinned. 'I could need to talk to you over – oh, I dunno – festival finances? In my new Snug?'

'What new Snug?' said Ben and Libby together.

'Formerly known as The Office.' Tim winked.

'No, you're all right,' sighed Libby. 'We'd better socialise. Fran and Guy will be down in a minute.'

'Where have you been?' asked Bel, as they pulled up chairs.

'Helping at the theatre,' said Ben. 'We had dinner at Harry's. Fran and Guy are in front tonight.'

Richard was frowning. 'In front of what?'

'In the audience,' explained Libby. 'Sorry, the jargon pops out now and then.'

'Ah.' Richard still looked puzzled, so Andrew, aided by Bel, took it on himself to explain the theatrical background of the Sarjeants and Ben himself.

'And here are Fran and Guy,' said Ben, standing up. 'You won't want to be bored by a lot of theatre talk, so we'll move.'

He firmly removed himself and Libby from the big round table to a small one by the window and went to help Guy with drinks.

'Thank goodness,' muttered Fran, taking her seat beside Libby. 'I really didn't want to be surrounded by academics again.'

'They can get a bit wearing,' agreed Libby. 'And Richard, despite being one of the family, knows next to nothing about theatre.'

'Not everybody does, Lib, and Ben was the first in his family to go into it, wasn't he?'

'Until architecture grabbed him.'

'I thought it was holiday jobs in the theatre while he was studying architecture that grabbed him.'

'Well, it was. Anyway, what did you think?'

They discussed the pared-down production of *Twelfth Night*, and agreed that the Olivia had managed to get the best out of the part, although still not as good, in Libby's

112

opinion, as the Globe's all-male production.

'Ian!' Ben stood up. 'It's not your usual night!'

'Just coffee, Tim,' Ian called over. 'On my way home.'
He sat down next to Ben. 'I wanted to ask you
something.'

They all became aware of the silent table full of people
by the fireplace.

'What I wanted know,' said Ian, lowering his voice,
'was: do you happen to know where the Shakespeare
forgery was?'

Chapter Fifteen

'Where it *was*?' echoed Libby. 'What do you mean?'

Ian frowned. 'Who had it? Duncan Lucas or National Shakespeare? I'm assuming they didn't, or I would have had it by now.'

'Lucas withdrew it from the V&A, you know that,' said Ben. 'So he had it.'

Ian sighed heavily. 'Well, he hasn't got it now,' he said.

'Oh, golly!' said Libby.

'Stolen?' said Fran.

'Presumably. Obviously the room where he was found was searched – and had been before we got there – so probably from there. It's certainly not in his car, or at his London address. No safe deposit boxes, or left luggage tickets or useful clues like that. I just had a faint hope that he might have left it with the management team, but I didn't really think so.'

'So it's gone.' Libby nodded. 'All the trouble it's caused. And now – murder. But why? Why steal a fake?'

'Perhaps someone didn't believe it was a fake?' suggested Guy.

Fran was frowning. Ian watched her. Libby turned towards her, then Ben and Guy. Eventually she shook herself and realised they were all staring.

'What?'

'Was that a "moment"?' asked her husband.

'I don't know,' she said slowly. 'Ian, I'd rather not talk about it here.'

'Not at the Manor, either,' said Libby, almost

114

whispering. 'The others might all go back there. Back at mine.'

They finished their drinks, waved goodbye to those at the other table and left.

'What was it all about, Fran?' asked Ian, as they walked down the silent high street. 'What didn't you want the others to hear?'

'You didn't want them to hear, either,' said Fran. 'You stayed away from them, too.'

'I did. So come on.'

'She's worried about all these new people turning up,' said Libby, when Fran didn't answer.

Ian's eyebrows rose.

'It just seems a bit suspicious.' Fran sighed heavily. 'They've all arrived unasked – Gilbert, Richard, Michael...'

'We've checked them all, Fran. Gilbert and Michael are both highly respected academics, as is your cousin Richard, Ben, in his own field. Michael's even been on television, if that's a recommendation.'

'Hmm.' Fran was still frowning. 'Still, that's all. We can go home, now.'

Libby stopped dead.

'What's up, Fran?'

Everyone else stopped, too.

Fran looked up and gave a crooked smile. 'I don't know. I'm just not happy. I haven't had any of these...well, "moments" for ages. Not sure how to deal with them.'

'I suggest we sit down and pick it apart, then,' said Ian. 'None of us will feel happy if it's wavering around in the ether unresolved.'

They resumed their walk. Ben let them in to Number Seventeen and Sidney shot out between their legs.

'That cat!' grumbled Ian.

'You told me last year you'd wondered about getting a cat for company,' accused Libby.

'I also told you I'd decided not to. Not fair on the poor animal, leaving it shut in all day.'

Libby opened her mouth and Ben and Fran dug her in the ribs from opposite sides.

'Drinks?' asked Ben, turning on lights in the sitting room.

'I won't, thanks,' said Ian, 'but you go ahead.'

'I can't,' said Fran, 'I'm driving, too.'

Libby, Ben and Guy all had whisky, while Fran frowned over her clasped hands.

'Honestly,' she burst out at last, 'I don't *know* what it is. You know when I've had pictures in my head before – like Aunt Eleanor dying? Or the woman under the Willoughby Oak?'

Everyone murmured agreement.

'Well, this isn't like that at all.' Fran shook her head, as if to free it from cobwebs. 'It's just like fuzz in my head, with this doubt in the middle of it.'

'Doubt? About a person or a situation?' asked Guy.

'I don't know.' Fran looked miserable. 'At first, when I told Lib the other day, I though it was about one of the people. I said how could they be sure that Richard was who he said he was, when they'd only found him through the internet, but it doesn't seem like that now. Not entirely, anyway.'

'So it could be one of them, still?' said Libby. 'They aren't right?'

'Maybe. But I don't know. I could be making it all up.'

'I've never known you make things up,' said Ian. 'You've always been spot on, even if you didn't know what you were talking about.'

'That sounds completely barmy,' said Libby, 'but I know what you mean. I didn't believe her when it first

116

happened, but Ben convinced me.'

'There's the whole situation surrounding the suspicious death,' said Ian. 'It could simply be that your subconscious is rebelling against the murder.'

'I sometimes see murders, or experience them,' said Fran, looking worried, 'but it's normally more of a direct threat. This is sort of – a – a vague, amorphous mess.'

'I think,' said Guy, putting down his glass, 'that it's what you said. You haven't had one of these for a long time, and you don't know how to deal with it. Or your mind doesn't.'

Fran smiled at him gratefully. 'I expect so. If I could stop worrying about it, it would resolve itself.' She stood up. 'I'm sorry if I've worried everybody else, too.'

Guy also stood and put an arm round her shoulders. 'Let's go and let them puzzle it out on their own,' he said. 'And thank them for a lovely evening.'

To Libby's surprise, Ian didn't leave with Fran and Guy, but sat back down when they'd gone.

'What do you think?' he asked.

'What about? Fran's niggles?'

'There's usually something in it, isn't there? I know I keep her involvement quiet as far as possible, but I'd be a fool to ignore her when she's had so much success.'

'If you can call it success,' said Libby.

'More whisky?' asked Ben. 'Sure you won't, Ian? Your room's ready over at the Manor. You look as though you want to talk it over a bit more.'

Ian looked undecided for a moment, then sighed and grinned.

'You've twisted my arm. Shall I call Hetty?'

'No – she's half expecting you anyway,' said Libby. 'So, what do you think you ought to do?'

'Have another look into all the backgrounds. Although I think I could ignore Gilbert. Andrew really did know him from years ago, and Michael really has been an advisor to the V&A as well as a fairly well-known expert on the history of theatre. I'm surprised you hadn't heard of him.'

'Where would I have done, though?'

'He's been on TV, I told you. I thought you would have watched programmes on the history of theatre.'

'Not always,' said Libby. 'I know we can watch anything any time these days, but I don't always hear about them.'

'So it's only my cousin who's doubtful,' said Ben.

'He's the only one we haven't got independent confirmation of,' said Ian, apologetically.

'But you have checked his credentials?' said Libby.

'Of course. Dr Richard Wilde, Senior Lecturer in Environmental Sciences.' Ian frowned at his whisky. 'What we haven't checked is if he really is your relation.'

'And, as Lib said, it's a common name. It could be another Richard Wilde.'

'That doesn't really make any sense,' said Libby. 'If there was a big prize to claim, yes, but there isn't in this case. What's he got to gain? If there was a real Shakespeare letter it would be different.'

'That's true,' said Ian. 'In fact, it's a mess. I think this murder may be nothing to do with the letter. Duncan Lucas may well be a career criminal.'

'And not old Nathan Vine's nephew after all?' asked Ben.

'He still might be,' said Ian. 'London are looking into that end. We should know tomorrow.'

Ian left shortly afterwards, but Libby continued to sit staring at the empty fireplace.

'Are you coming to bed?' asked Ben from the bottom of the stairs. 'You're not waiting up for Bel, are you?'

Libby looked up. 'Hardly! I don't think she'd risk

118

staying over at the Manor, however tolerant Hetty might be, but I can't see her coming home before the small hours. No, I'm just trying to decide what to do.'

'What do you mean, what to do?' Ben moved further into the room.

'I can't just do nothing, Ben. Someone's been murdered and our theatre and now your family are involved. Something's got to be done.'

'Yes,' said Ben, coming back to perch on a chair, 'and the police are doing it. What could you do?'

'Ask questions.'

'Of whom? Tristan's told us everything he knows, so have Gilbert and Michael, there isn't anyone else.'

'There must be someone.' Libby scowled at her other half. 'Where we can find out who knew enough to make the fake.'

'There are two strands to that,' said Ben. 'One – who knew enough technically, and two – who knew about the history of the house.'

'It would have to be someone who knew the history of the house, who could also lay their hands on a forgery expert.'

'Or, if it was the original owner, Nathan Vine, he could just have been persuaded to buy it,' said Ben.

'Which looks as if it would have to have been your uncle,' said Libby.

'Unless he also bought - or acquired - it in good faith,' said Ben.

'And – what? Sold it because he needed funds?'

'Well, he did need funds,' said Ben. 'He wasn't well off, and he resented Dad getting the Manor.'

'Suppose he got all the documents and archive material – and suppose - ' Libby sat up straight, eyes shining, ' – just suppose the letter was actually in there! In with all the archive material and your dad didn't know!'

Ben frowned. 'But how would it have got there? Dad had no interest in the history, and no one would have access to the archives to slip it in unnoticed.'

'Oh, perhaps not then.' Libby deflated.

'Leave it for tonight,' said Ben. 'Things might be clearer tomorrow, or Ian might have some news. And perhaps Fran's moment will have broken through.'

Libby gave him a wan smile. 'Perhaps. And perhaps not.'

Wednesday morning was flat and uninteresting. Ben had gone up to the Manor, ostensibly to work on the micro-brewery but, in reality, as he confided to Libby, to see what the quorum of academics were doing with the archive material. Andrew and Gilbert had arrived at nine thirty to join Michael and Richard in the dining room and a disgruntled Bel had appeared to join Libby over tea in the garden.

'No point in me going up there,' she told her mother. 'I don't understand half of what they're talking about and I can't actually *do* anything. I could go back up to the attics and poke about up there, I suppose, but I don't really know what I'm looking for. And they're waiting for this dendro-date or whatever it is which will tell everyone exactly how old the building is. So quite honestly, Ma, I think I might as well go back to London.'

'Not getting on as well as you'd hoped?' Libby ventured, never quite sure how much to ask her offspring about their private lives.

'Fine, as far as it goes, but all he's interested in really is all this archive material and the Shakespeare connection. I think they've more or less proved that he did come here, but they just want more.'

'Well, help me with our investigation then,' said Libby. 'I want to know more about this Duncan Lucas's murder.'

120

'Oh, you always do. But the police are looking into it and it might have nothing to do with this letter. Isn't Ian looking into other aspects?'

'Yes. The bloke might be a career criminal, he thinks.'

'And you can't do anything about that.' Bel stood up. 'I'm going to go up and see if Jeff-dog wants a walk. Want to come?'

'No, I've got some stuff to do here, and I'll give Fran a ring to see if her moment's got any clearer.'

'Sarjeant and Wolfe back on the trail again, eh?' Bel gave her mother an affectionate buffet on the shoulder. 'Go on then. See you later.'

Libby put mugs in the dishwasher, went upstairs and made the bed then went down to call Fran.

'No, nothing's clearer, but I feel a bit happier about it. I thought, if you don't mind, I might come up and see if I can latch on to anything up there. And we need to do something about the Summer Show, too, before it's too late.'

'Oh, golly, we do,' said Libby. 'I'd better start calling people and putting them off. I hope The Alexandria won't be too cross.'

'I'm sure they'll be a bit put out, but they've had a bargain for the last few years.'

'They can't really complain. Oh – hang on, the mobile's going.' Libby looked at the screen. 'It's Bel. I wonder what she wants? She's only just gone up to the Manor. Hello – Bel? What's up?'

'Ma – Jeff-dog's found a body!'

121

Chapter Sixteen

'What?'

'He – oh, Mum, can you call Ian? Please!' Belinda sounded almost hysterical.

'Just ring off and dial 999, darling. Quickest way. Where are you?'

'Near the huts. Will you come?'

'Yes, but ring the police Bel – now!'

Libby returned to the landline.

'Fran – Bel's found a body – yes, she was walking Jeff-dog, no, I'm going up there. Near the huts. No, I don't know any more. If you come up, go straight to the Manor.'

Libby felt as near to panic as she ever had in her life. Suppose the killer was still there? Was it murder? Could it be a tramp? If not, who? She grabbed her basket and keys and dived out of the cottage as fast as she could. She dithered for a moment wondering whether to go via the fields or round by the high street and the drive and opted for the fields, suddenly accompanied by Sidney. She found she was still clutching her mobile and rang Ben.

'All right, Lib, all right.' His calm voice soothed her. 'I'll go and find her and meet you up here. You did the right thing.'

By the time the huts came into view, she could also see a cluster of people a little further on and a police car, its blue light still flashing. Ben detached himself from the group and came towards her.

'It's all right, Lib, Bel's fine. The police car and I arrived at the same time – they sent someone who was

122

already here, down at the church hall.'

'Who is it?' Libby managed to get out.

'I don't know. They've called Ian and the whole circus, so we'll know soon. The officer says we can take Bel back to the Manor.'

Michael had appeared by now and had his arm round a shivering Bel. Jeff-dog was sitting, alert, by her feet. Libby practically fell over her own feet in her haste to get to her daughter, who promptly burst into tears.

'If you'd like to go back to the house, madam,' said the officer, looking somewhat out of his depth, 'someone will be over to see you shortly.'

Slowly, not looking towards the ominously shielded lump on the ground, the little procession made its way back towards the Manor, where Hetty waited by the big oak door. No one said anything.

In the kitchen they were met by Gilbert, Richard and Andrew, all looking worried.

'Is it -' began Richard, and Ben shook his head.

'Let Bel come to terms with it,' he said. 'Time for questions later.'

Hetty was already pouring tea. Jeff-dog, looking as relieved as a collie could, settled down by the Aga where he could keep an eye on the company. If there was any more excitement, he wasn't going to be left out.

Bel began to speak.

'It was so weird. You always hear about dog walkers stumbling across bodies, but you don't expect... I'd just let him off the lead, you see, and he went straight to this bush -' She stopped. 'I didn't know what to do.'

'Nothing else you could do, gal,' said Hetty gruffly. 'Right thing.'

Libby sat ineffectually patting her daughter's arm, while Michael stayed by her side, his arm still around her shoulders. Bel seemed to notice neither. Ben roamed round the kitchen frowning.

'What was someone doing up there?' he said. 'Richard must have seen something. I'll go and ask him.'

'No, don't,' said Libby. 'Leave it until Ian or someone else gets here.'

'Why?' said Ben. Libby scowled at him and he subsided.

It wasn't long before Fran arrived, followed very soon after by Ian and a female officer. Everyone stood up.

'Shall we go?' asked Libby.

'No, Ma, stay,' said Bel, the panic returning to her voice.

'Yes, Libby, stay,' said Ian. 'If the rest of you would -? Hetty, I'm sorry to turn you out of your own kitchen.'

'Be in my room,' said Hetty, giving Bel a final valedictory pat.

'And we'll wait in the dining room,' said Ben. 'Come on Michael.'

'This is DC Trent,' said Ian, smiling at the female officer and waving her to a chair. 'You won't mind her taking notes, Bel?'

Bel shook her head, glancing nervously at the notebook which had appeared in the officer's hand.

'So, tell me what happened?'

Bel repeated her story, only stumbling when she got to the body.

'And you'd never seen him before?'

Bel shook her head.

'Had you, Libby?'

'I'm afraid I didn't look,' she said. 'But as Ben said, what was someone doing up there? And why didn't Richard see it?'

'It was hidden,' said Bel. 'It was only because Jeff-dog sniffed it out…'

'Richard's staying in the Hoppers's Huts?' said Ian. 'I

124

shall have to talk to him.'

'Have you seen it?' asked Libby. 'Do you know who it is?'

'There's no confirmation as yet.' Ian stood up. 'I'll go and speak to Richard and send Ben and Michael back in.'

DC Trent gave them a vague smile and followed Ian from the room. After a moment, Ben, Fran and Michael came back in.

'He knows who it is,' said Libby.

'He didn't say that, Ma.' Bel sounded stronger.

'He said "no confirmation". That means he does, but the body has to be formally identified.'

'Someone we know, then?' said Ben.

'Bel would have recognised it,' said Fran. 'She's met everyone connected with this business.'

'Someone connected with Duncan Lucas who we don't know about then,' said Libby. 'Perhaps Ian was right. Lucas was a villain and his murder was nothing to do with the Shakespeare letter.'

'He's talking to Richard,' said Gilbert. 'Why is that?'

'Because Richard's staying near where the body was found,' said Ben. 'Ian wants to know if he saw or heard anything.'

'There's nothing much there to see or hear,' said Libby. 'You can't even see the huts from here, or from the top of my lane.'

'Is it a short cut to anywhere?' asked Michael.

'No. Just from here to, as Lib said, the top of our lane. Nowhere else.'

Richard came in looking shaken.

'I'm beginning to think it's not a good thing to be connected to this family,' he said.

'Something a lot of us have said for a long time,' said Andrew. 'But quite exciting, nevertheless.'

'If you can call murder exciting,' muttered Richard.

'I take it you didn't see or hear anything?' said Fran. 'Last night or this morning?'

'Nothing.' Richard shook his head. 'I came back here with Michael, then I went straight across to the hut. Had a nightcap and that was that. This morning I came over here, Hetty gave me some breakfast and I went straight to the dining room.'

'Will he ask us to look at the body?' asked Michael. 'In case we knew him?'

'I don't know,' said Libby. 'It all depends on whether he actually knows who it is.'

'That was a knock on the front door,' said Fran. 'Shall I go?'

'I will.' Ben was already out of his chair.

'That sounds like Tristan,' whispered Libby, as they all listened intently. 'Yes it is. Coming in here.'

Ben ushered a scared-looking Tristan into the kitchen.

'Well, at least it isn't him,' muttered Michael.

'I'll go and tell Ian,' said Ben.

'What's going on?' asked Tristan. 'There are police...'

'DCI Connell will explain,' said Fran. 'Don't worry.'

Ben came in with DC Trent.

'Mr Scott?' she asked. 'Would you follow me, please?'

'Did he send for him?' Libby asked, as Tristan left the room. 'Ian, I mean?'

'I don't know.' Ben shrugged.

They sat in silence for a few moments, then Andrew stood up.

'Do you think the police will want to talk to us any more? Only we might as well go back to Nethergate if we can't do anything here.'

'I'd wait a bit,' said Fran.

'In that case, shall I make coffee?' asked Libby.

There were murmurs of assent, and Libby went to the

Aga to start preparations. When the coffee was made, Ben took a cup to Hetty and everyone else waited once more in silence, until finally, Ian returned, without Tristan or DC Trent.

'I think I can tell you now. Tristan Scott has gone to identify the body, but we believe it to be Gideon Law.'

'The money man from National Shakespeare?' said Libby, amid gasps from the others. Gideon Law then had to be explained to those who hadn't heard the name before.

'We think so.' Ian looked round at the puzzled faces. 'I can't say much more now, so perhaps you'd like to go back home, or back to the dining room. We're going to set up a proper incident room in the church hall again, with Mrs Cole's permission.'

'Mrs Cole?' asked Richard.

'Our vicar,' said Ben. 'OK, Ian. Will you keep us informed?'

'As far as I can,' said Ian, with a smile for Bel. 'You did well, Bel. I might have to talk to you again, but you can go now.'

Michael, Richard, Gilbert and Andrew returned to the dining room, Ben went back to his brewery and Fran, Bel and Libby remained round the kitchen table.

'So, Gideon Law,' said Libby. 'Who the police have already spoken to.'

'Remind us,' said Fran. 'Now he's come firmly into the picture.'

'The theory – that we worked out, anyway – was that Lucas and Law had been in touch, apparently about the letter. Before Lucas submitted it to the V&A. Whether they hatched the plan for the tour between them or what, we don't know.'

'And Michael never heard of him,' said Bel.

'No. So as far as we know, he might have been in

127

touch with Nathan Vine in the past. But why was he killed?'

'Because he knew the letter was a fake?' suggested Fran.

'That doesn't work. Everyone knows the letter's a fake now,' said Libby.

'So,' said Fran frowning, 'he must have known who set it up. And therefore, who killed Lucas.'

'And that somebody,' said Libby, 'is down here in Steeple Martin.'

'Oh, God, Mother!' said Bel. 'How do you do it?'

'Oi!' said Libby. 'Nothing to do with me!'

'It really isn't, Bel,' said Fran. 'Really, nothing.'

'But you always manage to get mixed up in it!' wailed Bel. 'It's not natural.'

'No, of course it's not, darling. But I can't help that. I'm just sorry you got mixed up in it, too.'

'If only I hadn't come down here with Michael.' Bel swirled her coffee moodily. 'What do I need a man in my life for, anyway?'

Fran and Libby exchanged amused glances.

'Well, now,' said Libby. 'That *is* natural.' She stood up. 'Shall I go home and make some soup for lunch?'

'What about the men?' asked Fran.

'They can fend for themselves. There's a perfectly good pub, not to mention Harry's, and they're here on their own behalfs – behalves? So not our problem.'

'Well, they are trying to find out something for Ben's family,' said Fran.

'Not really,' said Libby. 'Neither Ben nor Hetty really care. Are you coming, Bel?'

'No, Adam's here today, so I'll go down and see him. He can cheer me up.'

'Gee, thanks.' Libby made a face. 'You're feeling better now, then?'

'Yes.' Bel looked down. 'It was just – a shock. You know.'

'No need to be ashamed of it,' said Fran. 'It's a horrible thing, finding a body.'

The three of them walked down the drive together after bidding farewell to Hetty and Ben, and left Bel at The Pink Geranium.

'What now, then?' said Fran, as they strolled towards Allhallow's Lane. 'There are an awful lot of police cars in Maltby Close.'

'Incident room again,' said Libby. 'Poor Beth. And the residents, of course.'

'Oh, I'm sure they love it,' said Fran. 'A bit of excitement.'

'That's true. Flo does, I bet.'

Flo Carpenter was Hetty's oldest friend, who now lived with Hetty's brother Lenny and kept the residents of Maltby Close, all over sixty, in order.

'So, you said what now,' said Libby. 'What do you think?'

'I don't know.' Fran stared up at the sky. 'We've no way in to the investigation. I know you wanted to ask questions, but that was before this latest development. We don't know anyone to ask.'

'And your psychic antennae aren't twitching?'

'Not in the slightest. It's shut down again.'

'Oh well,' said Libby with a sigh. 'Time to make soup. Lentil and tomato or leek and potato?'

It was halfway through the afternoon, when Fran was thinking about making her way home, when there was a knock at the door.

To Libby's surprise, Bel stood on the doorstep with Michael, both looking a little furtive.

'Why didn't you use your key?'

'Michael didn't want to just walk in,' said Bel. 'He –

er – he's got something to tell you. I think.'

'Sit down, then,' said Libby, as she and Fran resumed their seats. 'What's up?'

'It's a bit difficult,' said Michael, looking sideways at Bel. 'It's something I found.'

'Yes? Found where?'

'In the – er – archive material.' Michael cleared his throat.

'Richard's stuff? Or the county's?'

'Well, Richard's stuff, but I don't think he knows it's there.'

'What is it?' Libby looked from one to the other. 'Come on, tell me.'

'It's a draft. Of the Shakespeare letter.'

Chapter Seventeen

'The – what?' gasped Libby.

'Are you sure?' said Fran.

'Yes. It was in with a mass of other stuff tucked into a large manilla envelope.' Michael shook his head. 'It didn't look important at first, all the other papers were letters about household accounts and the accounts themselves dating from last century, when Ben's father was alive. They went back to the war.'

'And this was with them? So it dates back that far?' said Libby.

'I don't think so. There was some stuff that came from later – when Richard's father took the archive. I think it's from then. It hasn't been aged, or anything, it's simply a draft of what the letter says. It's obviously been researched – there are an awful lot of corrections.'

'You must take it to the police,' said Libby. 'This is evidence.'

'But it means Richard's father must have done it,' said Bel. 'That's why we didn't know what to do.'

'He's been so enjoying going through everything,' said Michael. 'It didn't seem fair.'

'Fair or not, it's got to be done,' said Fran. 'And you must tell Richard.'

'Yes, you really must,' said Libby. 'Go on, go now. Take the draft to the incident room, then go and tell Richard. I'm sure he'll be upset, but he'll be even more upset if you don't tell him.'

Looking miserable, Bel and Michael stood up.

'All right,' said Bel, 'but don't blame us if he's

furious.'

They left on leaden feet and Fran and Libby looked at each other.

'Well?' said Libby. 'What about Richard now?'

'He wouldn't be so idiotic as to leave evidence like that lying around,' said Fran. 'No, it can't be anything to do with him.'

'But if that's the case, how did it get there?' said Libby.

It was almost five o'clock by the time Libby had completed her round of phone calls apprising all interested parties that there wasn't going to be a summer show this year, and no word had been heard from Bel or Michael. Ben arrived back from the Manor with the news that Tristan had confirmed that the body was that of Gideon Law and that Ian had said he would meet them as usual in the pub later that evening.

'But he said nothing about the draft letter?' said Libby.

'Not a thing. I don't think he'd been back to the incident room, though. I expect he knows by now.'

'He'll want to talk to Richard again. Who won't be happy.'

'I don't expect he will,' said Ben.

'Oh, well,' said Libby, 'I suppose I ought to start thinking about dinner.'

Dinner, however, was interrupted.

'Have you heard about this letter?' Richard, accompanied by Bel and Michael, stood on the doorstep.

Suppressing a sigh, Libby stood back. 'Come in. We were just having dinner.'

'Oh, I'm sorry, Ma,' said Bel. 'We'll come back later.'

'No,' said Ben, coming up behind Libby. 'Come in. We'll have to talk about it. I'll put our plates in the oven.'

Once established in the sitting room, Richard spoke again.

'Did Michael tell you about the draft?' Libby nodded. 'What did you think?'

Ben looked at Libby. 'We didn't know what to think. Has Ian spoken to you?'

'Oh, yes.' Richard sounded bitter. 'He seems to think I must have known about it. How could I? I've never been through this stuff before.'

'I know,' said Michael. 'That was why I was so nervous about telling you.'

'It does look as though your father must have known, though,' said Ben. 'He was the one who was so interested in the archive.'

'You're accusing him now, are you?' said Richard.

'Not exactly,' said Libby, 'but surely he must have seen it. We're not saying he had anything to do with it.'

'Oh, it's a complete mess.' Richard put his head in his hands. 'I don't know what to do.'

'Will Ian let you go home?' asked Ben. 'No, I suppose he won't.'

'He wants to take everything we've got to a police expert,' said Michael. 'He thinks he should establish a link between Richard's father and Nathan Vine. Although I don't see how he can do that. They're both dead.'

'And Duncan Lucas is dead, too, so nothing can be tracked back from him,' said Libby.

'Well, they've got all sorts of resources,' said Bel. 'They'll go through Law's papers and stuff and be bound to find something. Don't suppose it'll link up with your father, though, Richard.'

'I hope not.' Richard turned bleak eyes on her. 'It's a nightmare.'

'Come on.' Bel stood up. 'We all need to eat. Let's go and get something at the pub.'

Richard and Michael nodded.

'And we might see you later,' said Ben. 'Try not to

worry, Richard.'

'I expect I'll go back to my hut after dinner,' said Richard. 'I don't feel like socialising.'

'Just as well, really,' said Libby, closing the door after them, 'if Ian's coming to the pub.'

After finishing their rather dried up dinner, Libby rang Fran to tell her about Richard's visit and the results of her Summer Show phone calls.

'The only one who was sticky was The Alexandria. She said – you know, that woman they've put in charge now – that we were already in the publicity and we should have let them know earlier.'

'Well, we – you – should, really.'

'But we haven't got a contract or anything,' said Libby. 'And now I feel that we've let them down.'

'Point that out and let them sort it out themselves,' said Fran.

'I have. And now we've said we'll meet Ian in the pub and Richard might be there. This could get very awkward.'

'I did have a thought on the way home.' Fran spoke slowly. 'That draft could have a different interpretation.'

'It could?'

'Couldn't it have been someone – Nathan, perhaps – writing it down to work out what it said? Remember, it's apparently in a crabbed hand and rather archaic language. Might you not write it out? And the corrections could be almost better explained that way.'

'Or Russell himself could have done it!' said Libby, excited. 'Oh, wow! Yes – suppose he found it in the archive material and tried to make sense of it.'

'And then – what? Passed it on to Nathan Vine?'

'Why not? Sold it, maybe, because, as we've said, he was hard up. And then Nathan took it to the V&A. That makes far more sense than any other interpretation.'

'But how did it get into the archive material in the first place if that's the case? Ben's father wouldn't have put it there.'

'Oh, I don't know. It's your theory, after all. Can I tell Ian?'

'If you think he'd be interested.'

'Oh, he would,' said Libby. 'He's still hoping you'll have a breakthrough with your moment. I suppose this wasn't that sort of thing?'

'No, it was just logical thought process,' said Fran. 'I do have them occasionally.'

On the way to the pub, Libby told Ben Fran's idea.

'She's right, you know,' he said. 'It makes more sense than the other interpretation. And could be that Russell, and possibly Nathan, both thought it was genuine.'

'That would relieve Richard,' said Libby. 'Can't believe Ian or his minions haven't thought of that, though.'

'No. I expect someone has. And now we have to decide how much we tell Patti and Anne.'

Every Wednesday, the Reverend Patti Pearson came to Steeple Martin from her parish down the coast to spend time with her friend Anne Douglas and catch up with Bethany Cole and Libby and Ben. Ian often called in on Wednesdays, and on occasion Fran and Guy would be there too.

'They'll know a fair amount already,' said Libby. 'Beth will have told them.'

'But the family connection,' said Ben. 'That's rather a private matter.'

'We'll see how Ian wants to play it,' said Libby. 'And if you want to keep the family connection quiet, we will.'

'It's not so much me as Richard,' said Ben, opening the door of the pub. 'Here we go.'

Patti and Anne had already arrived, fresh from dinner

at The Pink Geranium, sitting with Bel and Michael, who looked slightly ill-at-ease. Libby and Ben were greeted with relief.

'So how much have you told them?' asked Libby.

'Nothing,' said Bel, looking surprised.

'We didn't ask,' said Anne, swivelling her wheelchair to make more room for Libby.

'We often discuss things with Anne and Patti,' Libby explained to Michael. 'After all, we met when Patti had a particularly nasty murder in her church.'

'Another murder?' Michael looked bewildered.

'Par for the course,' said Ben, arriving with drinks. 'Even Ian doesn't mind them learning about – well, whatever's going on.

'I gather it's about this fake letter?' said Patti. 'And there's been a murder, too?'

'Has there been a lot about it in the press?' asked Libby. 'I haven't been following it.'

'Not that much,' said Anne. 'We've both looked, obviously, but it seems to be being kept low-key.'

'It's complicated,' said Ben. 'I don't think we ought to say anything until Ian's here. So how have you two been?'

A few pleasantries were exchanged and Michael's presence explained, then Bel stood up.

'I think Michael and I might go back to the Manor now, if you don't mind.'

Michael nodded. 'Richard was looking... I think I ought to check on him.'

They left and Anne turned bright eyes on to Libby.

'Richard? What's going on?'

'Shhh, Anne,' said Patti.

'No, it's all right,' said Ben with a sigh. 'Richard's my cousin. He's here for a visit.'

'And to see the play,' added Libby.

136

'That's not all, though, is it?' asked Anne. 'It's another mystery.'

'Let's wait for Ian,' said Libby firmly.

They didn't have long to wait.

'It's all right, Ben,' he said as he came in. 'I'll have beer. I'm staying over again.' He sat down and smiled at Patti and Anne. 'And you two are dying of curiosity, aren't you?'

'Well, Anne is,' said Patti.

'So are you,' said Anne. 'And they wouldn't tell us anything, Ian.'

Ian gave them a quick resume of his case so far, playing down any involvement of Ben's family.

'So this letter is a fake but based in reality?' said Anne when he'd finished. 'Shakespeare really came to your house, Ben?'

'Looks like it,' said Ben.

'When the house belonged to someone called Titus Watt,' said Libby. 'Have you heard of him, Anne?'

'Yes, but I didn't know he had a house here.' Anne worked for the big library in Canterbury. 'I'll look him up.'

'Andrew – remember Andrew Wylie? – he and a chap called Gilbert, also an academic, have been researching the archives at Maidstone,' said Ben. 'Just for interest's sake.'

'But Ben and Hetty don't want publicity,' said Ian. 'They don't want the house besieged by the public.'

'No, of course,' said Anne, looking disappointed.

'So your cousin's also interested in the archive?' said Patti. 'He's come to investigate too?'

'More or less,' said Ian. 'His father was the family archivist, although he – Richard - knew nothing about it.'

'Exciting,' said Anne.

'Or not,' said Patti, looking at Ben. 'I don't think we

137

should ask any more, Annie.'

'Oh, I don't know,' said Ian. 'A fresh perspective, perhaps? On the fake, at least.'

'Fran's had a thought about that,' said Libby. 'I was going to tell you.'

'Go ahead,' said Ian. 'Always ready to hear Fran's thoughts. Ben, do you want to tell Patti and Anne about the letter?'

'No, you tell them,' said Ben. 'You'll be clearer.'

Ian explained about the draft letter being found among the archive documents, managing to avoid planting suspicion on either Richard or his father.

'So you think this Richard's father made the fake?' said Anne.

'Well, probably not,' said Libby, hurrying in with Fran's alternate theory.

Ian smiled. 'A theory – no, a likely scenario – we'd come to ourselves. Do you agree?'

Ben looked relieved.

'It sounds far more plausible,' said Patti. 'Why didn't everyone assume that in the first place?'

Ben, Libby and Ian looked at one another.

'I think,' said Libby slowly, 'it was because Michael found it and jumped to the conclusion that it was proof of Richard's father's guilt. I suppose I accepted it and it went from there.'

'But I would have questioned it anyway,' said Ian. 'However, if you think Richard's mind would be set at rest by this, by all means tell him. Have you got his mobile number?'

'I have,' said Ben. 'Excuse me.' He moved away from the table, phone already at his ear.

'Well, that feels better,' said Libby. 'Thanks, Patti.'

'I didn't do anything,' said Patti. 'It was Ian who confirmed Fran's theory.'

'Well, we don't know for absolutely sure,' said Ian, 'no one was there at the time, not even Richard.'

'No,' said Libby. 'He said he didn't have much to do with his father, and Hetty said much the same. Russell didn't have time for children. Ben didn't know him.'

'On the surface,' said Anne, 'it just looks as if this Lucas person tried to get something out of the National Shakespeare tour. But what?'

'That's what puzzles me, Anne,' said Libby. 'He was only loaning them the letter, not selling it.'

'But it would have increased the interest, and then if he wanted to sell it the price would have gone up,' said Patti.

Ian nodded, smiling.

'Is that what you think, Ian?' said Libby.

'What I think doesn't matter,' said Ian. 'But as I told you, London are going through his affairs now.'

'Hoping they'll find criminal connections?' said Patti.

Ben arrived back at the table.

'Richard feels a lot happier,' he said, sitting down. 'Let's hope the police can confirm it.'

Chapter Eighteen

'You know what we've never gone into,' said Ben on the phone to Libby on Thursday morning, 'why Nathan Vine's number and address was in Dad's book.'

'So we haven't. Has Ian?'

'He hasn't said so.'

'We did try the number, didn't we?'

'No, we looked up the address. We didn't try the number, but I doubt if that's still in use. Certainly not by Vine.'

'In that case, we ought to investigate,' said Libby. 'How do we go about it?'

'We ought to leave it to Ian.'

'No, he's probably got too much to do,' said Libby. 'Especially now with Gideon Law's death as well.'

'That's your excuse for being nosy.'

'You mentioned it first.'

'All right.' Libby could hear the smile in Ben's voice. 'You and Fran have a go.'

Libby sat for a while thinking before ringing Fran.

'So how do we do it?' she asked, after bringing Fran up to date on last night's meeting with Ian and Ben's new idea.

'If Hetty doesn't know, I can't think.' Fran was silent for a moment. 'Unless there are any old friends of Greg's in the village who might know?'

'No one's come forward saying they know anything about the house,' said Libby.

'No one's asked, though, have they?'

'No, and it hasn't been made much of that it was the

house that Shakespeare visited,' said Libby. 'What about the old biddies' network?'

'I wish you wouldn't call them that,' said Fran.

'It's what Flo and Hetty call them. And – oh! I just remembered! Hetty said ask Flo, memory like an elephant. And Ben was going to ask Pete. I don't think he ever did.'

'Right, that's where you start,' said Fran.

'Aren't you coming?'

'I'm in charge of the shop today. Guy, believe it or not, is actually painting. Keep me posted.'

Libby sat thinking some more after Fran had rung off. The "old biddies" were, in fact, led by Flo Carpenter, Hetty's best friend, and included Hetty herself, plus two village ladies, Dolly Webley from New Barton Lane and Una Brent from Steeple Lane. Edie, the mother of a friend from out of the village, Lewis Osbourne-Walker, often joined them. Edie, a comparative newcomer, wouldn't be able to tell her anything, but the other three might. Even, thought Libby, Joe and Nella up at Cattlegreen Nurseries might know. He seemed to know about all the old houses in the area. She decided to start there.

As by now it was almost lunchtime, she decided to drive up to the Nurseries, where the 'boy', Owen, would be sure to offer her something. In winter it was always hot chocolate, which it might be today, but that was always comforting, and it wasn't the warmest of summer days.

As she drove into the yard, it was Owen who came to meet her with a wide smile.

'Hello, Libby!' He held her door open for her. 'You come to see Dad?'

'Yes, actually, Owen,' said Libby, a little disconcerted. 'Is he in the shop?'

'Yes. Come on. I'll go and make your chocolate.'

Libby followed him, grinning.

141

'So what is it this time, then, young Libby?' Joe, a large and comfortable countryman, perched on the edge of his counter. 'More anonymous letters? All those old houses?'

'Actually, yes, Joe. Old houses, the Manor in particular.'

'Ah. That'll be that letter, then.'

'What?' Libby was startled. 'What do you know about it?'

'All that about some letter and Shakespeare bringing one of his plays here. In all the papers, weren't it?'

'Well, yes it was, but -'

'Weren't true. But we reckon it was.'

'What?' Libby was more than startled now.

'Oh, not that letter. Someone pulling a fast one, that were, weren't it? No, but we reckoned... See, we remembered when old Greg had that bloke round.'

'What bloke? What are you talking about?' Libby automatically took the hot mug Owen offered her and winced. 'Ow! Sorry, Owen. Go on, Joe – what bloke?'

'Don't Hetty remember?'

'She says not. What was his name?'

'Oh, I never knew his name. But he made a bit of a fuss, see.'

'What sort of a fuss?'

'Far as I remember, he wanted to find out about the house, see. Its history an' that. He reckoned someone famous had lived there.'

'And what happened?'

Joe shrugged. 'Dunno. You want to ask old Flo. I was a bit young, see. She was Hetty's mate, wasn't she?'

'Still is,' said Libby. 'Hetty said to ask her. Said she'd got a memory like an elephant.'

'There you are, then. What do you want to know for?'

'Well, we didn't know anything about it, and if

142

Shakespeare really did come here – well, Ben would like to know.'

'I reckon you would, too, gal,' said Joe with a grin. 'Now, was you buying anything today?'

Libby drove back into Steeple Martin and parked in Maltby Close. Flo came to her door, ever-present cigarette in hand, and frowned at her.

'You didn't drive round here, did you, gal? Gettin' lazy?'

'No, I've come from the Nurseries, Flo. I wanted to have a word.'

'Ah. That'll be about that bloke, won't it?'

Libby, astonished as always by the osmosis by which information passed round the village, nodded. She had no doubt that Flo knew exactly which bloke she wanted to know about.

'How did you know?' she asked as Flo led her into the crowded sitting room. Lenny, Hetty's brother, sitting in his usual chair by the electric fire, on summer and winter, grinned at her.

'Thought we'd be seeing you,' he said.

'Go on, then, Flo. What do you know, and how do you know it?'

'Het rang me up the other day. Said did I remember some bloke who might have come to see Greg about the house. Course I did. Years ago, mind.'

'Why didn't she tell us?'

Flo shrugged. 'Dunno. Is it important?'

'It could be. Do you remember his name?'

'I didn't, but Het had it. Hang on, I wrote it down.' She fumbled for a notebook on the table by her chair. 'Keep this for me crosswords,' she explained. 'Ah, here we are. Vine. Nathan Vine. Funny name.'

'What do you remember about him?'

'He tipped up at the Manor, like, wantin' to know

about the house. Who owned it, see?'

'And Greg couldn't tell him?'

'No. Het fetched him from the office, and this Vine sat there with me in the kitchen, all toffee-nosed. I left when Greg came in, weren't my business. But Het said after he sent him away with a flea in his ear.'

'Why did he keep his address then?'

'I reckon he said he'd let him know if he found anything. Course, that weren't enough for him, was it?'

'What do you mean?'

'Went round the village, didn't he? Askin'.'

'Why has no one come forward with this?' asked Libby.

'Didn't know anyone wanted to know,' said Flo.

'But you must have heard about all the fuss? The fake letter?'

'Thought that was to do with them Shakespeare folk,' said Lenny. 'Not the Manor.'

'I see.' Libby reflected that the name Nathan Vine hadn't been publicised and the Manor connection played down, so that was probably true.

'Do you remember who he asked?' she spoke again to Flo.

'Not off the top of me head,' said Flo, 'but I tell you what, I'll call a meetin'.'

'A meeting?'

'The old girls. Una and Dolly an' them. You can come. You'll enjoy it.'

'Will they remember?'

'We all remember things back then better than yesterday,' said Lenny. 'None of us ain't senile yet.'

'I'll try and get 'em fer tomorrow,' said Flo. 'That all right for you?'

Libby left Maltby Close, parked the car at home and wandered back to The Pink Geranium. Harry was sitting at the table in the window staring blankly at an open laptop.

'No customers?' said Libby, opening the door.

'Calm before the storm,' said Harry. 'The hordes come in late afternoon. Special arrangement.'

'The Shakespeare lot?'

'Yes, them. Bloody luvvies.'

'Oh, go on! You love them.'

'Yeah, well.' Harry stood up. 'Want something to eat?'

'If there's anything going.'

'The usual try-it-out-soup.'

'Lovely,' said Libby.

When Harry had brought two bowls and a bottle of wine to the table, she launched into her story.

'So you see,' she concluded, 'we might actually be able to find out what the connection was with Greg and then with the archive material.'

'It's all a bit of a bloody muddle, if you ask me,' said Harry. 'How would the village know if this Vine got in touch with – what was his name?'

'Russell. Greg's cousin.'

'Yes, him.'

'I don't know, but we might get a clue. Everyone's flailing around in the dark.'

'Well, the dishy Ian will be looking into the victims' backgrounds, won't he? He'll turn up something there.'

'But will it help? Will it find a motive?'

'Will a motive help?'

'Well, of course. We've no idea who killed either Duncan Lucas or Gideon Law. Lucas's killer could be anybody, connected or unconnected, but Law was actually killed on Ben's land. That really has to be someone connected.'

'But connected to what?'

'To this case. And even if the fake letter isn't the

reason that Lucas was killed, the fact that he was in touch with National Shakespeare and Law was a member of the board, or whatever, means there has to be a connection.'

Harry sat back in his chair and scratched his head. 'Damned if I can see what, though. How's this Richard shaping up?'

'Shaping up? He seems really nice. Fran was a bit wary at first. A bit suspicious.'

'Was she now.' Harry raised his eyebrows and leaned forward. 'And what did we think of that, petal?'

'She's changed her mind now. It was just that Ben found him through social media and she wondered if he was really who he said he was. But Ian's made sure he is. And anyway, what would he have to gain? Technically, all the archive material belongs to Ben, even if he doesn't want it. Have you heard any gossip over the nachos?'

'Not much. The actors weren't really that interested as long as nothing upset their run. And the murders seem hardly to have impinged on their collective consciousness.'

'Poor Ben's getting bothered. It's a long time since his family were involved in anything – well, questionable.'

'It's not him, though, is it? Greg gave all the stuff to Richard's dad. Anything nasty comes out of that woodshed.'

'It looks as if the letter was forged knowing about the archive material, though.'

'Yes, pet, but while it was in Richard's dad's possession, not Greg's.' Harry waved the half empty bottle of red wine at her. 'Drop more?'

'Oh, go on, then,' said Libby with a sigh.

Libby wandered home after her impromptu lunch and called first Ben, then Fran to update them. Ben was dubious about the collective village memory, but Fran was enthusiastic.

146

'Just what we want,' she said. 'Remember how good they've been in the past. I bet they come up with something. Let me know.'

'If Flo organises a meeting tomorrow, will you be able to come? Or will Guy still be creating?'

'Even if he is, Sophie's on call tomorrow,' said Fran. 'Are you going to tell Ian?'

'I don't know,' said Libby. 'He might tell me to stop.'

'Why would he? You're just talking to the village. And Nathan Vine isn't a victim, is he?'

'I suppose not. Sounds as if he was a bit of a pain, according to Flo.'

'And she would know,' said Fran with a laugh.

But Libby got the chance to tell Ian about her investigations when he turned up with Ben at the end of the afternoon.

'Ben tells me you've been asking your village ladies,' he said, settling into a chair.

'Well, I started with Joe up at Cattlegreen,' said Libby. 'Remember him?'

'One of your network, yes, of course.'

'He remembered, although not the detail, and he suggested Flo. And she said Hetty had asked her about Nathan Vine. You remember she suggested asking Flo the other day? And,' she said turning to Ben, 'why didn't she tell us Flo remembered?'

'Probably didn't think it was important after we'd got in touch with Richard.'

'Anyway, she remembered and suggested this meeting with the village ladies. They've helped before.'

'Never underestimate a village,' said Ian. 'I should have thought of it before. And now, I have some news, too.'

Chapter Nineteen

'Duncan Lucas,' said Ian, 'was a well-known operator under a variety of aliases. I don't know why he didn't come up on someone's radar before this, but it doesn't look as if he was Nathan Vine's relative.'

'How did he get hold of the fake, then?' asked Ben.

'That we haven't confirmed yet.'

'Has no one seen a will? Didn't the V&A check when he presented it? They have to have valid provenance, surely?' said Libby.

'That's being looked into,' said Ian. 'The situation's opened up a bigger can of worms than anyone would have thought – it looks as if Lucas was part of an international art fraud ring.'

Libby gasped.

'Art fraud?' said Ben.

'They deal in forgeries, fake antiques – anything the customer wants. It looks as though that's what this is all about.'

'So he got hold of it for that specific reason?' said Libby.

'The Arts and Antiques Unit are looking into it. They'll have to look at Nathan Vine very seriously, now, so any information your ladies can come up with will be most useful.' Ian stood up.

'What about my dad?' said Ben.

'I should think any trail there is will stop with Russell Wilde,' said Ian. 'I really cannot imagine Greg Wilde being involved with anything even moderately fraudulent, can you?'

'That's bias!' said Libby with a grin.

'So it is,' said Ian. 'Now I'm off home. I can't keep taking advantage of Hetty, and besides, my emergency wardrobe has run out.'

'And we still don't know where home is,' said Libby, as they closed the door after him.

'The fact that we don't, even after all this time, means he really wants to keep his private life private,' said Ben. 'Don't pry.'

'I thought we were part of his private life,' said Libby mournfully. 'He's part of ours.'

Flo called just after the news had finished on television.

'Meetin' set up tomorrow fer eleven. All right with you? Arst Hetty along, even if she don't remember. It is her family.'

'Can Fran come?'

'Wouldn't expect otherwise. What about that Ian?'

'He knows about it, but the ladies would feel better without him there, wouldn't they?'

'All fancy 'im,' said Flo. 'Still, spect you're right. Carpenter's, then. Eleven.'

Carpenter's Hall was part of the original barn buildings in Maltby Close, now used as a meeting place and venue for occasional entertainments for the residents of the Close, and sometimes for the wider village.

'What do you think they'll remember?' asked Ben.

'No idea, but if Flo remembers him there might be something. Worth a try, anyway.'

Friday morning, and almost the end of The Glover's Men's run of Twelfth Night at the Oast Theatre.

'I've just remembered,' said Libby, when Fran arrived from Nethergate. 'Nathan Vine lived here, didn't he? In Steeple Lane. No wonder Una knew him.'

'What I'm wondering,' said Fran, 'is when he moved

here. From what you've told me, he didn't live here when he first made contact.'

'So he must have moved here afterwards,' said Libby. 'To make his search easier? But Greg wouldn't have been pleased. He didn't want anything to do with the history.'

'I expect that's why he handed it all over to Russell,' said Fran. 'You know, "here you are, you deal with this madman." That would make sense.'

'It would,' said Libby thoughtfully. 'I can't think why it slipped my mind.'

'There's been a lot going into it,' said Fran.

'Going into what?'

'Your mind.'

They turned into the high street and crossed the road just as a flotilla of Glover's Men crossed the other way. A couple greeted Libby.

'Meeting with the suits,' one explained. 'I think they want to ask for an extra performance.'

'Really?' Libby raised her eyebrows. 'Even after all the problems?'

'People got really interested,' said another actor. 'They've had more ticket requests than they could cope with, and we were already sold out.'

'Why don't people go to one of the other venues?' asked Fran.

'Because this is the one where all the interesting stuff has happened,' said the first actor, the irrepressible Feste. 'Will you say yes?'

'It will depend on what we've got coming in,' said Libby. 'You'll have to ask Ben in the office.'

'Not us, love,' said Feste. 'The suits!' And with a wave, he was gone.

'They'd better be bloody nice to us after the last time we crossed swords,' muttered Libby, as she and Fran turned into Maltby Close. As they did so, her mobile began to ring.

'It's me!' spluttered Ben.

'Oh, dear,' said Libby. 'The suits have been on.'

'Yes – how did you know? If by that you mean "management"?'

'Fran and I just bumped into the actors. They said they wanted to ask for another day.'

'Yes – and they had the bloody infernal cheek to summon me to their presence in the hall.'

'What did you say?'

'If they wanted to speak to me they could come up to the Manor and wait for me in the theatre foyer.'

'Excellent! And?'

'They blustered and said they'd get back to me. Honestly! Some people.'

'I suppose they think we'll go for the prestige.'

'Prestige my -! They've been nothing but trouble.'

'Well, they haven't actually, Ben. The acting company have been fine. It's the trouble they've unwittingly caused.'

'I suppose so,' said Ben with a sigh. 'Anyway, what do you think? Do we let them have another day?'

'What's coming in next week?'

'Nothing until Friday, then it's a one-nighter.'

'So we've got room? Well, why not? Make 'em pay through the nose, though.'

'So what happened?' asked Fran. Libby told her, and they both arrived at Carpenter's Hall laughing, just as Tristan Scott came hurtling from behind the church.

'Libby!'

'Here we go,' whispered Libby, and put on her sternest face. 'Tristan?'

'I was wondering,' he panted, skidding to a breathless halt in front of her, 'if you could pop up to see the committee for a moment?'

'No, Tristan, I couldn't. I'm just about to go into a meeting, and I believe Ben has already told your management team they will have to go to the theatre and wait until he has time to see them.'

Tristan opened and closed his mouth in fish-like distress.

'Don't worry,' said Fran kindly. 'I'm sure if they're polite and ask nicely Ben will be reasonable. But don't let them try and browbeat him. It won't go down well.'

'I told you before, Tristan,' said Libby. 'They may be good at making money, but as for people management, forget it. Chocolate teapots spring to mind. Come on, Fran.'

They opened the door of Carpenter's Hall and left him standing open mouthed outside.

'Do you think he'll toughen up eventually?' said Fran.

'I hope so, for his sake,' said Libby.

At one end of the hall, someone had pulled up a tea trolley, set with cups, pot, huge teapot and cakes.

'Come on, gal,' called Flo. 'We're waitin' for you.'

Dolly Webley, large and comfortable, sat in the biggest chair, knees wide apart, smiling benignly. Una from Steeple Lane, smaller and brighter, peered over the rim of a cup, while Edie from Creekmarsh sat, waiting to be entertained, next to Hetty, who looked slightly uncomfortable.

Flo opened proceedings. 'So, gal, you want to know about this bloke Vine. Well, I told you, he come bothering Hetty and Greg way back, and Greg sent him off with a flea in his ear.'

'Yes, you told me, Flo,' said Libby. 'But what I want to know is how come he ended up living in Steeple Lane?'

This obviously took the wind out of their sails. Hetty sent her best friend a slightly malicious look.

'How did you know that, duck?' said Una.

'I did tell Flo that Nathan's address was in Greg's old book,' said Libby.

'I thought you meant his address before!'

'No, we've no idea where that was,' said Libby. 'So what else do you know about him?'

Flo looked as if she wasn't about to say another word, but Una spoke again.

'Oh, nice enough bloke. Course, that house has gone now. He only rented it from old Terrance.'

'Who's old Terrance?' asked Fran.

'Farmer up beyond Steeple Lane,' said Dolly. 'Family knew him. Wanted to build new houses, see, so he wouldn't sell Farm Cottage, only rent it until he could knock it down. When that Nathan left, that's what he did. Only they wouldn't let him build, see?'

'How long was Nathan there, then?' asked Libby.

'No more'n a coupla years,' said Dolly. 'Was he, Una?'

'No. Spent most of 'is time over at the library or with that other chap what used to come down.'

'Russell Wilde?' suggested Libby.

'Dunno, duck. D'you know, Het?'

Hetty shrugged. 'Don't ask me. I didn't even remember him. All I know is whenever Russell came down I got out of the way.'

'He came round one day asking for Nathan,' said Una. 'He had all these papers with him. I showed him the way to Farm Cottage and he went off as pleased as punch.'

'Did Greg never say anything about this, Hetty?' asked Libby.

'Might have done. He got very fed up with Russell. I expect he got fed up with this Nathan Vine as well. Palmed 'em off on one another.'

'That sounds most likely,' said Libby. 'And then,

153

when Nathan had all the papers, he moved out of the cottage and went back to London, or wherever he'd come from.'

'You're assuming the man who went asking for Vine at Una's was Russell Wilde,' said Fran.

'Stands to reason,' said Flo.

'What happened after this man went to find Nathan, Una? Did he go back to London?'

'Stayed round here, didn't they?' said Dolly. 'Went up to the Manor, didn't he, Het?'

Hetty nodded. 'Told you 'is dad came round when Ben was little, didn't I, gal? Always pokin' about.'

'But Nathan didn't?' said Fran.

Hetty shook her head.

'And did you see him again?'

'No, gal. Russell went off after a bit. But we forgot about him.'

'Where did he go in the village, Dolly? Do you remember?' Libby leant forward.

'This Nathan bloke? Didn't see 'im much. He used to use that photo place a lot.'

'What, the Steeple Martin Studio?' Libby sat back in surprise.

Dolly nodded.

'I wonder why.' Libby frowned.

'To make copies of the documents,' said Fran. 'No handy smartphones in those days. When was it, by the way, Dolly?'

Dolly shrugged and looked at Una and Hetty.

'While Ben was living away,' said Libby. 'If the ladies knew, Hetty, why didn't you?'

'Het didn't go out in the village much,' said Flo. 'Not like us.'

Hetty nodded, and stood up. 'Seems to me you've got what you need, gal. I'll take Edie back for a cuppa, now.'

There was a silence after Hetty and Edie left. Libby looked round at the remaining three and raised her eyebrows.

'Always felt on the outside, like,' said Dolly.

'On account of marrying gentry,' said Una.

'But that sort of thing doesn't matter these days,' said Libby.

'It did when her and Greg got married. Don't forget she already had Susan. Took a time to live that down,' said Flo. 'But then I came down and it was a bit better after that.'

'I'm glad I didn't live in those days,' said Libby.

'Gawd, I'd've liked to see that!' said Flo.

Fran stood up. 'So would I, Flo. Come on, Libby. Let's go and think this over. Thank you ladies.'

'Tell you what, duck,' said Una suddenly, when they were halfway out the door. 'Sandra might know. Her and Elliot got quite friendly with 'im. That Nathan.'

'Really? Elliot was still alive then? Well, thank you, Una,' said Libby, surprised.

'Well, what about that!' she said to Fran once they were outside.

'Sandra Farrow, I take it she meant?' said Fran.

'That's the one! Fancy a trip over to Itching?'

'Where was it she lived? Perseverance Row, wasn't it?'

'I suppose so. Not today, though.'

'No, of course not. Meanwhile, what *did* you think?' asked Libby,

'I don't know. It looks as if Russell and Nathan were in touch and investigating the archive material, and Greg just handed the lot over.'

'But who got hold of who?' asked Libby ungrammatically. 'Were either of them crooks? Was one of them planning a scam?'

'Or did they genuinely find the letter and take it to the experts. Then were disappointed when it turned out to be a fake?'

'Do you know,' said Libby, as they turned into the high street, 'that's what it feels like to me. I suppose I don't want to think that Russell was a crook. And besides, we don't even know yet that Lucas wasn't Nathan's relative.'

Chapter Twenty

Libby sent Ian a text about the village ladies' revelations, then took Fran to the pub for a sandwich.

'Ladies,' said Tim. 'What'll it be?'

When he delivered their order, Libby asked him to sit down.

'I've got work to do, madam,' he said, sitting, nevertheless. 'What is it this time?'

'What do you know about previous tenants of the pub?' asked Libby. 'In the eighties, for instance.'

Tim looked suspicious. 'Not a lot. Why?'

'Not even a name?'

'Oh, I expect I've got the names. What do you want them for?'

'Nothing much.'

'No? Nothing to do with this fake letter that's turned up?'

'Not really,' said Libby, looking at him sideways.

Tim gave her a knowing look and slid off his stool. 'I'll see what I can find.'

'What do you want to know for?' asked Fran.

'To see if the landlord's still around. No one like a landlord for knowing the business of the village.'

'But I thought we'd got enough,' said Fran. 'We know Nathan was around in the village, and we know he was in touch with Russell -'

'We *think* it was Russell,' interrupted Libby.

'Who else would it be?'

'Well, anyway. Now we need to know if Lucas came here. If he met anyone.'

'Like who? He was in touch with National Shakespeare, not the Oast Theatre or the Manor.'

'But he was in Canterbury. He must have been keeping tabs on the progress of the tour.'

'Why, though? The letter was discredited. There was no point in him pursuing it.'

'Well, what about the Law person? He was actually on our ground! Ben's ground.'

'Look, Lib, the police are looking into both Lucas and Law's backgrounds. They'll find whatever evidence there is.'

Libby made an exasperated sound.

'Oh, eat your sandwich,' said Fran.

Fran went home and Libby went up to the Manor, where she found Ben in the estate office.

'We'll be ready to open in September,' he said, looking up from the desk. 'Bought in hops this year, but next year our own. Exciting, isn't it?'

'Yes.' Libby arranged her face into a suitably excited expression.

Ben lifted an eyebrow. 'Well, I'm excited. What happened at your meeting?'

Libby told him.

'So it looks as if Russell was here, got all the stuff from your dad and took it to Nathan up at Farm Cottage.'

'Old Terrance's place? He was living there?'

'That's right. Did you know him?'

'Everyone knew him. Dad wanted to buy the cottage, but he wanted to build new houses and wouldn't sell.'

'Yes, that's what Una said. But they wouldn't give him planning permission.'

'Everyone knew that except Terrance. So Nathan was in the village for some time?'

'Until he'd seen all the archive stuff, anyway,' said Libby. 'Did the Shakespeare suits ask you for an extension, by the way?'

'They did.' Ben grinned. 'I made them pay through the nose. Two performances on Sunday, which means get-out on Monday. Apparently the whole debacle has been extremely fruitful for them. I also pointed out that there was absolutely no reason for us to be accommodating when they had been so rude at the beginning of the run. They had the grace to apologise.'

'So I should think,' said Libby. 'Now I'd better go and tell Hetty to mobilise her work force on Tuesday instead of Monday.'

'Already done. She came in to see me when she came back from Flo's. She remembered things a bit better after talking it over with the others. She's taken Edie into the kitchen for some lunch now.'

'What has she remembered?'

'She just said she remembered now. She didn't say what. But it looks as if not only Nathan but Russell actually stayed in the village, doesn't it? I wonder why I don't remember?'

'Because Hetty told you that Russell didn't have much to do with children, even his own. Nathan was obviously the same. And he would have seen your dad in this very office, wouldn't he? Not in the kitchen or the sitting room.' Libby looked round the room as if expecting to see something imprinted on the walls.

'He would. And I never came in here unless there was a very special reason.' Ben pulled a face. 'Like a punishment.'

'Like the headmaster's office,' said Libby with a grin. 'By the way, did Michael and Bel find anything in the fabric of the building when they were looking?'

'I don't think so. Except that they took samples for dendro-dating.'

'Which they haven't had back yet,' said Libby. 'So we

don't know, still, who had the knowledge to make that fake.'

'Presumably, Nathan had. I doubt if Russell had, or he wouldn't have taken the material to Nathan.'

'It's a shame. Lucas sounds a much nastier type than Nathan. I want it to be him who made the fake,' said Libby.

'And it can't be, because Nathan took it to Gilbert.'

'Oh, well.' Libby got up from her perch on the desk and sighed. 'I can't think of anything else I can do. I can't look into the backgrounds of any of these people, so I'll have to find something else to do.'

'If you're not going to run the Summer Show this year, you could start planning the pantomime,' said Ben. 'You haven't thought about that yet, have you?'

'Oh, the endless grind,' groaned Libby. 'All right, I'll think about it.'

That evening, after an afternoon of slogging through old pantomime scripts and falling asleep over them, Libby was just dishing up fish and chips for supper when the phone rang. Ben answered it and came into the kitchen looking surprised.

'That was the theatre. They said they had a friend of ours in the audience tonight who wanted to know if we could go up and meet him for a drink in the interval.'

'Who?'

'Edward!'

By the time the interval came round, Libby and Ben were sitting at one of the little white wrought iron tables in the foyer bar. Two members of the semi-permanent Oast Theatre Company were manning the bar, and Libby had to restrain herself from telling them how to do the job. Edward came through the auditorium doors and was waved towards Libby and Ben by the bar staff. He greeted Libby with a kiss and shook Ben's hand.

'Here I am then!' he said, sitting down. 'I heard Libby's Loonies were in need of help, so I came along.'

Edward had been delighted when Harry included him in what he called Libby's Loonies, after helping to solve a mystery.

'Did Andrew call you?' asked Libby.

'Yes, he did. Although I don't know that I shall be any use. The house isn't my period, and I'm certainly not a Shakespeare buff.'

'But you were interested anyway?' said Ben. 'Do you want a drink, by the way?'

'No thanks, I've got to sit through the second half yet.' Edward grinned at them both. 'Well, it is nice to see you again. Will you have time to see me afterwards?'

'Of course,' said Ben, 'won't we, Lib? Why don't we wait for you in the pub? Perhaps Harry can come in after he's finished service.' Harry had taken a distinct shine to Edward.

'Great. Trinity term's just finished, so I'm off the hook for a while. Going back to Leicester to see friends, but I don't have to get up in the mornings.'

'Excellent,' said Libby. 'We can see a bit more of you, then.'

'I hope so,' said Edward. 'And now tell me more about the current mystery.'

Between them, they told him the story of the fake letter, Nathan Vine, Duncan Lucas and Ben's family.

'And Gideon Law, don't forget,' said Libby. 'Although we have no idea how he fits in.'

Edward was frowning into the distance.

'Have you thought of something?' asked Ben.

'Maybe,' said Edward slowly. 'Probably means nothing. But we come across it in our side of the business. Remember the things we found in Dark House?'

'The Celtic cross and the ring? What was it? A gunnel

ring?'

'Ginnel ring,' corrected Edward. 'Well, as you found out, they were valuable, and there is a huge market in antique jewellery. An illegal one. And the same goes for paintings and documents. Your policeman must have told you this?'

'He has. And even I thought maybe our forgers might be trying to create some kind of provenance for themselves in order to gain some traction in the underground market,' said Ben.

'We both did,' said Libby.

The five-minute bell rang.

'We'll continue this in the pub,' said Ben. 'Will you have a drink when you get there, Edward?'

'Just coffee.' Edward pulled a face. 'I have to drive back to my digs in Medway.'

Libby and Ben helped clear the bar area and wash up glasses, then strolled down the drive towards the pub.

'Edward's thinking of a scam, isn't he?' said Libby.

'A scam gone wrong,' said Ben. 'Do you think it was originally? When Nathan got hold of the stuff from Russell?'

'Or Russell got hold of it from Dad? Is that how it started? To make money?'

'We have thought of that before,' said Libby.

'But not seriously. If Russell had the idea -'

'But it looks as if Nathan was on the trail of the archive material before Russell,' said Libby.

'I'm not sure,' said Ben. 'I think possibly Russell wanted the stuff, and when he couldn't get it, set Nathan onto Dad. He found the forger, Nathan I mean, but when the V&A rejected it, they decided it was too risky to carry on.'

'Which of them paid for the forgery, then, do you think?' asked Libby.

'No idea. Share of the profits, maybe?'

'Heaven knows. And where does Gideon Law come in?'

'Well, Edward's hardly going to speculate on that, is he? He doesn't know anything about Gideon.'

'Come to that, neither do we,' said Libby gloomily.

'Do you think your visit to Sandra Farrow will help? Have you rung her, by the way?'

'No – do you think I ought to?'

'Of course you should. As I remember her, she was a very proper lady.'

'Who played the ukulele and was a whizz at darts,' said Libby, with a grin.

'You're spending a lot of time in here at the moment,' said Tim as they arrived at the bar. 'Fed up with Allhallow's Lane?'

'No, we're meeting someone,' said Ben. 'A university professor who's here to see the play.'

'Another one?' said Tim. 'You know an awful lot of clever blokes, don't you?'

'We just stumble across them,' said Libby. 'They litter the ground round here.'

Tim's eyes did widen a fraction when Edward entered the bar some half an hour later, but he smilingly produced a cup of coffee and brought it to the table.

'Never knew such people for having tee-total friends,' he said.

Edward laughed. 'Not me! I've just got to drive back to Medway tonight. I really should think about moving to Steeple Martin, shouldn't I?'

His three listeners chorused agreement.

'Didn't you mention something about that before?' said Libby.

'I think I might have done.' Edward flashed his brilliant smile. 'But when I actually started at the

University, I realised how much further away it was than I'd realised. If I'd been based on the Canterbury campus it would have been different.'

'Don't they shunt you around between the two?' asked Ben. 'I rather thought they would.'

'Occasionally,' said Edward. 'But we're not here to talk about that. Tell me more about your Shakespeare Mystery. You see, the more I thought about it, the more I thought the Arts and Antiquities squad at Scotland Yard should be involved.'

Chapter Twenty-one

'I agree,' said Libby. 'In fact, they are.'

'You're right.' Ben frowned into his beer. 'They should have been from the beginning, shouldn't they?'

'Ian said he'd been on to them,' said Libby. 'He told us.'

'I suppose,' said Edward thoughtfully, 'when the original approach was made to the V&A, to – what was his name?'

'Gilbert Harrison,' supplied Libby.

'To Professor Harrison, then, there was no suggestion of any fraud taking place, as the article was withdrawn as soon as doubt was expressed.'

'Exactly,' said Libby, 'which is why I'm disinclined to blame Nathan Vine for anything illegal.'

'Except,' said Ben, 'that he deliberately came down here, rented a cottage and hung around.'

'So did your Uncle Russell,' said Libby.

'And they were in collusion,' said Ben.

'And it looks like a scam,' said Edward. 'I don't know whether the original plan was to palm it off on an organisation like National Shakespeare – I doubt it – but certainly to sell it to the highest bidder. Don't you think so?'

'It looks like it,' said Ben despondently.

'You can't find out anything more about this Nathan Vine?'

'We can't, although I'm hoping to talk to someone who might have known him over the weekend,' said Libby. 'Although I doubt if they'd know about anything dodgy in his background.'

'And even if it was a scam,' said Ben, 'it would then have to be carried on by Duncan Lucas, who said he was Vine's nephew, although we have no proof.'

'Well, surely you know that he was a criminal?' said Edward. 'He was murdered, for goodness' sake!'

'Every murder victim isn't a criminal,' said Libby. 'But he was. Ian said he had various aliases – aliae? – and operated on a large scale. He was surprised that hadn't come up before.'

'But everything points to him being involved in something – well -'

'Dodgy?' suggested Libby. 'Yes, it does. But then we've got Gideon Law being done in, too. And on Ben's land.'

'Well, I must say I can't see how he fits in,' said Edward with a frown, 'but then, I don't know anything about the National Shakespeare set-up. You said he was part of their board?'

'A money man, apparently,' said Ben.

'So concerned with any potential loss of revenue?'

'Suppose so,' said Libby, 'but when he was found, all that had been ironed out. They'd not lost any money, and were capitalising on the Titus Watt connection.'

'Explain that to me again, please?' said Edward. 'Briefly!'

'Titus Watt was an Elizabethan apothecary like John Dee,' said Ben, before Libby could launch into the story, 'and probably, like him, a member of Elizabeth's spy network. There is a genuine reference in the archives to Shakespeare's company coming to the house to perform on one of their tours.'

'And we think,' interrupted Libby, 'that this is the basis for the forged letter. No one could have known about it, because it was in the private archive of Ben's family home until his Dad let his cousin Russell have it, as he was much more interested in the history.'

'And your father didn't want it?' Edward turned horrified eyes on Ben.

'Because it wasn't our family house. We only bought it in the mid-eighteen hundreds,' said Ben, amused.

'Ah.' Edward lapsed into silence.

'And that's why we're uncomfortable,' said Libby. 'Because this Russell might have turned criminal, and not just been interested in the history.'

'Well.' Edward roused himself. 'I can see why Andrew got on to me.'

'You can? But you said it wasn't your period and you weren't a Shakespeare buff,' said Libby.

'Ah.' Edward grinned. 'But I am one of the Arts and Antiquities special advisors.'

Ben and Libby gaped at him.

'Why didn't you say?' said Libby at last.

'Can I get you another drink?' asked Edward standing up. 'You look as though you need it.'

Ben and Libby agreed to another drink, and waited, slightly bemused, for Edward to resume his story.

'I'd already been approached when we looked into the Dark House business,' he continued after setting down the glasses, 'and by the time of the Hellfire tunnels I was on the list. They have resident experts, as it were, but they need a fleet of us who specialise in certain areas. Obviously.'

'So Andrew got in touch with you because he knew you were an Arts and Antiquities advisor. Why?' asked Ben.

'He thought it should have been brought in to Arts and Antiques, and he thought I could find out if it had, and what the findings were.'

'Well, yes, I can see that, but it's not your field,' said

167

Libby.

'Ah, but I know the people to ask,' said Edward, flashing his beautiful smile once more. 'However,' he said, suddenly serious, 'I shall have to tread very delicately, or I might upset your handsome Detective Connell.'

Libby frowned. 'That's a point.'

'And we don't want to do that,' said Ben,

Libby frowned at her drink. 'Should we ask him?'

'No!' said Ben and Edward together.

'That's just what might annoy him,' said Ben.

'Oh.' Libby gave a disconsolate sigh. 'Well, it's all down to talking to Sandra Thingy, then.'

'Apart from Edward going in to bat on our behalf,' said Ben.

'Well, yes, but there's nothing I can do about that.' Libby picked up her drink, thought about it, and put it down again. 'What *are* you going to ask?'

'I shall ask if they've been approached by the Kent Constabulary, and if so, what the outcome was.' Edward looked at his watch. 'And now I'd better go.' He stood up and looked round the bar. 'Such a nice place. Sorry I won't see Harry and Peter, but I'll arrange to come over next week some time. Will Hetty have room at the Manor by then, Ben?'

'Yes, the actors will have gone by Monday – I hope.' He and Libby both stood up and Libby kissed the smooth black cheek.

'See you next week, then,' she said. 'And thanks for agreeing to look into it.'

Tim had called time before Harry and Peter skittered in, Harry looking dishevelled and Peter his immaculate self.

'Gawd, what an evening!' said Harry, collapsing into a chair. 'Don't throw us out yet, love. I need sustenance.'

He waved a languid hand at Tim, and Peter, with a rolling of the eyes, went to fetch drinks.

'You've just missed Edward,' said Libby.

'Oh – my black beauty!' said Harry, sitting upright and beaming. 'Why didn't he wait?'

'He had to drive back to Medway. But he said he'd be back next week.'

'He's working down here now, then? I remember he said he was going to be.'

'Yes, one of the Medway campuses. Shame he's not in Canterbury.'

'Who isn't?' asked Peter, coming up with drinks.

'Edward – you remember him? The magnificent professor?'

'Oh, yes, I remember,' said Peter, amused. 'You do a good line in magnificent professors, Libby, don't you?'

'Only Edward and Michael. Gilbert and Andrew are a bit long in the tooth,' said Libby.

'And there's my cousin,' said Ben. 'Although I wouldn't call him magnificent. More bear-like.'

'And they're all hanging around,' said Peter. 'Like a symposium.'

'Are they hoping for cultural crumbs?' asked Harry. 'Attracted by the whiff of scholarship?'

'I'm not sure.' Libby frowned. 'Michael's attracted more by a whiff of Belinda, if you ask me.'

'And Gilbert wants to see justice done,' said Ben.

'And Andrew and Richard are just curious.' Libby nodded. 'So are we all.'

'And Edward? What attracts him?' asked Harry. 'Not me, I suppose.'

'Sadly no,' said Libby. 'Much the same as Gilbert, really. An interest in justice. Andrew asked him.'

'So where, if one may ask, are you *à ce moment-là*?' asked Harry. '*En investigation*?'

169

'No idea,' said Ben. 'Nobody seems to know why the fake letter was made, or by whom.'

'Or why the two murders were committed. And by whom,' added Libby. 'Oh, and do you remember Sandra Thingy?'

'Thingy?' repeated Harry and Peter.

'Oh, you know. Used to live up in Steeple Lane.'

'My ma knew her quite well. Didn't she remarry?' said Peter.

'Yes, and used to belong to the ukulele group.'

'Farrow,' said Ben with a sigh.

'Yes, her. Lives over in Itching now. You remember she got quite involved over the ukulele murder. Apparently, she and her Elliot also knew Nathan Vine quite well.'

'The original fakery person?' said Harry. 'Well, well, well!'

'That doesn't surprise me,' said Peter. 'Sandra and Elliot were always dashing off to concerts and theatre in London. A nice Shakespearean collector, or whatever he said he was, would have appealed to them.'

'That's a point,' said Libby. 'I wonder what he said he was? Why he wanted the archive?'

'I don't believe he would have asked Dad for it,' said Ben. 'He might have asked for a look at it...'

'So he asked Russell to ask for it,' said Libby.

'We've been over this before,' said Ben. 'Either Nathan asked Russell to get it, or Russell asked Nathan to fake the letter. We're no nearer knowing which way round it was.'

'Well, if Mrs Thingy knew Nathan, she might be able to tell you,' said Harry. 'And now tell me what Edward said.'

The following morning, Libby searched her contact list for Sandra Farrow's number. When she found it, she called Fran.

'I don't know what to say,' she said.

'Oh, for heavens' sake! Tell her the truth. She knows perfectly well what sort of situations you get into, she won't be surprised.'

'This isn't my situation!' said Libby, indignant. 'It's landed on me!'

Fran sighed. 'Yes, Lib. They always do.'

'So what do I say?'

'Do you remember a man called Nathan Vine who used to live in – what was it called?'

'Farm Cottage, was it?'

'Farm Cottage, then, in Steeple Lane.'

'Hmm. A bit bald.'

'Well, elaborate then. But not too much, or she'll get confused. She must be getting on now.'

'Oh, like Flo and Hetty get confused, you mean?' said Libby scornfully. 'Some hopes!'

'Not all old people are like them, Lib, and, as I remember, she was younger than the rest of them so I suppose she isn't likely to get confused. She might refuse to help after the last time, though,' said Fran. 'Well, go on, ring her then. Might as well give it a go.'

'Are you coming with me?'

'Depends when it is.'

'OK.' Libby heaved a huge sigh.

'You were hoping I'd volunteer to ring her, weren't you?'

Libby stifled a snort.

'Well, I'm not. Go on. Off you go.'

Libby wandered round the house for a while finding jobs to do, and eventually took the phone into the garden and made the call.

'Good lord, Libby! Yes, of course I remember. Have you got another murder?'

171

Libby choked.

'Er – yes!' she gasped. 'Sort of.'

'Is it to do with the Shakespeare letter?'

Libby spluttered.

'You see, we're coming over tonight to see the play – really looking forward to it – so we were following all the reports about the forgery. And there was a murder connected to that, wasn't there?'

'Yes, there was,' said Libby, recovering. 'And I did want to ask you something connected to that. I'm sorry.'

'Heavens above! What could we have to do with it?'

'When you lived in Steeple Lane, you knew a man called Nathan Vine, Una said.'

'Yes.'

'It was about him I wanted to talk to you. It wouldn't be very convenient tonight, so I wondered if I could pop over some time?'

'How intriguing!' Sandra sounded delighted. 'Yes, of course. You could come this afternoon, if you like. Alan won't be here, but you don't need him, do you?'

'No, that's fine, thank you,' said Libby weakly. 'I don't want to hold you up, though, if you've got to get ready to go out.'

'No problem, Libby. Sid Best's cooking for us at The Poacher.'

'Ah. Well, would two thirty be all right?'

'Yes, of course. Will Fran come with you?'

'Oh, you remember Fran?'

'Of course. Will she come?'

'I doubt it,' said Libby, slightly miffed that Sandra appeared keener to see Fran than herself. 'It's a summer Saturday, and she works in her husband's gallery on Nethergate seafront.'

'What a lovely thing to do,' said Sandra. 'Well, I'll see you later, then. Looking forward to it.'

Libby remained looking at the phone in some puzzlement. Why was Sandra so keen to see her? So pleased to hear from her?

She reported to Fran, who, as she had predicted, couldn't come to Itching with her, and to Ben, who sighed a bit.

'Well, you could come, too, if you wanted.'

'If her husband was going to be there, maybe, but not just with you two women.'

'That's a very old-fashioned view,' said Libby.

'I *am* old-fashioned, or hadn't you realised?'

So at two o'clock Libby got into the silver bullet and set off towards Itching and Perseverance Row. Itching was just down the hill from Shott and a little over a mile from Bishop's Bottom. All the villages, which Libby thought sounded like something out of *Cold Comfort Farm*, shared churches ministered to by the Rev. Patti, and therefore shared gossip, but Libby found it very useful on occasion, as Patti frequently knew the right people to talk to in certain circumstances.

Sandra led her through to a neat garden as manicured as she was herself, her silver hair swept back in a French pleat, her make up immaculate. Libby, some years her junior, would never aspire to the same style.

'Now,' she said, seating her guest on a comfortable garden lounger, 'Nathan Vine. What did you want to know? I haven't seen him for years.'

'You didn't know he was dead?' Libby asked hesitantly. She needn't have worried. Sandra merely looked surprised.

'I had no idea! But we never kept in touch after he left the village, although Elliot and he became quite close for a time. I didn't even have an address to let him know when Elliot died.'

'Ah.' Libby paused to collect her thoughts. 'Well, we

173

were wondering, you see, how he became acquainted with Ben's father. We found his address in Greg's address book.'

'That was our fault.' Sandra smiled.

'Oh?'

'He moved in to Farm Cottage to do some research into historical houses in the area.'

'Yes, we thought so...'

'And he went to see dear Una to ask if she knew who owned the Manor. Well, she knew of course, but couldn't introduce him, and it wasn't open to the public – still isn't, I gather?'

'No.'

'And so she sent him on to us. And I said I'd ask. We knew the Wildes, and Elliot was quite friendly with Greg. So we did. But I don't think he got very far.'

'No, I don't think he did, either.' Libby gave a small smile. 'So what was he looking for?'

'Looking for?' Sandra's eyebrows rose. 'The history of local houses, he said. Nothing in particular.'

'Oh.' Libby was puzzled. 'Not Shakespeare?'

'No. I can't see what he would have had to do with that business, you know.'

'Well.' Libby thought for a moment. 'It was him, you see, who had the forged letter in the first place.'

Sandra frowned. 'Nathan? But when was this? When he lived in Steeple Martin?'

'Actually, I'm not sure. But quite a time ago.'

'So what does it have to do with the business over this Shakespeare letter now? And the murder?'

Libby sighed. 'It's actually quite complicated.'

'In that case,' said Sandra, standing up, 'let's have a cup of tea.'

Libby followed her into the house.

'Nathan showed the letter to the V&A, you see, years

ago,' she said, as Sandra filled a kettle in her immaculate kitchen. 'And after a while they got in touch to say it was a fake. So he took it back, and that was that. But last year – I think it was last year – it turned up again at the V&A, sent by Nathan's nephew.'

'Nephew?' Sandra turned round. 'But how could he have had a nephew? He didn't have any brothers or sisters.'

Chapter Twenty-two

Libby let out a satisfied "Yes!" and hit the work surface.

'I said that,' she said. 'We didn't know if he was really Nathan's nephew.'

'Who?' Sandra looked bewildered.

'Duncan Lucas. I don't suppose you know if he visited Nathan?'

'No idea.' Sandra turned to pour boiling water on to tea bags in mugs. She always used to make proper tea in a teapot, Libby reflected. And served in proper teacups. How people change. 'We didn't see many of his visitors. Oh, we went round for drinks, sometimes, and he came to us, and we all went to the theatre together a few times, but we didn't meet many other people.'

'Well, this chap sent the letter back to the V&A, and, more or less at the same time, he got in touch with National Shakespeare, who were making plans to do this booth stage tour to the same places as the Lord Chamberlain's Men. Then, to cut a long story short, the V&A confirmed that it was a fake, and Lucas took it away and disappeared from view. By which time, National Shakespeare had built a whole publicity strategy around it, particularly as the letter had referred to Steeple Martin and we now had a theatre there.'

'So was it this Lucas who was murdered?' Sandra handed over a mug.

'Yes, it was, but not then. He was found after they'd arrived here – in Steeple Martin, I mean – and no one knew he was here, or why.'

'And he said he was Nathan's nephew?'

'Yes. But we did think Nathan was also a friend of Greg Wilde's cousin Russell Wilde. You don't happen to know if he was?'

Sandra was frowning again. 'Let's go back outside,' she said. 'Now, when Nathan was hoping to find out something about the Manor, Elliot happened to mention that he knew there were some old household documents there, but that Greg wasn't that interested in them.'

'That's right. But this cousin, Russell, was.'

Sandra resumed her garden seat.

'I've got a vague idea that someone went to see him.' She sipped her tea. 'He got quite excited about it. That's it!' she put down her mug. 'He told Elliot he'd been fobbed off!'

'Fobbed off?'

Sandra laughed. 'Yes. He wasn't upset about it, quite the reverse. He said Greg Wilde hadn't wanted to be bothered and he'd sent someone else. Could that have been this cousin?'

'It sounds like it,' said Libby. 'But you don't know anything else?'

'No, dear.' Sandra shook her head. 'He wasn't around for long after that. Oh, he went to see old Colonel Feathers at Old Hall, but I don't suppose he had much joy there. He wouldn't have known much of the history of the place.'

'No,' said Libby. 'He'd been out in India, hadn't he? His wife didn't know how to wash a floor, it was said.'

'That's him. Expected the locals to kowtow.'

'So I heard. And no doubt thought India had been better off under the British.'

Sandra looked at her doubtfully. 'Maybe...'

Libby smiled. 'Sorry, one of my hobby horses. Well, that's been very helpful, Sandra, thank you. And you've got a lovely garden.'

177

'Thank you.' Sandra looked round complacently. 'Although the house is smaller than the one in Steeple Lane.' She sighed. 'I was sorry to leave there.'

'But Itching's a very pretty village.'

'Not so much going on, though.' She sighed. 'I'd go back like a shot. And I miss Una.'

'I think she misses you, too,' said Libby. 'Have you kept the old house?'

'Yes. Alan says it would need doing up before we sell it, but...'

'I know,' said Libby. 'Ben wanted to move into Steeple Farm now it's been done up, but I didn't want to leave my cottage, and I'd have to keep it as a bolthole, I think.'

Sandra pulled an expressive face. 'I'm afraid I'm a bit like that.'

They went back through the house and Libby stepped out into Perseverance Row.

'Is the ukulele group still going?' she asked.

'No,' Sandra said with a laugh. 'We all felt a bit dispirited after the murder, and as you know, a lot of people had already left, so we gave up. I believe the Canterbury group are still going, though. Why, did you want to join?'

'Good heavens, no! The strings still hurt my fingers. And what about the darts? Are you still Ladies' Team Captain at The Poacher?'

Sandra laughed again. 'Still playing, but not Captain any more. I'm too old, and my eyesight isn't what it was. We haven't been to Steeple Martin for a long time, though.'

'We've got a new landlord, Tim. Very forward-looking. He helped organise our Beer Festival last year.'

'I heard,' said Sandra. 'You won't be having another one, will you?'

'Oh, I don't know. Did you know Ron Stewart came to help us?'

'Yes, I did hear. I expect that was quite a draw, wasn't it?'

'Much as it was for the concert that time,' said Libby. 'Well, I'd better get on. I expect I'll see you tonight, won't I?'

'I expect so. Last night, isn't it?'

'No, actually, they've asked for another day, so they're doing two performances tomorrow.'

'Oh! Well, good for you, I suppose,' said Sandra doubtfully.

'Except for having to find staff for tomorrow,' said Libby. 'I think I shall be working the bar for both performances.' She pasted on a bright smile. 'See you later.'

She drove back through Shott, past The Poacher with its creaky sign hanging over the door, and back up the hill towards the Canterbury Road. So what had that conversation told her?

Well, only one thing, really. That Duncan Lucas couldn't have been Nathan Vine's nephew. *But*, how could Sandra actually know that? How did she *know* Nathan didn't have brothers and sisters? Presumably he'd told her or her husband, but why? Libby scowled at the road ahead. That posed more questions than it answered.

It did look as though Russell had been in touch with him, though. It also looked as if contact had first been made by Russell, not the other way round. She sighed and gave up. Her brain was full.

When she got back to Steeple Martin, she found Ben asleep in the back garden of 17 Allhallow's Lane and a message from Sandra on the landline answerphone.

'Sorry, I meant to tell you that Nathan had another friend in the village – well, several really. Elliot introduced him to the Chess Club, and he got to know a couple of them really well.'

'And who were they?' Libby asked the unresponsive phone.

'Who were what?' said a sleepy voice.

'Sandra left a message. She forgot to tell me something.'

'Couldn't it wait until tonight? You'll see her at the theatre.'

'Yes, but as I said to her earlier, it wouldn't be very convenient to talk there. Not privately, anyway.' She sighed. 'Still, I might as well wait, now. Do you want to hear what she said?'

Ben did, and made tea while she told him.

'You're right,' he said when she'd finished. 'How did she know that for a fact?'

'It's not the sort of thing that comes up in conversation, is it?' said Libby. 'You don't suddenly come out with: "I've got no brothers and sisters, you know," do you?'

'It might,' said Ben. 'I can think of lots of conversations where it might come up. Talking about families in general, you know.'

'I suppose so,' said Libby grudgingly. 'She did seem very definite about it. Anyway, I suppose I should have asked.'

'And the Chess Club.' Ben was frowning. 'Who was a member of the Chess Club?'

'Not your Dad, then?'

'No, I never knew him to play chess. I didn't, either.'

'Who would know?' Libby scowled at her mug. 'I bet Flo doesn't.'

'I wonder if it's still going?' said Ben.

'Yes, but no one will remember Nathan Vine.'

'Why not? Sandra Farrow does.'

'That's true – and so did Una and the ladies.'

'And you've asked Tim about old landlords – although I don't suppose you'll have much luck there – and Edward's going to ask the Arts and Antiques squad. So unless you go knocking on every door in the village, I can't see that there's much else you can do.'

'No, you're right. What a pity the photo shop isn't still there. Russell used it, the ladies said.'

'Was it a photo shop, then?' asked Ben.

'According to the ladies he used it, so it must have been. But I remember Ian telling us it had been closed for years, though obviously after that time.' She frowned. 'So was Russell here twice?'

'He used to visit, Mum said, didn't she?' said Ben. 'So he must have been here more than twice. I mean, he was coming when I was a boy, and the whole business with Nathan was far more recent than that.'

'Was it?'

'Must have been. Sandra Farrow wouldn't have known him otherwise.'

'Oh, yes! I must say, the whole timing aspect of this has me confused. Shall we ask Hetty? I mean, did he stay at the Manor? Or somewhere else?'

'Well, don't ask her now, she'll be resting. I'll pop in when we go up to the theatre later. I take it we are going?'

'I said I'd see Sandra. And if the cast want the bar open after the show I suppose we ought to offer to man it.'

'We'll be doing it tomorrow, anyway,' said Ben, with a sigh. 'Oh, the joys of running a theatre...'

They arrived at the theatre half an hour before the interval and told the bar staff the good news that they could go home early. Libby helped finish off the pre-ordered interval drinks while Ben went over to the Manor to quiz Hetty. He arrived back just in time to start collecting glasses as the interval bell sounded.

'Yes, she remembered,' he said, unloading glasses from a tray. 'You remember she said that the other day? It's jogged her memory.'

'Go on, then. What?' asked Libby, loading glasses into the dishwasher.

'Wait a minute. I'll finish this first.'

Libby managed to contain her soul in patience until Ben had collected all the glasses.

'What she said was that Russell used to come down when I was a boy and sometimes stay at the Manor, although he and Dad never got on. She didn't really know what they talked about, but Dad always seemed to want to get rid of him. Then – and this is the interesting part – she actually remembered Dad inviting Russell down many years later "to get that other one off my back".'

'Nathan!' said Libby.

'Looks like it. She didn't remember meeting him until Flo reminded her, which was why she didn't recognise the name when we found it the other day. But it looks as though Nathan went to see Dad, and then Dad asked Russell to deal with him. "Fobbed him off", as Sandra told you.'

'So did he give Russell all the documents then or when he came down before?'

'I would think then, wouldn't you?'

Libby nodded.

'Oh – and she remembered the Chess Club.'

'No!'

'Yes!' Ben grinned. 'Not that she or Dad were members, but they met in the pub, apparently, and – get this – they still do!'

'Oh, good lord. And this was when?'

'Oh, she doesn't remember that. But it was before I moved back, obviously, and she thinks before Peter and

Harry came back, too.' He sighed. 'What a pity Mad Millie isn't slightly more – well, with it.'

'What about,' said Libby, suddenly struck with inspiration, 'your sister Susan?'

'Susan? What, a member of the Chess Club?'

'Or maybe her – er – husband.' Libby swallowed nervously. 'Do you think...?'

'Despite what happened when we put on *The Hop Pickers*,' said Ben, with a wry smile, 'I suppose Susan and David *were* upstanding members of the community. I could ask her.'

Libby breathed a sigh of relief. Susan was rather a tricky subject in the Wilde family.

'Where is she now?' she asked. 'I lost track.'

'London, believe it or not,' said Ben. 'Mum's family are still up there, or some of them are, and she went to stay with Great-Aunt Bessie. Then, when the dust had settled, so to speak, and she had some money, she bought herself a little flat and got a job. Mum couldn't believe it.'

'Gosh!' said Libby, who couldn't imagine strait-laced countrywoman Susan living and working in London. 'One of Betjeman's businesswomen in Camden Town, eh?'

'Overlooking the railway lines?' Ben smiled. 'Maybe, but it's more Canning Town than Camden.'

'Goodness! She hasn't got one of those smart Docklands flats, has she?'

'No, it's a Victorian conversion. I popped in to see it once or twice when I was up there.'

'You didn't tell me!'

'Well, no. Not the happiest memories, are they?'

'No,' conceded Libby.

Luckily, the cast of *Twelfth Night* had no desire to party long and hard after the show now they had two more performances on Sunday, and Libby and Ben were able to get down to the pub as soon as Libby had spoken to

Sandra, who didn't appear to be keen to stay and chat.

'She said Dr Dedham *was* a member of the Chess Club,' she told Ben triumphantly, 'so perhaps you needn't ask Susan now.'

'But she might know other members,' said Ben. 'It wouldn't hurt to ask.'

Libby raised her eyebrows at this. Ben wasn't usually keen to get involved in investigations, although this did touch on his own family.

'Well, anyway, let's ask Tim about the current Chess Club and the old landlords. You never know,' she said, tucking her arm through Ben's.

The pub was as full as it always was on a Saturday night, and it was some time before Tim had time to answer Libby's questions.

'Now that's funny,' he said when Libby mentioned the Chess Club. 'It was old Tony Turner who started that. He was landlord from the early seventies until the mid-nineties. After that, as I expect you remember, they had managers in here because they couldn't sell it, then we bought it when it went back on the market. Made it a proper free house again. Only way to go with all the micro pubs springing up.' He sent Ben a darkling look.

'I'm not opening a pub!' protested Ben. 'Only a brewery. You can sell the beer if you like.'

'Have to see what it's like first, won't I?' Tim grinned slyly. 'Anyway, yes. The Chess Club still meets here. Upstairs, now we've cleared that function room.'

'Every week?' asked Libby.

'More like once a month. I get a phone call asking if it's free on such and such a day and that's that.'

'Who runs it?'

'That barrister chap who lives up the Nethergate Road, Philip something. Know him?'

'No,' said Libby, 'but someone will. What about this

Tony Turner? Where do we find him?'

'Heaven, love. Or hell, being a landlord. Died years ago.'

'Oh.' Libby's face fell.

'What is all this, anyway?' Tim turned away to serve someone in the other bar. 'Writing a history of the pub?'

'Trying to find out about someone who lived here a few years ago,' said Ben. 'Do you know any of the other members of the Chess Club?'

'Johnny Darling,' said Tim. 'Know him? He's always in here. I'll point him out next time he's in when you are.'

'I know him,' said Libby. 'He's a friend of Joe's.'

'Oh, I know. Builder, isn't he?' said Ben.

'Was,' said Tim. 'He's retired, now.'

'Will you point out this Philip person, too?' asked Libby.

'Always comes in of a Sunday evening, if you're around tomorrow,' said Tim.

'We're working the bar again tomorrow,' said Ben. 'We might get in late.'

'Oh, he doesn't stay late,' said Tim. 'Still, there'll be other times.'

'Trouble is,' said Libby, as they carried their drinks over to the window, 'We don't want to wait until another time, do we?'

As it happened, they didn't have to wait for long. Cousin Richard took himself for a pre-lunchtime drink on Sunday morning and bounded into the Manor kitchen a little later announcing that he'd been introduced to Philip Jacobs.

'Who?' asked Michael and Belinda.

'The barrister who runs the Chess Club, isn't it?' asked Libby.

'That's it.' Richard beamed at her. 'Tim said you'd been asking. And you'll never guess what!'

'What?' said Ben, obediently.
'He knew my dad!'

Chapter Twenty-three

There was a short, stunned silence.

'You mean in London?' said Belinda eventually.

'No, no! Here. Philip joined the Chess Club not long after it started, and one of the members brought Dad along several times. He was good, apparently.'

'Who took him along?' asked Ben, kicking Libby under the table.

'Oh, he wasn't sure about that. But he knew Dad was your dad's relative. Very interested in the history of the area, he was, according to Philip.'

'You don't remember that, do you, Mum?' Ben turned to Hetty, who was impassively carving a monstrous leg of lamb. She shook her head.

'Remember the Chess Club, though,' she said.

'Do you? Neither you or Dad played, did you?'

'No, son, I said, didn't I? I just remember it starting. People weren't sure it was right for our village. A bit posh, like.'

'When was it? After I'd left?'

'Blimey, years after! When Richard's dad started coming again.'

'Again?' said Ben, Richard and Libby together.

Hetty looked surprised. 'Told you that, too. Well, he used to come when you were a boy, then I reckon him and Greg had a bit of a row and he stopped. Then yer dad asked him down here – I told you – and he came back.'

'What, though?' Richard was frowning. 'What would my dad have that your dad wanted? It was the other way round, surely?'

'We think he might have wanted Russell to – er – get Nathan off his back,' said Ben.

'Didn't he tell you *anything* about it, Hetty?' asked Libby.

'No, gal. I reckoned it was business, so I kept out of it.' Hetty pushed the platter of carved lamb into the centre of the table. 'Help yourselves.'

Conversation became relaxed and somewhat desultory after this, everyone concentrating on Hetty's magnificent Sunday roast, but when the fruit crumble and cream had been demolished and Hetty banished to her sitting room, the clearing-up began and speculation resumed.

'So we think,' said Libby, 'that what your dad wanted, Ben, was for Russell to take Nathan over, so to speak, to get him off his back?'

'Of course it was. That was the fobbing off, wasn't it?'

'What fobbing off?' asked Michael, flapping a tea towel in the direction of Hetty's crystal wine glasses. Belinda rescued them.

'Yes – what are you talking about?' added Richard.

'Sorry, I should have explained,' said Libby. 'I went to see an old friend yesterday.'

And she told them about her visit to Sandra and the subsequent revelations.

'So Duncan Lucas wasn't Nathan Vine's nephew,' said Michael.

'And was a career criminal,' said Libby.

'So how did he get hold of the fake letter?' asked Michael.

'That's what we don't know,' said Ben.

'But Ian – or his London counterparts – will be going through Lucas's life with a toothcomb,' said Libby. 'They'll find out. And Gideon Law's, too.'

'I'm not absolutely sure I know where this Law person fits into the story,' said Richard. 'I know you've told me, but...'

'We don't know, either,' said Ben. 'We can only speculate. We know that he was obviously in touch with Lucas as the police found – was it correspondence, Libby? – in his flat, or house, or whatever it was.'

'And I found him,' said Bel with a shudder. 'Or Jeff-dog did.'

'Quite near the Hoppers's Huts, actually,' said Libby. 'You were asked about it, weren't you?'

'Yes, but I'm still in the dark about most of it,' said Richard. 'And I really don't like being this close to murder.'

Libby was tempted to say "Go home, then" but realised a) it sounded rather rude and b) the police probably wouldn't let him. Instead, she said 'Do you think this Philip would still be in the pub? Tim said he goes in on Sunday evenings, but we're being bar staff tonight.'

'At the theatre?' asked Michael. 'I used to love working the Union bar at Uni.'

'Did you?' Ben looked interested.

'No, don't ask him,' said Libby. 'That's taking advantage.'

'I could, easily.' Michael looked at Belinda. She grinned and nodded.

'We could do it, Ma. Make a change. And you were there last night, weren't you?'

All eyes turned to Libby and she gave in.

'All right, but one of us had better come up and show you the till and the stock, and make sure the beer's OK,' she said. 'I made sure there was lemon in the fridge and -'

'Stop it, Lib,' said Ben, laughing. 'Bel's done it before, and I'll go up about a quarter to seven and make sure everything's OK. Thank you both – very much.'

They decided to pay their usual visit to Peter and Harry before going home, but to call on Tim to find out if

189

Philip Jacobs was expected that evening. He had, in fact, gone home, but told Tim he would see him later "as usual".

'So will I tell him you want to see him? Although I think your cousin did that.' Tim grinned. 'Seemed Phil knew his dad.'

'So he said. Coincidence, eh?' said Ben. 'No leave it, and we'll see what happens. He might not want to talk to us.'

Peter and Harry were, as usual on a Sunday afternoon, on the sofa in their living room, Harry's feet in Peter's lap.

'So how are things going, petal?' Harry asked, waving Libby towards an array of bottles on a side table. 'No more bodies?'

'No, but we've discovered a few more links in the chain,' she said holding up a brandy bottle.

'Not for me,' said Ben. 'If we're committed to the pub tonight...'

'I thought you were doing the bar?' said Pater.

'We were,' said Libby. 'Shall I make some tea while you explain, Ben?'

When Ben had finished his explanation of recent events, Libby brought in Harry's old decoupage tray with an assortment of mugs.

'Did you hear that, Lib?' asked Ben. 'Pete knows Philip Jacobs.'

'So does Hal,' said Peter. 'He's a regular at the caff.'

'And Johnny Darling,' said Harry. 'He did the flat up before Fran lived there. And put up the spiral staircase.'

'Why didn't we think to ask our nearest and dearest?' said Libby. 'I made tea for everyone – but I'll drink them all if you two are on the bottle.'

Peter accepted a mug, but Harry waved it away. 'I've been working, dear heart. Now, explain again why the

Chess Club is important? I didn't entirely follow it all.'

Libby started to explain.

'OK, I get it – the first person to have the fake lived here for a bit,' said Harry, 'and he hounded your dad, Ben.'

'But we want to know about Uncle Russell,' said Libby. 'We're sure he and Nathan cooked it up between them.'

'Well, *you're* sure,' said Ben.

'And the Chess Club helps how?' persisted Harry.

'Because Nathan joined, and we think he might have made friends there.'

'Even if he did, he would hardly tell them about his nefarious goings on, would he?'

'No, but we might find out a bit more about him.'

'And Uncle Russell? Doesn't Richard really know any more about him?'

'He wasn't very child-friendly,' said Ben. 'I barely remember him, yet Mum says he came to visit when I was a kid, and then again later. Which we didn't realise.'

'What, when you were grown up?' asked Peter.

'Apparently. That would have been when Nathan was pestering Dad.'

'So Greg introduced them to each other?' said Peter.

'That's what we think,' said Libby. 'But we've got no proof.'

'Do you think Russell belonged to the Chess Club as well?' said Peter.

'He didn't live here, so I doubt it,' said Libby.

'But he could have gone along as a guest,' said Harry. 'I'd ask if I were you.'

'We're going to,' said Ben. 'Subtly.'

'What? With *'er* around?' said Harry, with a witchlike cackle.

'What about coming to the pub with us this evening?'

said Libby, ignoring this sally. 'It would be much easier to get into conversation with you there.'

'What about it?' Peter asked Harry. 'Or do you want to stay in and put your feet up?'

'I spend so much time in the pub it's almost like being at home anyway,' said Harry with a theatrical sigh.

'You go in after work,' said Peter. 'And it's almost always nearly closing time.'

'Oh, all right. What time?'

'Eightish?' said Ben. 'We don't want to be too late – it's Sunday and *most* people have work tomorrow.'

Harry beamed. 'Then *most* people aren't as sensible as me!'

Libby and Ben went home to Allhallow's Lane, where Libby fell asleep on the sofa. Ben went up to the theatre at a quarter to seven and made sure the bar was ready for business, then showed Michael and Bel what they needed to know before going back to wake Libby and go to the pub.

'Blimey,' said Tim, as they walked in. 'You again!'

'We've come to meet this Philip person,' said Libby. 'Harry and Peter know him, too, so they'll be in soon.'

'Suppose he's with someone?' said Ben, as they took their drinks to the table by the fireplace.

'We'll have to wait and see, won't we?' said Libby. 'Look, here's Hal and Pete.'

It was while Peter was collecting drinks at the bar that Tim announced the arrival of Philip Jacobs in the other bar.

'Shall I send him in?' he called.

'No!' Libby went pink with embarrassment.

But Peter had made eye contact and was holding a conversation across the bar.

'Coming in,' he said returning to the table. 'He's on his own, so happy for some company.'

192

'He won't be for long,' said Harry, sotto voce, as a cheerful looking man, with a tweed jacket stretched over an ample paunch covered with a mustard waistcoat, came to join them.

'Philip – I don't think you know Ben Wilde, do you? Or Libby Sarjeant?' said Peter.

'Only by reputation,' said Philip Jacobs, shaking their hands. 'And I met your father, of course, Ben.'

'I suppose you would have done,' said Ben. 'I'm sorry our paths don't seem to have crossed.'

'I don't do as much in the village as I used to.' Philip beamed round the table. 'But I'm a frequent visitor to The Pink Geranium, of course, and this is my local.'

Now it came to the point, Libby couldn't think what to say. Ben, Peter and Harry all looked at her quizzically. She cleared her throat.

'Er – do you ever come to the theatre?' she began weakly.

Not noticing any atmosphere, Philip replied enthusiastically. 'Oh, yes! I absolutely loved *Twelfth Night*. How clever of them to use the booth stage – really added something to the performance, don't you think?'

Relieved, Libby plunged into a discussion of Shakespeare's plays, and in particular the various productions of *Twelfth Night* she had had seen, happy to find that Philip shared her opinion of the Globe's all-male production.

'And you met Ben's uncle, too, didn't you?' said Peter eventually, when he could get a word in.

'Oh, yes!' Philip turned to Ben. 'I met your cousin this morning. He said he's staying down here? Like his father used to do.'

'Er – yes,' said Ben. 'How did you meet him?'

'Your cousin? In here!'

'No – his father.'

193

'Oh, right! He seemed impressed with that. Well, he was brought along to the Chess Club. It was before I was chair, of course, some years ago, now.'

'Who brought him, can you remember?' asked Libby, finally plunging in.

'Oh, yes, of course – a particular friend of mine. Nathan Vine.'

Chapter Twenty-four

Harry gave a little crow and Philip looked surprised.

'Did you know him, too?'

Ben scowled at Harry. 'No, but my father did. We wondered if it might have been him.'

'Oh?' Philip was now looking slightly puzzled.

'We think my father introduced them, you see.'

'Ah! Well, I believe that was the case.' Philip looked round the table. 'Another drink, anyone?'

There was a deal of good-mannered jostling for position over the buying of the next round and Ben won.

'Did you meet Nathan when he moved down here?' Libby asked when Ben returned to the table.

Philip once more looked surprised. 'Good Lord, no! In fact it was my suggestion that he came down here.'

'Your -'Libby was gobsmacked. This was more than she'd bargained – or hoped – for.

'You knew him before, then,' said Ben, giving her a headmasterly look.

'In London, yes.' Philip nodded. 'I did my pupillage in London, after university, and we were in the same chambers.'

'He was a lawyer?' Peter's eyes were up to his hairline.

'He was.' Philip smiled. 'Older than me, but we became friends. We shared a love of Shakespeare.'

This time, Libby choked on her lager.

Philip frowned. 'There's obviously something about him you want to know?'

'Well, yes,' said Harry, 'although it's them, not us.'

195

Ben sighed. 'I'll try and explain as Libby's obviously incapable.'

Libby, still recovering, wiped streaming eyes and glowered at him.

As well as he could, Ben explained the situation and the reason they were trying to find out about Nathan Vine. Philip's eyes grew rounder and rounder.

'I wish I'd known!' he said, when Ben finally wound down. 'I thought when the *Twelfth Night* tour was announced how much Nathan would have enjoyed it. But before I tell you any more about him, I can assure you that he most certainly didn't have a nephew.'

'Yes, Sandra Farrow said that.' Libby nodded.

'Who?'

'Oh, sorry. She was Sandra Brown back then. Lived next door to Una on Steeple Lane.'

'Oh, yes, I knew Sandra – and Una.'

'How long had you been down here, then?' asked Harry.

'Oh, I come from Steeple Martin.' Philip smiled. 'I went away to university, then to chambers in London, and finally came back to work out of Canterbury. My mother was pretty old, then, so I moved back home to help her, and after she died, I stayed.'

'That's amazing,' said Libby. 'So what else can you tell us about Nathan? I didn't know him at all, but I sort of like him at a distance.'

'He was a very nice man. Single, like me, and, like me, inclined to become obsessed by hobbies.'

'And one of his was Shakespeare?'

'It was. He spent most of his spare time researching him, or what's known about him, I swear he knew all the plays and most of the sonnets off by heart and he eventually became certain of the theory that Shakespeare was a spy.'

Libby, Ben, Peter and Harry all registered astonishment in different ways.

'Well, bugger me,' said Harry.

'Hal!' reproved Peter.

Philip looked innocently round the table. 'It's not an unknown theory, you know. There've been books written about it. And in fact, that was one of the reasons I suggested he might come down here.' He turned to Ben. 'I suppose you know all about Titus Watt owning your house?'

'We do now,' said Ben. 'We didn't before all this started.'

'Oh?' Philip looked as though he couldn't believe anyone would remain ignorant of this. 'Well, I expect you know now that he was an Elizabethan spy?'

'Like John Dee,' said Libby.

'Exactly,' said Philip, 'only not as well-known, either then or now. I had the fanciful idea that the spying connection might link somehow to Shakespeare. It was very tenuous, but when Nathan started to look into it, he thought there might have been a link as The Lord Chamberlain's Men toured the area in 1597. He worked out that this was after Shakespeare had reappeared in London, and after he stopped being mentioned by Dee.'

'He was mentioned by Dee?' Now Peter was frowning.

'Not exactly. There's a theory that someone Dee talks about was, in fact, Shakespeare, but, as I said, that person disappears from Dee's diaries in the mid-nineties, or thereabouts. It fits in with Shakespeare's rise to fame in London.' Philip laughed. 'Don't take me for an expert! I just had to sit and listen to Nathan raving on about it.'

'So that was why he wanted to see any archive documents,' said Libby.

'Yes. I suggested he tried to get in to meet the owner – your father, Ben – and Elliot Brown took him up to the

Manor and introduced him. I'm afraid he wasn't very complimentary about your dad, Ben.'

'No, I'm not surprised,' said Ben. 'Dad thought he was a nuisance, I think. And he wasn't interested in the history of the house.'

'So he said. But then your uncle came down. And I don't know exactly what happened, of course, but Nathan brought him to the pub one night and said he was celebrating being "fobbed off". That was how he put it.'

'Yes, Sandra said the same thing,' said Libby. 'So what had happened? Greg unloaded all the archive stuff on to Russell and told him to go and deal with Nathan?'

'That's how I read it,' said Philip. 'Anyway, the next thing I knew was that Russell had rented a room somewhere in the village, and Nathan brought him to the Chess Club.'

'Well!' said Ben, sitting back in his chair.

'Blow me down,' said Harry.

'Good Lord,' said Peter.

Libby didn't say anything.

'Come on, Lib! What have you got to say?' said Harry.

Libby seemed to come back from a long way away. 'Why didn't more people know him, then?'

'That's a point,' said Ben. 'And why doesn't my mum remember Nathan, at least?'

'She probably would if she tried hard enough,' said Peter. 'And she does remember Richard's dad. But if both Nathan and Russell were living in the village for a while, it does seem odd that they aren't remembered.'

'Had Nathan retired by then?' asked Libby. 'Did he and Russell spend a lot of time going over the documents?'

'I think so.' Philip looked doubtful. 'Although they didn't exactly take me into their confidence. They appeared to have got very close, and I only saw them at the pub.'

'Was Russell retired by then, too?' asked Harry.

'I don't know, but I assumed he was. I don't even know what he did for a living.'

'We were also told that Nathan spent a lot of time at the library – in Canterbury, or Maidstone I suppose – and used the photo shop a lot,' said Ben.

Philip nodded. 'He did. I think he was photographing documents. No phone cameras then. Funny, isn't it? It wasn't that long ago, yet it seems like centuries away. And I think he was looking at the Maidstone archives. Russell used to go with him.'

'I expect that was why the villagers didn't know much about him if he was always away,' said Libby. 'They don't always know much about the commuters.'

'That's true,' said Philip. 'I've never understood why people commute from here to London. It's not exactly close to the station, is it?'

'Where did Russell rent his room?' asked Ben.

'Somewhere down Lendle Lane.' Philip stood up. 'And now I must go. It was lovely to meet you all. Perhaps we could have a meal together at Harry's restaurant soon?'

There was general assent to this suggestion, and they parted with expressions of mutual esteem.

'Well, that was a turn-up,' said Harry, leaning back and crossing his ankles.

'Didn't tell us much that was new, though,' said Libby.

'But we got confirmation of a lot of things we suspected,' said Ben. 'And it looks as if Nathan wasn't the bad guy, as you hoped.'

'I wonder why they didn't come into the restaurant,' said Peter.

'Perhaps you weren't open then,' said Libby. 'We still

haven't pinned down when all this happened.'

'And what we still don't know,' said Ben, 'is how Lucas got hold of the letter.'

'And why, when they were both apparently staying in the village, neither of your parents came across them. Nathan seems to have been known, if only vaguely, but Russell's even vaguer.'

'If you ask me,' said Peter, 'they were avoiding your parents. And probably my mother, too. She was obviously still up at Steeple Farm then.'

'And Susan,' said Libby, looking at Ben. 'Have you called her?'

'Not yet,' said Ben, looking uncomfortable.

'Susan?' Peter looked horrified. 'Oh, you can't – poor Susan!'

'I'll be tactful,' said Ben. 'And I've seen her since she got settled in London, don't forget.' He glanced across at Libby. 'Even Mum has.'

'You didn't tell me that!'

'Oh, yes.' Ben nodded. 'Susan didn't feel she could come here, for obvious reasons, so I've taken Mum up once or twice. And they speak on the phone at least once a week.'

'That's a relief,' said Peter. 'I always felt bad about Susan.'

'So did I,' said Libby. 'In fact, I felt bad about the whole thing.'

'Just think though, petal,' said Harry, 'it set you off on your adventures *and* got you together with the lovely Ben.'

'Hmm,' said Libby.

'Mixed blessing,' said Ben.

'Shut up, Hal,' said Peter.

They sat in a silence for a moment or two, then Ben said 'Come on, Lib, it's early yet. Let's go and give the youngsters a hand. The cast may want to let their hair down tonight.'

'God forbid,' said Peter. 'Rather you than me.'

But Belinda and Michael didn't want any help.

'They're a bit subdued tonight,' said Bel. 'We haven't even got any orders for after the show. We offered, but they said they're going back to the Manor for an early night. And their company manager locks up, doesn't he?'

'Yes, and he's been very good about it,' said Ben.

'So we might as well go home?' said Libby. 'If you're sure?'

'Oh go on, do!' said Bel. 'We wouldn't have offered in the first place if we weren't sure!'

So Libby and Ben strolled back to Allhallow's Lane.

'And do we do anything now?' asked Libby. 'Do we tell Ian? Is there anything there he doesn't know?'

'I don't know,' said Ben. 'He's been going through their lives, hasn't he? Lucas, Russell and Law. He probably knows it all, now.'

'Not necessarily about the locals in the village. You remember he said the village ladies would be helpful? I don't suppose Lucas, Vine and Law – or Russell – made notes in their diaries of meeting neighbours.'

'Unless they were useful to them,' said Ben. 'But honestly, I don't see how we can find out anything else. We know now about where they lived and at least some of the people they knew, and it doesn't seem as though either Russell or Nathan talked to anyone else about the archive documents.'

'No.' Libby shook her head sadly. 'And Gideon Law doesn't seem to have had any involvement in the village.'

'Except being killed here,' said Ben, unlocking the door of number seventeen.

On Monday morning Ben went straight to the theatre after a breakfast of tea and toast to help with the get-out, and Bel appeared moodily downstairs with her little case.

'Oh – you off?' Libby raised her eyebrows in surprise.

'I've stayed longer than I intended to,' said Bel, picking at a slice of toast Ben had left on his plate.

'And you were prepared to stay longer.'

Bel sent her a sideways look. 'Yes, well...'

'So, he's going back to London?'

Bel nodded.

'And what's the problem?' said Libby, sitting down at the table. 'Don't you think he'll want to see you in London?'

'I don't know. It won't be the same.'

'No.' Libby looked thoughtful. 'And no one can do anything to force the issue. I'd help if I could.'

'God, no, Ma!' exclaimed Bel in horror. 'Don't help!'

Libby grinned. 'No, dear.'

She did, however, accompany Belinda up to the Manor to say goodbye to Michael.

'Of course I'm taking her back!' he said, in answer to Libby question. 'And I'll bring her back down when we're required.'

Belinda brightened considerably at this, and gave Hetty an enthusiastic hug.

'Just as well we're out of your way before all the actors start milling about,' she said.

Hetty gruffly agreed.

'Do you think we ought to wait and say goodbye to Richard?' asked Michael.

'We'll do that for you,' said Ben, appearing from across the courtyard. 'You get off. We'll be overrun with traffic soon. You don't want to get caught up in it.'

'Say goodbye to Andrew and Gilbert for us,' said Bel, giving her mother a hearty kiss. 'See you soon.'

'Should we go and winkle out Richard?' asked Libby, as they stood in the courtyard waving Bel and Michael off.

'Why, though?' asked Ben. 'He doesn't have to go, as long as he caters for himself and doesn't get in the way.'

'That's just what he might do,' said Libby. 'If he carries on investigating.'

'Oho! Pots and kettles, there, don't you think?' Ben gave her a friendly buffet on the arm.

Libby smiled reluctantly. 'I suppose so. And quite honestly, it does look as though we've come to the end of the line, doesn't it?'

'It does. Come on, let's walk down to the high street and see how the incident room's doing.'

'Eh? Why?'

'Well, if it's winding down we know there'll be nothing more to do.'

'And what about the stuff we found out last night?' asked Libby.

Ben shrugged. 'We'll test the water.'

As they crossed over the high street, someone hailed Ben from Maltby Close.

'Johnny!' Ben smiled and put out a hand. 'Do you know Libby?'

'Oh, aye.' Johnny, a friendly looking middle-aged man wearing overalls, held out a hand to Libby. 'Friend of young Harry's.'

'Among other things,' said Libby with a grin. 'Are you the Johnny who did the flat and the spiral staircase?'

'That was me.'

'We were only talking about you last night,' said Ben. 'Or the Chess Club actually.'

'Oh?' Johnny raised his eyebrows in interrogation.

'We were asking Philip about Nathan Vine,' said Libby.

'Him!' Johnny Darling's face darkened ominously. 'Bastard!'

Chapter Twenty-five

'Beggin' your pardon, ma'am.' Johnny bobbed his head towards Libby who was temporarily deprived of speech.

'Didn't like him, eh?' said Ben. 'We haven't heard anything bad about him.'

'No?' Johnny pulled a face. 'Well, I'll tell you. A right chiseller, 'e was.'

'Why? What did he do?' asked Libby, finally finding her voice.

'Got me to do a load of work on that Farm Cottage and then wouldn't pay me.'

'Really?' said Ben. 'I thought it belonged to Terrance and he let it fall down in the end?'

'Old Terrance,' said Johnny, settling comfortably on one hip, 'didn't know his ar – er – bum from his elbow. Thought he was going to build posh houses, when everyone else knew he'd never get planning permission. So he wouldn't sell Farm Cottage.'

'So Nathan Vine got it on a repairing lease?' said Libby.

'Aye, and got me to do the repairin'!'

'And why wouldn't he pay?' asked Ben.

'He just didn't want to,' said Johnny. 'Made all sorts of excuses, said it wasn't worth it because Terrance would let it fall down. Then in the end he did a flit.'

'Really?' gasped Libby. 'Left without even paying his rent?'

'Nor me neither. Tried to find him in London. Never did.'

'What work were you doing?' asked Ben.

'Patching up at first. Bit of plumbing. Then he had me build this shed in the garden. More like a – I dunno – a security shed. No windows,'

'What did he want it for?' asked Libby.

Johnny shrugged.

'And Terrance wouldn't pay you, either?' said Ben.

'Him! Never.' Johnny hitched his bag on to his shoulder. 'Well, good luck if you're trying to find him.'

'Oh, Vine's dead,' said Libby.

'Oh?' The eyebrows went up again. 'Well, good riddance. I'll be seein' you.'

'Well, that was a surprise,' said Libby, watching the stocky figure disappear into the eight-til-late.

'And what did he want that shed for?' murmured Ben.

'Locking something up,' said Libby. 'Something he couldn't hide in the house?'

'But, surely, a brand new security shed would look suspicious?' said Ben. 'And even odder that no one mentioned him.'

'Yes – you'd think someone would have said: "you know, the bloke with the shiny new shed", wouldn't you? It would stick out like a sore thumb. And Johnny wouldn't have kept quiet about it, would he?'

'Why don't you ask Sandra and Una if they know anything about it?' suggested Ben. 'They might.'

'I bet Pete's mum would have done, too, living up there.' Libby tucked her hands in her pockets and turned to face the church. 'Come on, let's go and see if Ian's in residence.'

But Ian wasn't in the incident room, which was, as Ben suspected, winding down.

'I'm sure I can't tell you,' said nice DC Trent. 'I think most of the investigation's going on in London.'

'Oh, all right,' said Libby with a sigh. 'Well, we just thought we ought to tell him that Belinda – you know, who found the body? – and Michael Allen have gone back to London, and ask if the rest of the visitors could go home.'

DC Trent looked confused. 'I'm not sure,' she said. 'I suppose it's all right if we have their addresses. Are they material witnesses?'

'Don't you know?' asked Libby. Ben dug her in the ribs.

'Not all of them,' he said. 'Don't worry about it, we'll send him a text.'

DC Trent opened her mouth and then obviously didn't know what to say, so smiled weakly. Libby and Ben left.

'That went well,' said Libby.

'You were rude,' said Ben. 'It isn't up to us to criticise.'

'Well, she should have immediately said that they would rather not have their witnesses leave, shouldn't she? Or at least ask someone.'

'You could have been more polite about your reply,' said Ben.

'Oh, how?' Libby stood still, hands on hips.

Ben turned and looked her up and down. 'Do you genuinely not know?'

Libby lifted her chin. 'No.'

Ben regarded her solemnly for a moment, then shook his head. 'Do you know,' he said, 'sometimes I really don't like you.' He turned and walked off down Maltby Close, hands in pockets.

Libby felt as if she'd been punched in the solar plexus and the heart simultaneously. She felt colour seeping up her neck and into her face and took a deep, if shaky, breath.

''Ere, gal!' Flo appeared at her door. 'You all right?'

Libby turned slowly and cleared her throat.

'Yes, fine,' she said, then remembered. 'Flo, do you

know if Una's at home today?'

'Bound to be, gal. Monday's wash day, see?'

'What? Even now?'

'Things don't change much at our age,' said Flo. 'Sure you're all right?'

'Yes, I said, I'm fine. I must get off now, I need to see Una.'

Flo raised her eyebrows and pursed her lips, but didn't say anything else, and Libby hurried on down Maltby Close, her head still feeling like a badly balanced washing machine.

What had happened? Why had Ben turned on her? Why now?'

Because that's what you're like, whispered a voice in her head. You're rude, nosy and you like your own way. And so far you've got away with it.

She came to the end of Maltby Close and couldn't see Ben anywhere. She hesitated, then decided to do what she'd said she would to Flo – go and see Una. She turned left and went towards Steeple Lane, glancing across the road to the Pink Geranium, closed today as it was Monday, and relieved to see no one in there. She couldn't go in there for refuge today. Today she wasn't lovable, scatty, nosy Libby, the version of herself she'd been accepting for over ten years now. Today, she was quite a different person.

As she began the steep walk up Steeple Lane, she remembered when she had been brought up short on a previous occasion by Fran. This was worse. It was one thing, your best friend letting you know you weren't as good as you thought you were, but quite another having your life partner telling you you weren't a very nice person. She felt an uncomfortable ache in her throat which presaged a bout of uncontrollable crying, and swallowed hard. She stopped and turned to look over the little hollow into which the little River Wytch ran in a desultory trickle.

'Come on, Libby, pull yourself together.' She spoke out loud, annoyed to hear her cracked voice. She turned back to face up Steeple Lane towards Una's cottage and came face to face with Steeple Farm and it's creepy thatch eyebrows. Uttering the worst swear word she knew, she took in a bushel full of air and stomped off up the lane.

''Allo, me duck! And what's rattled your cage?' Una had come to the door wearing a large apron and wiping her hands on a striped towel.

'Oh, just the walk up the hill!' Libby tried to laugh it off. 'Not as fit as I was.'

'I don't do it at all these days,' said Una. 'I allus get someone to give me a lift. But you ain't as old as me, me duck. You should be fine. Come you away in.'

Seated in Una's cheerful sitting room, Libby began to recover her equilibrium.

'What I wanted to ask, Una,' she said, 'was - when Nathan Vine was your neighbour, did you see the shed he had built?'

'Shed?' Una looked bewildered. 'No, me duck. Builders, 'e 'ad – that Johnny Darling for one – but I dunno what they were doing. Why? Who says he had a shed?'

'Johnny Darling,' said Libby. 'A security shed, he said.'

'Well, I wouldn't know. But there was bad blood between Nathan and Johnny, mind.'

'Do you know what about?'

Una looked shifty. 'Not my place to say.'

'Come on Una. Nathan's dead now, so it doesn't matter.'

'Money.' Una shut her mouth tightly.

'Nathan owed Johnny?'

'That's what was said.'

'By whom?'

'Eh?'

'Who said he owed Johnny? Johnny?'

'And others.' Una looked round as though afraid someone was listening. 'We didn't say before, but there was talk going round that he wasn't payin' up for lots of things. 'Im and that other bloke.'

'The other bloke – Greg Wilde's relative?'

'Don't rightly know. They was different from us, see. Went out with Sandra and Elliot and belonged to the Chess Club.' Una looked thoughtful. 'Mind you, Johnny belonged to the Chess Club, too. P'raps that's where they met.'

'You don't think Sandra would know any more about it?' asked Libby.

'Might do, duck. You already asked her though.'

'Yes,' said Libby, refraining from saying she'd already asked Una, too. 'Oh, well, it was worth a try.' She stood up. 'Now I've got my breath back I'll go back down the hill.'

'All right, me duck, if you're sure that's all?'

'Yes, it was just something Johnny said when we saw him this morning.' Libby smiled and kissed the smooth old cheek. 'Thanks, Una. I'll see you soon.'

Feeling marginally better, Libby walked away down Steeple Lane, glancing as she did so at the low cottage next to Una's that had belonged to Sandra Farrow and her first husband. Suddenly, she stopped. Where had Farm Cottage been?

She turned round slowly. Beyond Una's cottage, they'd said. But it had fallen down. Been left to rot.

Libby sniffed the air like a retriever. Time to go a-hunting.

Beyond Una's cottage the land flattened out. On her

left, it still fell into the small wooded cut where the Wytch had finally petered out, but on the right it was a wide expanse of agricultural land, planted with some kind of wheat crop. Libby wasn't well up on crops. Rounding a slight bend, she came across a few buildings, most looking abandoned. And beyond them, what appeared to be the shell of a small house.

'Farm Cottage!' Libby whispered to herself, and strode on towards it.

Half of it had indeed fallen down, into a pile of brick at the back, but the front still looked reasonably intact. She stopped at the gate.

Once it had been a charming cottage with a green-painted front door in the middle, a sash window either side and two above, with a chimney in the middle of the roof, exactly like a child's drawing. Now you could see through the windows to open farmland beyond. And, Libby noticed, another building.

She pushed open the gate, which objected a bit, and stepped through into the overgrown garden. She managed to navigate her way through fallen masonry and vengeful vegetation to the side of the cottage where she came to a halt, prevented from going any further by the remains of a high fence. Between the broken palings she could see what looked like a reinforced large coal bunker, presumably the "security shed" Johnny had built. But it certainly didn't look big enough to house people, so whatever it was for, it was more for storage than anything else. Libby scowled at it, noting the heavy – and shiny – new padlock attached to the hasp of the door.

She tried to see if there was any sign of recent activity but couldn't, and finally, after acknowledging that she was beginning to feel a little nervous, she clambered her way back out of the garden and began to retrace her steps.

Now she was wondering what to do. Go back home?

Go to the Manor? Go and see how the get-out was going? She hadn't had any lunch, and she wondered if Ben had. Should she go back and send him a text saying lunch was ready? Pretend nothing had happened? Or should she wait for him to get in touch? And do what, she wondered. Apologise? No. She shook her head. She should be the one to apologise, if anyone. Possibly for years of bad behaviour.

When she reached the bottom of Steeple Lane where it turned back into the high street, she rang the Manor.

'Hetty, is Ben there? Has he had any lunch?' An odd request, she knew, but Hetty was unlikely to ask questions.

'He's just had a sandwich in here with me,' said Hetty. 'He's finishing off in the theatre with that Tristan.'

'Ah,' said Libby. 'Thanks, Het. Tell him it's curry tonight.'

She hoped, anyway. As long as she had all the ingredients...

As she passed the Pink Geranium, Harry popped out like the genie in Aladdin.

'Something tells me,' he said, 'that someone is in the mood for try-it-out soup.'

Libby looked up at him blankly. 'What?'

'Lunch, dear heart. Ben's up at the theatre and you're wandering the streets like a lost soul. Come along.'

He took her arm and piloted her into the restaurant, pushing her down in a chair at the table in the window, which was already set for two, including a bottle of red wine and a basket of fresh bread.

'How -' she began. Harry tapped the side of his nose.

'Pour the wine, woman. I'll fetch the soup.'

This was one of Harry's standards, a soup made at times when the Geranium was closed and there was a surfeit of leftover vegetables. Libby was often the

211

beneficiary of these bouts of creativity, although today it had revived the weepiness that had come over her in Steeple Lane. Harry ignored it, merely passing her a handful of paper napkins before fetching the soup bowls. Neither of them spoke until Libby had almost finished her bowlful.

'Thank you, Hal,' she said. 'How did you know?'

'Ben came out of Maltby Close looking aloof and aristocratic and you followed ten minutes later looking hot and bothered. Then Ben disappeared up the Manor Drive and you went haring off up Steeple Lane. I could be making five out of my simple sums, but I don't think so.'

'No, you're quite right,' said Libby, scooping up the last of her soup. 'And that was gorgeous. I won't ask what was in it.'

Harry gave an artistic shudder. 'No, don't, dear heart.' He topped up their glasses.

'Aren't you going to ask?' said Libby.

Harry shrugged. 'I will if you want me to, but if it's private, and I guess it is, then you won't want to tell me.'

'Well, I do want to tell you, because you're always honest. Remember when Fran got the hump about me?'

'Yes, and quite right, too.'

'Well now Ben's done it.'

Harry sat back in his chair and regarded her thoughtfully.

'Out of the blue, or for any particular reason?'

'To be honest, Hal, I think he might have had more than he could take.'

Harry nodded and rested his chin on his hands. 'We rather wondered how long it was going to take,' he said.

Chapter Twenty-six

Libby gaped.

'Have you all felt the same way about me for ages?' she asked eventually, in a small voice.

'What way?' Harry put his head on one side.

Libby closed her eyes. 'That I'm a rude and nosy old cow.'

Harry snorted. 'Well, yes, obviously.'

Libby's eyes flew open. 'Eh?'

'Well, you asked.' He leant forward and patted her hand. 'Come on, you old trout, it's part of your charm.'

'That's what I've told myself. Excused myself,' said Libby. 'But I do always like my own way, and I am rude to people. I was horrible to the young DC up in the incident room.'

'Look, Lib. Yes, you are – or can be – rude. Sometimes you speak without thinking and don't put things as tactfully as you should. But hell – so do I! And that's why you leap into situations, as well, and why you get into trouble with so many investigations. But listen.' He pushed her glass towards her. 'Why do you think Ian lets you carry on poking your nose in? Why do people come and ask you to investigate? Why did I?'

'I don't know.' Libby looked at him doubtfully.

'Because you're actually quite good at all this, you daft bat! And if Ben gets fed up now and then – well, I'm not surprised. I expect he sometimes feels a bit responsible for you, and he does, after all, bear the brunt of the whirlwind.'

'Whirlwind?'

'You, idiot. So drink up, go outside and have one of your increasingly rare fags, and cheer up.'

Libby gave him a tremulous smile and stood up. 'I always said you were my best friend.'

'Notwithstanding the elegant Mrs Wolfe?'

'Even her,' said Libby, and gave him a huge and rather damp hug.

Eschewing the suggested cigarette, Libby took her courage in both hands and walked up the drive towards the Manor and the theatre. The forecourt was full of vehicles, including the lorry that transported the collapsed booth theatre and people. As she hesitated, wondering whether to try and enter the theatre through the front or the back, Ben appeared pushing a wheeled flight case. He saw her, stopped and grinned. Libby's insides did something peculiar.

'Have you had any lunch?' he called.

'Yes, thanks. Just wondered how things were going. Can I help?'

Ben looked surprised. 'No we're fine, thanks. They'll be gone soon, then I'll do a quick look round and pack up. Tristan's already checked out of Steeple Farm.'

'Is he here? Should I say goodbye?' Libby realised they were going to treat this morning's episode as if it hadn't happened and felt obscurely cheated. Oh, well, she'd deal with that later.

'He's in the house rounding up his last actors. I'll just finish up here and be home in about half an hour.' Ben resumed his pushing.

Libby went in to the Manor and found Tristan in the large sitting room Hetty gave over to visitors.

'I came to say goodbye,' she said. 'I hope it hasn't been too traumatic.'

'No.' Tristan gave her a sheepish smile. 'I think we've been a lot more trouble than we were worth, and I'm

214

sorry. But in the end it's turned out well for us, and we appear to have got more work out of it.'

'Just don't let those people on your board loose on the cultural side of things,' said Libby. 'They're hopeless.'

Tristan sighed. 'They are, rather. Gideon was the only one who understood the theatrical world. And he was very keen on Shakespeare.'

'Well, I would imagine anyone who worked for National Shakespeare would be,' said Libby.

'Oh, no. He's just a commodity to them. Most of them couldn't tell you a thing about him.'

'Heavens.' Libby shook her head. 'Well, good luck with the rest of the tour. Where are you off to next?'

'West, now. Marlborough next weekend.'

'Few days off, then.'

'There'll still be stuff to do,' said Tristan. 'More publicity.'

'Of course.' Libby held out her hand. 'Well, it was nice to meet you, despite everything else.'

'And you.' Tristan shook her hand. 'And again – sorry.'

Libby went home. As she passed The Pink Geranium she gave Harry a thumbs up and received a wink in return.

Now she could start thinking about her revised picture of Nathan Vine and his security shed.

The landline was ringing as she came through the door and Sidney shot out.

'Hello?'

'You sound breathless,' said Fran.

'I've just come in – I was outside when the phone began to ring.'

'Oh, sorry. Do you want to get your breath back?'

'No, it's OK, I've got some news for you.'

'I did wonder,' said Fran.

Libby sat down on her favourite step and proceeded to

bring Fran up to date with everything that had happened over the last two days, leaving out the situation between her and Ben.

'So you see, things have changed somewhat,' she finished, 'and Nathan doesn't look like a good guy anymore. But I can't fathom what that shed is for.'

'Shouldn't you tell Ian?' said Fran. 'It could have a bearing on the case.'

'It was Nathan's, not Duncan Lucas's,' said Libby.

'Didn't you say, though, that there was a new padlock on the door? That couldn't have been Nathan, could it? Could it have been Lucas? Before he was killed? We know he was in Canterbury.'

'Yes.' Libby chewed her lip. 'Oh, all right. I'll report it in. And don't you think it's funny that the villagers didn't say anything about Vine? Or Russell Wilde, come to that.'

'Apart from knowing everything by osmosis, villagers can be remarkably close-mouthed,' said Fran. 'You know that.'

'I know.' Libby sighed. 'And Fran -'

'Yes?'

'Oh, nothing. I was just -'

'Just what? Come on, Libby.'

'Just wondering.'

'Wondering what? For goodness' sake, Libby. You're not usually so reticent.'

'No, that's the trouble, isn't it? I'm not. Ever.'

Silence fell, and Libby's solar plexus began to play up again.

'What's happened?' said Fran at last. 'Who have you upset?'

'How -? Oh. Well, Ben, actually.'

'*Ben*?' Fran gave a shout of laughter. 'What was the straw that broke the camel's back?'

'Oh, so you've been expecting it, too, have you?'

'You've been talking to Harry.'

'Yes. He ambushed me in the high street.'

'Did he give you a good talking to?'

'In a way,' said Libby with a reluctant smile. 'But he made me feel better. And Ben was perfectly normal when I went up to say goodbye to Tristan.'

'Tell me what happened.'

Libby told her.

'I wouldn't wonder if he didn't think anything of it,' said Fran. 'Looked at rationally, he didn't do much, did he?'

'He told me off.'

'And some of us have wondered why he hasn't done it before.'

'That's more-or-less what Harry said.' Libby sighed. 'Do you really think I'm making too much of it?'

'I do, so stop dwelling on it, but take it as a warning.'

Libby instinctively bristled, then realised that what Fran was saying was right.

'OK, boss, I will. Now I'd better get on and leave a message for Ian. I did actually tell that nice DC I was rude to that I'd leave him a message about Michael and Bel leaving.'

'Go and do it, then.'

Libby went into the kitchen and put the kettle on before sending Ian a text about Bel and Michael and "another matter" on both his mobiles. Up to him, now. She had had just poured boiling water into the teapot when her phone rang.

'Go on, then,' said Ian. 'What do you want to tell me?'

'You didn't have to ring me back,' prevaricated Libby.

'I know, that's why you sent me a text. But I have, so what is it.'

Libby repeated all her information and waited to be told off for trespassing in the garden of Farm Cottage.

'And you want to know what's inside?' was all Ian said.

'It's a new padlock,' said Libby weakly.

'And a new hasp?'

'It looked it.'

'In which case, we will definitely look into it. And no, you can't come with us.'

'What about Johnny Darling and Philip Jacobs?'

'What about them?'

"They knew Nathan Vine and Russell Wilde.'

'Yes, they did. And yes, I shall probably talk to them. But again, you can't come along.'

'No.' Libby pulled a face at her mug. 'But it's interesting, isn't it?'

'Yes, it is. And now, Libby, I must go back to work.'

'Sorry. Will you -'

'Yes, I'll keep you informed where I can.' The phone went dead.

Libby, realising that Ben would be with her shortly, fetched another mug and poured out her own tea.

'Go on, then,' said Ben coming in to the kitchen from the back garden and making her jump. 'What's been happening?'

Libby told him what Una had said, and what she'd seen in the garden of Farm Cottage.

'So I reported it all to Ian, and about Philip and Johnny of course. And he's going to look into it. So that's good, isn't it?' She poured out his tea and pushed it over, eyeing him warily.

'Excellent. And what do you think about it?'

'Me?'

'Yes, Lib. You.' Ben looked at her quizzically, then laughed. 'Look, I'm sorry if I upset you earlier, but sometimes you do get my goat. I still love you, though.'

'Do you? Really? Only I'm such a rude nosy old

cow...'

'But you're *my* rude nosy old cow.'

'And people are always making allowances for me -'

'Well, perhaps we'll have to pull you up a bit more often,' said Ben, taking her hand in his.

Libby wisely didn't mention her chats with Harry or Fran and went round the table to give him a kiss.

On Tuesday morning, Ben went to open up for the small army of local people who cleaned the theatre and the Manor. A couple went in every morning during performances, but the whole place needed a deep clean after a run like this.

Libby forced herself to go into the conservatory and do some work on the sadly neglected painting that Guy had wanted for the shop at least two weeks ago. She was just starting to glare at the badly sketched-in cliff line when her phone rang.

'Libby, me duck – do you know what all them police are doing up the road here?'

'Er – not exactly, Una, but I can take a guess.' Libby sighed and put down her charcoal.

'Go on then. Is it something to do with what you was talking about yesterday?'

'Yes – it's that shed I asked you about. Although I didn't know they were going to send a squad up there. Are there many of them?'

'Looks like it. I can't tell, properly, they're round the bend, but there's a couple of police cars and a minivan effort.' Una sounded excited. 'And I don't want to go out and look nosy!'

Libby laughed. 'I promise I'll tell you as soon as I hear anything.'

She cut the call and phoned Fran.

'So Ian's taken it seriously,' said Fran.

'I wonder if that's because the police have found something suspicious in their background checks,' said Libby. 'Or maybe in Russell's?'

'Would they have checked with Richard if that was the case?'

'I don't know. In fact, I don't really know why he's still here.'

'Who's got all his father's papers? Him, or Andrew and Gilbert?' asked Fran.

'I've no idea. They were all looking at them in the Manor dining room, but now Michael's gone home they seem to have come to a dead stop. And for all I know, Gilbert may have gone home, too.'

'He'd have told you, surely?'

'I would have thought so,' agreed Libby. 'I suppose I could ring round and see who's still here.'

'Will you be having a meal at the caff tomorrow with Patti and Anne?'

'I hadn't thought of it, no. Why?'

'You could ask all your academics to come for a farewell meal. That'll give them a hint.'

'Well, yes, but Gilbert's no trouble – we hardly see him, staying down in Nethergate. And to be honest, Richard isn't, either, but I suppose we shouldn't allow him to live rent-free in his hut for much longer when he's got a perfectly good home to go to. I'll see what Ben says.'

In fact, it wasn't necessary to ask Ben or the academics, as both Richard and Gilbert got in touch with her.

'I'm going home, Libby,' said Richard, standing uncomfortably on her doorstep. 'The police appear to have finished with me, and say if they've any more questions they know where to find me.'

'Come in for a moment,' said Libby, holding the door

wide. 'Did they tell you anything else?'

Richard shook his head. 'No. They're still trying to find out who forged the letter, and apparently they've managed to track my father down here, where he stayed for a time in touch with Nathan Vine. I suppose that's relevant.'

'I suppose so,' said Libby, refraining from saying "I know." 'Well, we'll keep you abreast of any developments as we hear of them, although I don't suppose there'll be much now. Unless they find the murderer.'

'Or murderers,' said Richard. 'Well, I hope they do.' He bent and kissed her cheek. 'Thanks for your hospitality, Libby, and I'm delighted to have met you.'

'Drive safely,' said Libby, watching him cross the road and climb into his old sports car.

She had barely closed the door behind him when the phone rang again.

'Libby, it's Andrew.'

'Oh! I was going to ring you to ask if you and Gilbert fancied coming for a sort of farewell meal at Harry's?'

'Two minds with but a single and all that,' said Andrew, 'but Gilbert's going home today. He feels he's trespassed long enough on my hospitality, and now Richard's taken all his father's papers back home with him -'

'Has he?' Libby was surprised. 'He didn't tell me that.'

'Yes.' Andrew sounded faintly annoyed. 'He just turned up here out of the blue yesterday afternoon and asked for them all back.'

'How did he know where you lived?'

'Oh, he had my address, and presumably he's got satnav. Everybody has these days, haven't they?'

'Or an app on their phone,' said Libby. 'That is,

everyone except me.'

'Oh, well, there you are,' said Andrew with a sigh. 'And I know Michael's gone, too – he called to say goodbye. I gather he and Gilbert will be getting together in London. They said something about going through the V&A paperwork.'

'Oh, that's a good idea,' said Libby. 'And they'll let us know, won't they?'

'I expect the police have already done it,' said Andrew, 'but yes of course they will. And Edward will be in touch, too, I expect, won't he?'

'Oh, yes, I'd forgotten Edward,' said Libby. 'What a lot of academics.'

Andrew laughed. 'I'm taking Gilbert to the station here shortly and he can link up with the main line at Canterbury. And I was wondering, do you still meet for a meal on Wednesdays sometimes?'

'Why, yes -'

'Well, how about tomorrow, then? I know Patti and Anne go too, but they wouldn't mind, would they?'

'No, of course not, and in fact, I was going to suggest it myself,' said Libby. 'I'll book it with Harry.'

She ended the call, thought for a moment and then called Ben.

'And I wonder why he wants to come up?' she said. 'After all, he's seen us quite a lot over the last week or so.'

'Normality?' suggested Ben. 'After all, it's all been a bit odd recently, hasn't it? And however exciting it's been, it's also been stressful, and the older you get the more that takes it out of you.'

'How would you know?' laughed Libby. 'You're nowhere near Andrew's age.'

'Thank you, kind lady. And now get on and phone Harry. Oh, and you'd better phone Guy and Fran, too.

And Patti and Anne to warn them.'

'It's on,' said Libby to Fran, 'but only Andrew. All the others have gone voluntarily. So, do you want to come up?'

'Yes, and I think it's Guy's turn to drive. How I wish we had a train line between us.'

'There is a bus,' said Libby.

'Twice a day and takes hours,' said Fran.

Chapter Twenty-seven

By the time Libby had warned Patti about the invasion and booked a table with Harry it was time for lunch and while she was dithering about what to have Ben called with an invitation from Hetty.

'She's made an enormous tuna salad which she says won't keep, so can we help her eat it. I think it's an excuse to find out what's going on.'

Libby happily abandoned her easel for her latest basket and set off for the Manor.

'Golly!' she said surveying the huge bowl of salad sitting in the middle of the kitchen table. 'We'll never get through that lot.'

'Give it a try, gal,' said Hetty. 'Want a drop of wine with it?'

'I'd better not,' said Libby. 'or I'll never get anything done this afternoon.'

'Right, Mum. What did you want to ask us?' Ben fixed his mother with a shrewd eye.

'Had Una on the phone,' said Hetty, completely unruffled. 'About the police.'

'Ah,' said Libby. 'Yes, she called me, too, but I don't know anything about it.'

Hetty nodded and forked up a mouthful of tuna. Ben and Libby waited.

'Just wondered if it had anything to do with that Richard.'

'*Richard*?' echoed Libby and Ben.

'Why he went so sudden, like.'

'Did he?' Libby looked at Ben, who shrugged.

'Don't ask me. He just appeared in the theatre foyer earlier and said thank you for the hospitality and he thought he ought to get back.'

'He came to see me and said the same thing,' said Libby. 'So he didn't explain it to any of us? And now Gilbert's gone too.'

'Funny, if you ask me,' said Hetty. 'All of 'em going at once.'

'I think Michael going was the catalyst,' said Libby. 'Andrew said he called to say goodbye this morning, and I suppose Gilbert thought there was no point in staying. They're going to get together in London, anyway. Oh – and Richard took all his father's papers back.'

'Did he?' Ben looked at Hetty. 'Did you know, Mum?'

Hetty shook her head.

'Technically, of course, they're my papers now,' said Ben. 'They belong to the house.'

'But you've never wanted them before,' said Libby.

'Well, no, but they're rather important now, aren't they?'

Libby gave him a dubious look. 'They were Greg's to give away – technically.' She turned to Hetty. 'Did he know about the police in Steeple Lane?'

'No idea, gal.'

'I didn't tell him anything about the shed,' said Ben. 'Or about seeing Philip Jacobs last night.'

'So he won't know, then.' Libby frowned down at her plate. 'Can't have been that, then.'

'And why would it have been, anyway?' said Ben. 'According to him, he knew nothing about his father's jaunts down here. He only knew about his interest in the history of the house when he was older.'

'Oh, I know,' said Libby with a sigh. 'It was just Hetty wondering...'

'Sorry, gal.' Hetty looked up and gave her a tight

smile.

'And how would he have known about the police in Steeple Lane, come to think of it,' said Libby, 'unless one of us told him. He doesn't know Una, and the police wouldn't have told him.'

'Just had enough, then,' said Ben.

'Hmm,' said Libby.

After lunch she was tempted to wander up Steeple Lane and see what was going on, but decided to curb her curiosity until she could ask Ian.

"And when that'll be, heaven knows," she told herself.

On Wednesday morning, giving in to temptation, Libby called Una and asked if the police were still there.

'No, me duck. I saw all the police cars drive away last night, and I toddled up the road meself this morning. They've left some of that stripy tape you see on the telly across the gate and the fence at the side, but no people.'

Police tape! That meant a crime scene, thought Libby. Aloud, she said, 'Oh, that's all right then, isn't it? We haven't heard anything, so probably nothing to do with our business.'

And if you believe that, you'll believe anything.

'Bit of a coincidence though, innit?' said Una thoughtfully.

'Certainly is,' agreed Libby. 'OK, Una, look after yourself. I'll see you soon.'

She ended the call and phoned Fran.

'Crime scene! Can't believe it. No police presence, though.'

'How odd.' Fran sounded as though she was frowning. 'An old one, do you think?'

'From when Nathan lived there? Maybe. Do you think Ian will come to the pub tonight?'

'So that you can grill him?' said Fran. 'If he's got any sense he'll stay away.'

'Johnny Darling might know,' said Libby. 'I told Ian about him, so he's bound to have asked him, isn't he?'

'I would have thought so, but honestly, Lib, you can't just go and ask him.'

'Can't I? Oh, no, I suppose I can't. Oh, how annoying it is being on the outside.'

'You aren't exactly on the outside,' said Fran.

'I know,' said Libby. 'I'm going to take Jeff-dog for a walk. He's good at sniffing out things.'

'He can't go into Farm Cottage, Lib, you know that. And they might have had dogs up there already.'

'I'm still going to,' said Libby.

'You'll look suspicious,' said Fran.

'Who to? Una? She wants to know what's going on anyway.'

Hetty was so suspicious when Libby turned up wanting to take Jeff-dog out she refused to let them go unless she went with them.

Libby sighed. 'I'm going up Steeple Lane,' she said.

'Thought so,' said Hetty. 'Good excuse to see Una, then. Come on.'

She put Jeff-dog's smart red leather collar on and clipped on his lead. Apart from looking rather puzzled when he was led down the Manor drive rather than the other way over the fields, he seemed happy enough, and Libby congratulated herself on having found and adopted such an amenable dog.

'What you looking for, then?' asked Hetty as they walked down the drive. 'Nothing to see, wouldn't have thought.'

'No, I know, and as Fran said I won't be able to go inside the gate like I did the other day.'

'What we going for, then?'

'I don't know. Sheer nosiness,' admitted Libby. 'You didn't have to come.'

227

'Stop you getting into trouble,' said Hetty gruffly. Libby grinned.

To her surprise, when they reached Una's cottage, Hetty carried on walking.

'I thought you said you were going to see Una.'

'Will after. Want to see Farm Cottage. We tried to buy it.'

'Yes,' said Libby, sending her a curious look. 'Is he dead now? The owner?'

'Terrance, yes.'

'I thought he must be.' Libby nodded.

They rounded the bend and came up to the cottage. Police tape fluttered along the fence and across the gate in front, and across the door and side access inside the fence.

'I'm going round the back,' said Libby, handing the dog lead to Hetty. Neither side of the cottage looked particularly accessible, but one side looked slightly less impeded than the other, so, glad she was wearing jeans and trainers rather than sandals, she tackled that side. However, once she was there she found more fencing and more tape, and although it would have been fairly simple to climb over it, she decided not to. Not because she was scared, she told herself, but because it was the right thing to do.

She clambered back to Hetty and Jeff-dog waiting patiently in the lane.

'Can't see anything,' she said, and bent down to stroke Jeff-dog's head. 'Do you know, he's the most laid-back dog I have ever met.'

They turned and walked back to Una's cottage.

'Well, hello, me ducks!' she said with a delighted smile as she opened the door. 'What a lovely surprise! Come on in.'

'Gal's been snooping,' said Hetty. 'Can I bring the dog in?'

'Course you can. Never seen such a well-behaved dog.'

'That's what I just said.' Libby smiled a proud smile.

When Una had provided tea, she asked why Libby had wanted to look.

'I thought I might get an idea of what the police found.' Libby heaved a disappointed sigh. 'But nothing. Can't understand why there's no police presence if there's something worth protecting there.'

'Well, I told you, I didn't even know there was a shed there,' said Una. D'you reckon it's something they found in the shed worth protecting?'

'Must be,' said Hetty. 'Cottage is all open.'

'I wonder if Johnny knows what it is?' said Libby.

'Don't you go pokin' your nose in,' said Hetty. 'Leave him be.'

'That's what Fran said.'

'Sensible woman, that Fran.' Hetty nodded pointedly.

'I know, I know.' Libby sighed. 'Well, if there's nothing more to see, I should probably go home.' She stood up.

'I'll stay here a bit,' said Hetty. 'You go on.'

'All right. Thanks for the tea, Una.'

'Well,' she said to herself out loud once she was back in the lane, 'that was a bit pointless.'

She began walking back down the lane when she suddenly became aware of someone behind her. At the same time she became aware just how isolated it was up here. The cottage next door to Una's was empty, Steeple Farm, a little way along, was also empty, there was nothing else between there and the high street and nothing except woodland and the dewpond on the other side. She swung round to confront her follower.

'I bet you bin up to look at the cottage, too, ain't yer?' Johnny Darling was grinning at her and Libby felt herself sag with relief.

'Yes, Hetty and I were out with the dog.' Libby stood and waited for him to catch up. 'She's gone in to see Una now.'

'Course she has. Thick as thieves all our oldies.'

'Yes, well, I suppose they'd be like that in any community,' said Libby. 'Johnny, we were wondering why the police have put police tape round Farm Cottage. Do you know? Did they come and see you yesterday?'

'Certainly did. Asked me what was in the shed when I put it up.'

'And what was?' asked Libby.

'Nothing except shelves. All metal they was, like the shed itself. They had me put these concealed air bricks in, too. Well, they wasn't bricks exactly, more vents, like.'

'They?'

'That Vine and his mate. Both went to the Chess Club.'

'Russell Wilde?'

'I dunno his name – never did. He weren't local, like, although he stayed for a bit down Lendle Lane. Old Mrs Evans's place. I never saw him much, and he'd gone by the time Vine went.'

'Did you tell the police?'

'Course. No point in keepin' it to meself, was there?'

'No, I suppose not,' said Libby. 'Did you see there was a new lock on the shed door?'

'I did. And it weren't me what put it there. New hasp, an' all.'

'Yes, I noticed that. Looks as though someone's been using it again, don't you think?'

'Dunno who. Old Terrance's been dead for years, now, and no one's been lookin' after that cottage.'

'What about his farm itself? Do those buildings next to it belong to it?'

'Them buildings are only used for storage, but yes, they belong to the farm. See, it was only bought a year or so ago. 'Ad to go through the law, first.'

'Probate?'

'Aye. Reckon Terrance's son got it in the end and sold it.'

'Does he still live here? The son?'

'No, shot off years ago. Couldn't be doin' with farmin', see. Well, I'll be off, then.' Johnny stopped at the end of the high street. 'I'd like to know what's goin' on up there, though. Give us a shout if you find out? Leave a message with Tim at the pub.'

Libby said she would and watched him turn up the Nethergate Road. And then remembered a question she'd wanted to ask Andrew and Gilbert. She took out her phone.

'Andrew, sorry to bother you, and I know I'm going to see you later, but I just remembered. Did you ever ask that person's advice? What was his name – Harrold?'

'Jim Harrap. Yes, we asked him a few questions. He actually knew quite a lot about both The Lord Chamberlain's Men and the spy network, but I don't know how useful it would have been. I mean, what exactly were we trying to find out?'

'I suppose basically – where would the knowledge have come from to make the forgery in the first place,' said Libby. 'But only tangentially to do with the murder.'

'Or murders,' said Andrew. 'Look, I've got to go now, but if you like I'll bring down my notes of what he told me this evening.'

'Oh, good, thanks,' said Libby.

And Andrew was right to ask, she thought, as she walked slowly home. What exactly *were* they trying to find out? And just how important was it?

Chapter Twenty-eight

Once at home, Libby sat down at the table in the sitting room window with the laptop and a notebook to make notes. What was the problem here?

The first thing was the letter which was linked to the Manor. Then the discovery that it was a fake. The link to The Glover's Men she dismissed as irrelevant, except that it had brought them to Steeple Martin and the Oast Theatre. Then the discovery of Duncan Lucas's body, which was linked to The Glover's Men tour, so perhaps it wasn't irrelevant. And because he had been the person both to show the letter to the V&A and offer it on loan to National Shakespeare, it was felt that here was the motive for his murder.

But looked at like that it didn't seem a very sound reason to kill someone, Libby thought. Just because he was trying to pass off a forged Shakespeare relic? And despite all her ferreting round there was no connecting Lucas with the village, despite him having the tour flyer on his person. Naturally he was interested, he'd more or less caused this stop on the tour. But nothing more. As for Gideon Law, they knew nothing at all about him, and had nothing to connect him to anyone or anywhere else. Libby sighed.

And then Nathan Vine, who wasn't even related to Duncan Lucas after all, and Russell Wilde, who were both interested in the history of the Manor, who both looked into the archives and stayed in the village, yet didn't seem to do anything of interest except build a shed.

So what does all that add up to, she asked herself. The

answer – very little. Vaguely nefarious goings on, but I've made more of them than there actually is. As usual. And I've taken everybody else with me.

Well, she argued, there's the interest side of things, and the fact that we've found out that Shakespeare really *did* come here. And of course, Titus Watt. She looked up from her notebook and surprised Sidney, who had come on to the table to assist. Was that behind it all? Titus Watt, the Elizabethan Spy? But no one seemed to know much about him, either, and he'd hardly be a problem today, would he?

In fact, the whole case looked as though it had been blown out of all proportion – a spider's web of half-truths. There was obviously a case to be investigated, but it was Ian's case, and nothing to do with Libby, Ben, the Manor or the Oast House Theatre. She sighed and shut the laptop.

Later in the afternoon, Harry phoned.

'You've got an extra at dinner tonight,' he said. 'Mind you, he's only coming to see me.'

'Edward? He said he'd come this week.'

'Yes. He said he was killing two birds with one stone.'

'Oh? What did he mean?'

'I don't know, chuck, do I? He'll tell you later.'

The Wednesday night gathering, somewhat augmented, now consisted of Libby, Ben, Fran, Guy, Patti, Anne, Andrew and Edward. Everyone greeted Edward like a long-lost friend and wanted to know about his new job and digs.

'It's the digs that are the problem,' he said, as they settled round the big round table in the right hand window. 'I'm too old to be living in what are effectively student halls.'

'Are you a full professor now?' asked Anne.

'Yes – although it's more an honorary title than anything else. I'm still a Doctor.'

'It's very hit and miss, isn't it? Academia?' said Libby.

'It is, a bit,' said Edward, flashing his grin at her.

'So come on, Libby said you were killing two birds with one stone,' said Fran. 'Which birds?'

'I'm going to buy a house in Steeple Martin!' Edward beamed round at the delighted expressions from the assembled friends.

'I know you said you thought about it, but you also said it was too far from the Medway campus,' said Libby.

'I've changed my mind. I can stay up there a couple of nights a week, or when I need to, and spend the rest of the time down here. Better life-work balance.'

'And where's the house?' asked Guy.

'That's where I need your help, all of you. I need local knowledge. I've got some details from agents, but I don't know exactly where they are, or anything about them. I probably need Fran in her former capacity!'

'Actor?' said Anne.

'No! Investigator for Goodall and Smythe in London,' said Ben.

'Aren't they the posh estate agents?' said Anne.

Fran was scowling by this time.

'Yes,' said Patti, hurrying in to save the situation, 'but Libby would be better as a local informant, surely?'

'That was what I was thinking,' said Edward apologetically, 'but I hesitated to suggest it.'

'Oh, I'd be delighted,' said Libby. 'It'll get me away from thinking about this Shakespeare business.'

'Why?' asked Fran. Everyone looked surprised.

'Because it's pointless,' said Libby, and outlined her reasons. To her disappointment, everyone reluctantly agreed with her, and no one protested.

'I did find out a bit more about Titus Watt, though,' said Andrew, 'just for interest's sake.'

'Oh, I wondered about him,' said Libby, 'just in case

he was the whole reason for the fake and the murders. But I don't see that he could be.'

'No, I don't think so.' Andrew took a sip of wine. 'And the main reason for the connection with Shakespeare is that he appears to have visited Trebona with John Dee and Edward Kelly, when it's thought that Shakespeare was the other mysterious gentleman who visited.'

Most of the others gathered round the table were now looking confused.

'That's during the Lost Years?' asked Libby.

'Yes. It's speculation, but very persuasive. Several writers of the period were used as spies – Marlowe for one. And Dr John Dee went abroad with Edward Kelly, who claimed to be able to perform transmutation, but he was still in Elizabeth's pay. Shakespeare was thought to visit under a false name to take and bring back messages. It stopped when he came back to Mortlake. Shakespeare visited there once, but when his theatre career took off he appears to have given up his spying activities. However, it looks as if he and Watt encountered each other through Dee, and when the Lord Chamberlain's Men left London for their tour, Watt suggested he bring them to Quinton St Martin. There is also a suggestion that at this time, a year after the battle of Cadiz, the Earl of Essex was no longer in favour, and that Robert Cecil had both John Dee and Titus Watt looking into his affairs. Shakespeare, out touring England, would be ideally placed to nose out any further problems.'

'Right – I'm lost,' said Guy. 'I don't even know all the names.'

'Well,' said Libby, amused, 'I know the names, if not the detail, but I can tell you one thing. Quinton St Martin is Steeple Martin, and as far as we can see, it more-or-less consisted of the Manor and the church, although the Manor didn't look like it does now, and the church was rebuilt in the Victorian era.'

'The things we learn!' said Patti admiringly. 'Did you know all this, Anne?'

'No! I knew Titus Watt had a house here, as I said, but absolutely nothing else.'

'I'm still a bit worried that people will find out about it,' said Ben. 'We don't want to be a showplace.'

'You don't look like a showplace,' said Harry, coming up behind him. 'Come on, let's be 'avin' you. I haven't got all night.'

Edward smiled up at him. 'It's good to see you, Harry.'

Harry, to Libby's astonishment, went a gentle shade of pink.

Orders placed, the conversation reverted to Edward's future home.

'Shame Farm Cottage is in such a state,' said Libby, and had to explain Farm Cottage to the rest of the table.

'Isn't the photo shop still empty?' asked Fran. 'That was a lovely flat upstairs, wasn't it?'

'I don't think Edward would want that,' said Libby. 'Bad connotations.'

Immediately, Edward wanted to know what connotations.

'Connected to one of the investigations,' said Ben, 'but as it happens, it is empty, and it's also been approved for change of use.'

'How do you know?' Libby raised her eyebrows in surprise.

'Aha!' said Ben, and tapped the side of his nose. Libby snorted.

'Can I go and see it?' asked Edward.

'But it's a shop!' said Libby.

'It was a house originally,' said Ben. 'And there's access from the back, from Lendle Lane, so you could

236

have parking space, without using the high street.'

'Stop the sales pitch!' laughed Guy. 'You can find out about it tomorrow.'

It was only when coffee had been served to those who wanted it that Libby found out why Andrew had wanted to talk to her.

'I got myself into a tricky situation, actually,' he said.

'You did?'

'Yes. Gilbert.'

'*Gilbert*?'

'Don't look so horrified.' Andrew looked amused. 'I just wished I hadn't asked him to stay. It was his interest in the whole situation – it began to strike me as a bit unhealthy.'

'Unhealthy – how?'

Andrew sat back in his chair and looked at her. 'How was he when you first met him?'

'Worried. Flustered. He didn't want National Shakespeare to go ahead with the whole forged letter thing.'

'No, exactly. That's what he told me, but why was he so bothered? It hadn't got anything to do with him anymore.'

'Well, it was his professional reputation, I suppose.'

'Anything else?'

Libby frowned. 'I don't know why. Why? He isn't a fake himself, is he? No, he can't be – you knew him, and so did Michael, at least by repute.'

'No, he isn't a fake. But why did he stay here?'

'You asked him!' said Libby in surprise.

'May I butt in?' asked Fran.

'Please do – I'm flummoxed,' said Libby.

'You said he was excited.' Fran looked at Andrew. 'Is that it?'

He nodded. 'And the further we delved into it the more

frantic he got.'

'Frantic?' repeated Libby and Fran together.

'It looked like it.' Andrew twirled his coffee cup in his hands. 'I began to get a bit uneasy, especially when he started making suggestions.'

'Like what?' asked Libby.

'About trying to get Ben and Richard to part with the family archive. It seemed almost – I don't know – underhanded. Not illegal, exactly, but...'

'Oh, dear,' said Libby, looking worried. 'I shouldn't have introduced him, should I?'

'I don't see how you could help it,' said Fran. 'Under the circumstances.'

'Exactly,' said Andrew. 'It was my fault for inviting him to stay. If I hadn't, he wouldn't have got involved with the family, would he?'

'I suppose,' said Fran slowly, 'it was a bit odd anyway, his coming down here on spec to try and talk to Tristan.'

'Come to think of it,' said Libby, suddenly sitting up straight, 'how did he know about Tristan in the first place?'

'Didn't Tristan tell you that Gilbert got in touch with him to say the letter was a fake?' Ben, who'd come in on the end of this conversation, joined in.

'Yes, so I guessed Gilbert was genuine, so to speak, and took him for granted.'

'Well, he was who he said he was,' said Andrew. 'He had worked for the V&A, and he did work on the letter first time round. It was Edward who put me on to him.'

'Edward? How?'

'You're an advisor to the Arts and Antiques squad, aren't you?' said Fran to Edward, who nodded.

'And they didn't use Gilbert?' said Ben.

'No – and he's an Elizabethan expert who works – or worked – for the V&A. I found that odd.' Andrew finished his coffee. 'Do you think Harry would bring me some more coffee?'

'Nothing stronger? Oh, no you're driving, aren't you.' Libby waved at Adam and indicated coffee.

'We could have brought you,' said Fran. 'How silly, I didn't even think.'

'Neither did I.' Andrew smiled at her. 'Anyway, do you think we should do anything about the Gilbert situation?'

By this time Patti, Anne and Guy had all joined in.

'There's no actual evidence of him doing anything – well, odd, is there?' asked Patti.

'No. It was just his attitude.' Andrew sighed. 'I'm probably making a mountain out of a pimple, and of course, it may be that I was simply becoming uncomfortable having someone permanently in the flat. I'm not used to it.'

'No, I don't think that's it,' said Libby. She turned to Fran. 'You weren't very happy right at the beginning, were you?'

Fran looked surprised. 'That's right – I wasn't. I'd forgotten that. We decided that I was fed up because I was left out, didn't we?'

Guy snorted. 'Oh, come on! You've never been like that in your life!'

'It does sound unlikely,' said Anne. 'Now, if it was me...' She turned to Patti. 'Now there's a thought, Pats. We could team up like Libby and Fran. What larks!'

Patti looked horrified and everyone else laughed.

'Mind you, I can see you doing it, Anne,' said Fran. 'You can do it when I take a holiday.'

'You're on!' said Anne happily. 'And now – what were you saying about being left out?'

'Fran wasn't very happy about Gilbert – or Richard, come to that, were you?' said Libby.

'No, but Ian had them checked out, and Michael, too. I think I was just worried about all the academics gathering round.'

'Like vultures?' Andrew grinned. 'Yes, that happens sometimes. And we all try and find things out – and beat each other to it. And argue about it.'

'So let's go back a bit,' said Libby. 'Edward told you the Arts and Antiques people didn't use him, or hadn't heard of him?'

'I'm not absolutely sure if they'd heard of him, but they don't use him. And by the way, the police *had* called them in over this, but of course they haven't got the actual letter,' said Edward.

'Well, I can't see that there's anything to be worried about,' said Guy. 'He hasn't got away with anything precious, has he?'

'Nooo...' Andrew was frowning. 'I don't know, really.'

Libby continued to look at Andrew thoughtfully while the others started up the conversation again.

'Do we mention this to Ian if he's in the pub?' she said, as Adam arrived with the bill.

Andrew laid his bank card on top of it. 'My treat,' he said, amid protests. 'I don't know. Do you?'

'I would think so,' said Ben. 'I know I complain sometimes when these women go ferreting things out, but this is a bit close to home.' He looked across at Guy. 'Sorry, mate.'

Guy grinned at him. 'I'm used to it,' he said.

Chapter Twenty-nine

Just as they were leaving the caff, the door opened.

'Come on, Anne,' said Ian, holding the door open. Anne gave him a delighted smile and manoeuvred her chair through the door.

'We wondered if you'd be here,' said Libby, following the wheelchair into the high street.

'It looks as though it's a good job I am,' said Ian. 'What is it, a council of war?'

'No, just a normal Wednesday, and Andrew joined us to celebrate being back to normal And Edward..'

Ian smiled. 'Must have been hard for him to have someone living in his flat with him for such a long time.'

Andrew tapped him on the shoulder. 'Wasn't that long, you know!'

'Over a week,' said Ian. 'How did you find him?'

'Well...' began Andrew.

'Let's wait until we get inside,' said Libby, as they arrived at the pub. Ian lifted a quizzical eyebrow.

Somehow, their favourite round table was free and they managed to distribute themselves around it while Ben and Guy went to buy drinks. Patti, as usual, tried and was refused.

'Something to tell me?' asked Ian, once drinks had arrived.

'Ask you, really,' said Libby. 'We were wondering about Gilbert. And it sounds as if you were, too.'

'What were you wondering?' Ian looked from Andrew to Libby. With a resigned sigh, Andrew told him.

'Very vague,' he finished, 'but I was a little

uncomfortable.'

'I can't say that I have anything more concrete,' said Ian, after a moment, 'but I tend to agree with you.'

'Really?' Libby was surprised. 'You don't usually agree with me.'

'I'm agreeing with Andrew,' said Ian. 'And I'm trained to be suspicious. I wondered from the first why the esteemed Professor Harrison came haring down here desperate to see Tristan Scott when there was really no need to.'

'No, there wasn't, was there?' said Ben. 'Michael and his team had already told Lucas it wasn't genuine and he'd removed it.'

'I suppose he might not have known that,' said Libby.

'Oh, he did,' said Andrew. 'And if he was that worried he would have called the V&A and checked. He kept his links there – and as I said to you, old academics never retire!'

'I think I need to talk to Michael Allen and see if there are records of when Nathan Vine submitted the letter to the museum,' said Ian. 'Or someone does.'

'And find out when,' said Libby. 'The dates have been terribly vague. At first I thought we were talking about when Ben was a boy, because Hetty said Russell used to visit then, but it looks as though it was only a few years ago.'

'The more recent it all is, the more likely we are to find records,' agreed Ian. 'Duncan Lucas's tablet, which he had with him, had very few emails, neither did his phone.'

'Maybe if he used a dedicated email server they would be on his laptop?' suggested Fran. Libby looked bewildered

'Oh – and another thing,' said Libby. 'Farm Cottage. Why is there police tape round it?'

'So that people won't go into it,' said Ian blandly. 'Like you.'

Libby opened her mouth to protest indignantly and shut it again when everyone laughed.

'No really, Ian,' said Ben. 'Did you find something up there?'

'We think so. In the shed.' Ian shot Libby a sly smile. 'Possibly printing materials. And don't you dare say anything to anyone.'

'Printing materials?' Guy looked interested. 'You mean for forging fake documents, don't you?'

'I might.' Ian grinned. 'As I said, not a word to anyone.'

Anne was practically falling out of her chair with excitement. 'Who was it lived in the shed?' she said breathlessly.

'The original owner of the fake letter,' said Guy. 'So, you see...'

'Not in the shed exactly,' said Libby.

Ian was watching them all with amusement. 'Well, I'm pleased you're all so interested,' he said, 'but no more – er – helping, if you don't mind. And try and steer the family away, Ben, if you wouldn't mind.'

'Hardly family,' said Ben. 'Only Richard. My other family are on Mum's side.'

'And you were going to ask your sister about Russell and Nathan, weren't you?' said Libby.

Ben shot a quick look at Ian. 'Yes, I was. Is that allowed?'

'What were you going to ask?'

'If she remembered Russell and Nathan. If she or her husband were in the Chess Club.'

'If I remember rightly,' said Ian, 'not that I was involved back then, but I would have thought she might not have done.'

'But, you see,' said Libby, 'I don't remember the Chess Club, or Russell, or Nathan. And I would have thought I would.'

'I think it was just before your time,' said Ben. 'I hadn't moved back, either.'

'Hmm.' Libby thought about it. 'So there's been quite a gap.'

Ian finished his coffee. 'Well, I must get off.' He stood up. 'Try not to let anything else happen in Steeple Martin, won't you?'

'I don't know what he thinks we can do about anything,' said Libby, as she watched Ian's tall figure go quickly out of the door. 'And why's he gone off so early?'

'He's still got to drive wherever it is he goes,' said Fran, 'and he has to get up in the morning.'

'What about this Gilbert, then?' said Anne. 'What are you going to do about him?'

'Nothing, I suppose,' said Libby.

'I agree,' Andrew nodded. 'If Ian, and by extension, the police, know that there might be some doubt about his -' he clicked his fingers impatiently.

'Integrity,' supplied Libby. Everyone looked at her in surprise. 'I can be intelligent sometimes,' she said.

'Integrity, then,' said Andrew with a grin, 'I don't think we need to worry. And after all, he isn't trying to steal anything from Ben's family, is he?'

'Or from anyone's family,' said Ben. The only things there are to steal are the original house archives, which strictly speaking don't belong to the family anyway.'

'But the family own the house,' said Andrew, 'and therefore, the documents that go with the house. If the family that owned the house back then still existed it would be different.'

'Very complicated, this family history, isn't it?' said Guy. 'Glad I haven't got any.'

'Well,' said Edward, 'it's all very interesting, but I don't think I've managed to contribute much. If you could keep an eye on the property market for me, Libby...'

The following day Libby suddenly had nothing to do. The Glover's Men had gone on to their next stop, the incident room had shut down and there wasn't even the summer show to prepare for. The cleaners had been in to prepare the theatre for Friday's one-nighter, Ben was back at the microbrewery and Harry and Guy were preparing their businesses for the summer rush. Libby mooched round the conservatory trying to decide what to do and felt depressed.

'I ought to get a job,' she told Sidney. 'I've said it before. There must be something I could do.'

The paper currently being stretched on the draughtsman's board in front of her mocked silently. 'All right, I know I've got painting to do,' she grumbled. 'I just don't know what to paint.'

Eventually, she gathered up sketch book, charcoal and pencils and set off for Nethergate. The seascape always inspired her, and she had a fancy to go round the bay and perhaps have a go at the lighthouse on the northern tip.

At the top of the high street, she turned left to drive along the top of the downs, and dropped down to where the lighthouse stood guarding its few coastguards' cottages, which Guy had told her would one day fall in the sea, as they were getting closer and closer to the eroding cliff edge. Very sad, she thought, turning into the car park by the lighthouse.

Inevitably, the sun had gone in. She climbed out of the car, pulled on her emergency jacket, gathered her materials, and set off to look for a suitable vantage point. The chalk cliffs were alive with insects and offered nowhere to sit safely, so she walked slowly along until she came to a bench she remembered from a previous visit here with Ian and Fran and sat down with relief. She now looked down on the harbour, The Sloop Inn, Mavis's Blue Anchor cafe and away to her right, Fran's Coastguard Cottage.

And immediately below her, at the bottom of the cliff path, Richard Wilde.

Libby nearly fell off the bench.

For a moment, she couldn't actually make sense of what she was seeing. Richard had gone home, hadn't he? Yesterday morning. And he didn't know Nethergate – or she assumed he didn't. So what was he doing here? She stood up, intending to hail him, and then sat down again. No – if he wanted to see her or Ben he would have told them he was here. Andrew? Was he here to see Andrew? And, she thought, he didn't know where Fran lived, or he wouldn't be walking nonchalantly along Harbour Street.

She found her phone in her bag and called Ben.

'Why didn't he tell us he was going there?' Ben sounded as puzzled as she was. 'Nethergate's got no connection to the family, or to the murders, has it?'

'Not as far as I know,' said Libby. 'Do I go down and speak to him? He's sitting down outside Mavis's now. Or will it embarrass him?'

'I expect it will, but it would be best for him to be aware that this is our stamping ground and he's likely to trip over at least one of us if he stays here.'

'And I'm in full view of Mavis and not far from the gallery, so I'll be quite safe.' Now why had she said that?

'Safe? Well, of course you'll be safe. Yes, go on then. I'm very interested to know what he says.'

So am I, thought Libby, so am I.

She made her way over to the cliff path and scrambled somewhat inelegantly down it to where it debauched on to the small car park behind the cafe and pub. Richard was now nursing a tall mug and staring out to sea, where one of the two tripper boats was chugging towards the harbour.

'Richard!' she called brightly. 'Whatever are you doing here? I thought you'd gone back to Norfolk.'

Richard, who had started violently at the sound of his name, now turned and stared at her in what looked to Libby like horror.

'I -' he began, stopped and cleared his throat. 'I could – er – say the same thing.'

'Hardly!' said Libby with a laugh. 'This is our local seaside town, and Fran and Guy live here – just along there – and Andrew lives at the top of the hill. You obviously didn't know?'

'Er – no. I – um – just felt like a break.'

'Your stay in the huts got you in the mood, did it?'

'Yes, it did.' Richard stopped squirming and pulled himself together. 'I just thought I'd like a proper holiday, so I stopped for lunch in Canterbury and investigated the area. This looked like a nice quiet seaside town.'

'It is.' Libby pulled a chair out from the table and sat down. 'Where are you staying?'

Richard nodded towards the other end of Harbour Street. 'The Swan. It's very comfortable.'

'What do you plan to do while you're here?'

'Just relax. Try a few different places to eat. Thought I'd check out the pavilion place.'

'The Alexandria? That's been recently restored. Our company usually put on a summer show there, but we're not this year.'

'Oh, pity,' said Richard without conviction. He put down his mug and stood up. 'Well, I must be getting on.'

Libby raised her eyebrows. 'Must you?'

Richard reddened. 'Don't want to waste the day,' he muttered. 'Nice to see you, Libby.'

Oh, no it wasn't, she wanted to retort, but instead

simply stood with him. 'I'm going this way, too,' she said, although this was fairly obvious, it being the only way you *could* go.

They walked uncomfortably together along Harbour Street until they came to Guy's gallery.

'Fran's husband's place,' said Libby. 'Come and have a look round while you're here.'

'Er – I will,' said Richard. 'Cheerio for now.' He turned and shambled smartly off towards The Swan.

Libby turned to face an open-mouthed Fran.

'What was he doing here?'

'He *says*,' said Libby pointedly, 'he's here having a quiet break.'

She explained how she had seen him completely accidentally.

'Not very likely, is it?' said Fran, taking her place behind the counter. 'Guy's out the back painting again.'

'It just might be true,' said Libby, 'but he seemed very uncomfortable. What would he be doing here, though? As Ben said, Nethergate has no connection to the family business or the murders.'

'Then his visit isn't connected, either,' said Fran.

Libby paused and stared hard at Fran. 'That means that you think he *is* connected.'

Chapter Thirty

Fran looked puzzled. 'Did I say that?'

'You said he's connected to the business and the murders. And Nethergate isn't. Well, that's what it amounted to.'

Fran stared down at the counter. 'Yes, I think he is. But I don't know how.'

'The same as you were worried about him at first?'

Fran looked up. 'I don't know. I think I was more worried about him not being who he said he was then, but Ian's checked that out, hasn't he?'

'As he did with Gilbert. Who you also weren't sure about.'

'Pull up that stool,' said Fran. Libby pulled. 'Now, let's work out what he could be doing.'

'Doing here, or doing in respect of the – er – case?'

Fran smiled. 'The case first, of course.'

'Actually, I don't know.' Libby sighed. 'After all, there's nothing valuable in those archive documents, although I do wish he'd left them with Ben. He had no right to go off with them. And it wasn't him in Steeple Martin with Nathan Vine, it was his father, and according to him and Hetty he didn't get on particularly well with his father, and left home for good before Russell started going down to meet Vine.'

'And knew nothing about the whole letter business until Ben got in touch through social media,' said Fran.

'Well, he says not, but I wouldn't mind betting he'd read or seen something about it in the press. He would have noticed because of the name.'

'But he knew nothing of the Shakespeare connection to the Manor?'

'He says not. And that he'd not gone through all his father's old papers.'

'He probably hadn't,' said Fran. 'They wouldn't have meant anything to him, would they? And he hadn't even been to the house. Hadn't he asked his father to bring him, but his father didn't – or wouldn't?'

'That's true,' said Libby. 'Well, in that case, he really is nothing to do with the archives and the fake letter. And following from that, nothing links him to either of the murder victims.'

'Unless he knew one or other of them in a completely different capacity – which would be a hell of a coincidence.'

'So,' said Libby, 'just what *is* he doing here?'

'He was embarrassed, you said,' said Fran.

'More horrified, actually.'

'Shall we,' said Fran, after a moment, 'take a stroll down to the square? He might be sitting at one of the tables outside.'

'Not if he thinks I'm in danger of coming out of here and seeing him. Anyway, you're working.'

'Sophie's upstairs. I can call her down.'

'Well, we could walk along Victoria Place or Cliff Terrace, I suppose. We might spot him from there, although I would think he'd be in hiding now.'

'But why?' Fran frowned. 'And, you know, my instincts aren't working properly any more. I was wrong about him and Gilbert in the first place, and I'm wrong again.' She sighed, then went over to the door to the flat above and called Sophie.

Five minutes later, they were walking along Harbour Street towards the square, then, keeping their eyes on The Swan, the venerable old inn that stood on the seaward side, they climbed up to Victoria Place. At the end of this, where it opened on to the cliffs was a small car park and a couple of benches, where Fran and Libby decided to sit.

'Nothing much going on down there,' said Libby. 'I don't know what you expected to see.'

'I don't know, either.' Fran shook her head. 'I'm trying to force things that aren't there.'

It was pleasant sitting there in the sun, but after a minute or two, Libby began to get bored.

'Oh, come on,' she said. 'He's not going to emerge just to please us. We might as well go. Or Jane will see us and wonder why we haven't come in.'

Their friend Jane Baker lived in Cliff Terrace, just above Victoria Place, and was the assistant editor of the *Nethergate Mercury*, part of a group of local newspapers, although that was almost a misnomer these days when they were mostly online feeds.

'All right.' Fran sighed and stood up, shaking out her skirt as she did so. 'It was a silly idea anyway. Oh!' She stopped and put her hand on Libby's arm. 'Look at that!'

'What?'

'Down by The Alexandria – where it goes round to the back.'

Libby peered down. A sort of mini-promenade led from the front of The Alexandria round both sides, lit with the same coloured lights as the square and Harbour Street at night. And here, leaning on the railings overlooking the beach, was Richard Wilde.

'He's got someone with him!' said Fran. 'Who is it?'

'How should I know?' said Libby, then 'Oh! I do, though. It's Philip Jacobs. Well!' She turned to Fran. 'They only met on Sunday.'

'It looks,' said Fran, squinting into the sun, 'as if they've met several times since then.'

'It does.' Libby smiled. 'Do you know, Harry's

251

famous gaydar didn't scent this one out. Is that why he was embarrassed, do you suppose?'

'Oh, I expect so,' said Fran, with a grin. 'Poor bloke. Perhaps his home circle isn't quite as liberal as ours.'

'Do you think,' said Libby, as they began to retrace their steps back to the gallery, 'they really only met on Sunday?'

'From what we could see up there,' said Fran, as they passed the front of The Alexandria, 'it looked a newish friendship. And it explains why Richard was in such a hurry to get away. He would be wary of exposing himself to anyone else, wouldn't he? Better to come down here and hide it away.'

'Not knowing we have eyes everywhere!' said Libby.

'Poor Richard,' said Fran. 'I don't know how you're going to tell him we know and it's fine with us.'

'Well, we won't have to, unless he comes back to Steeple Martin,' said Libby. They came to a stop outside the gallery and she groaned. 'Oh, blimey – I forgot! I've got to walk all the way up the cliff path to the top to get to the car.'

As soon as Libby got back to Steeple Martin, she drove straight up to the Manor and made her way round to Ben's microbrewery.

'You'll never guess!' she said, as she burst in.

'No, I won't. What?' He turned from a table full of charts and catalogues.

'I think Richard might be gay.'

Ben blinked. 'Really? Why?'

Libby explained about seeing him with Philip Jacobs.

'Well, that doesn't mean anything!'

'No, but it looked very much as if they were – well, you know, a couple.'

'But they've only just met.'

'Well, maybe they haven't. But it does explain why he

252

wanted to leave Steeple Martin. After all, they met on Sunday, didn't they, and if they both spotted something then... And remember, he left quite early in the evening. Suppose he went to the Huts, or Richard went down to his house?'

'It's possible, but a bit of a leap of faith,' said Ben.

'Anyway, Fran's decided that all her fears about him were unfounded. So I suppose we just forget all about the whole letter and murder thing and get on with real life.'

'Yes, except that I would like all those papers back. I've got really interested in old Titus Watt now, and I'd like to get someone on to it. Make sense of it all. Someone like Andrew, maybe?'

'Oh, I think it would be a bit much to ask Andrew. It would be a huge job. You might have to pay someone.'

'Gilbert, then?' said Ben. 'He was really interested, and it was his period.'

'But Andrew wasn't very happy about him at the end, was he?' said Libby. 'Even Ian...'

'Well, why don't I ask Ian if he's made those further enquiries?' said Ben. 'Despite what we were saying last night, it could simply be that he was very interested in the subject and wanted to see if he could find out more about it, having been drawn into it originally by Nathan Vine.'

'Maybe,' said Libby doubtfully.

'Oh, come on, Lib. Let's leave Ian to his murders and - as you said - get on with real life.'

Real life consisted of Libby starting a new painting later that afternoon, only not of the lighthouse after all, and on Friday evening she and Ben went to the monthly quiz at the pub.

'Look,' whispered Libby, as they went into the main bar to find a table. 'There's Philip.'

'Now don't start asking questions,' Ben whispered back. 'Leave him alone.'

But it seemed Philip was going to be the one asking questions.

'Hi!' he said coming over to them beaming. 'Glad to have bumped into you – I was hoping to ask you something.'

'Oh?' Libby had slight difficulty getting the word out and Ben nudged her in the ribs.

'What can we do for you?' he replied pleasantly.

'Well,' Philip's beam turned to a frown, 'it's about your cousin Richard.'

Libby choked on her lager.

'Richard?' Ben raised an eyebrow.

'I wondered – is he likely to be coming back here?' Philip looked uncomfortable.

'There's no reason for him to,' said Ben. 'We aren't close. In fact we didn't know each other until last week.'

'That's what I thought.' Philip frowned and fell silent.

'May I ask why?' said Libby eventually.

'He called me on Monday.' Now Philip looked slightly shamefaced. 'I gave him my number when we met on Sunday, you see...'

'OK...' Ben was frowning. 'Quite normal, I would have thought.'

Philip was silent again.

'Philip – what's the problem?' asked Libby. 'You seem to be having one with this, whatever it is.'

'He asked to meet me, you see,' said Philip in a rush.

Definitely impatient now, Libby nodded. 'In Nethergate yesterday.'

Philip's mouth dropped open. 'How did you know?'

'I met him, didn't he tell you? And then my friend Fran and I saw you together at The Alexandria. She lives there, you see.'

'No, he didn't tell me any of that.' Philip suddenly relaxed. 'Well, that's a relief, in a way. I couldn't understand what he was being so secretive about when he called on Monday when it was obvious he hadn't told you he was coming. And he was still saying not to mention it to you if I saw you in the village yesterday.'

'So why did you want to know if he was coming back?' asked Ben.

'Quite frankly, so that I could avoid him,' said Philip with a crooked grin. 'I liked him when I first met him, but his phone call on Monday worried me a bit and then, yesterday, he made me feel really uncomfortable. I couldn't make him out.'

'I'm going to ask you an embarrassing question now,' said Libby.

'Libby!' said Ben sharply.

'No, go on,' said Philip. 'It's all right, Ben.'

'Did he – um – how can I put this… come on to you?'

Philip nodded. 'Yes, he did. And it was just so odd. I'm not gay, and I had the feeling he wasn't either, so what was he playing at? Did he think I was?'

'What did he want, though?' said Libby. 'Not a sexual encounter, obviously.'

'He was asking me virtually the same questions you were on Sunday evening. I'm afraid in the end I got rather sharp with him and asked why he hadn't discussed it all with you. He rather tried to gloss over the issue and then bought me lunch in The Swan.' Philip shook his head. 'It was one of the oddest meetings I've ever had – and I've had some odd ones, believe me! He was like two different people.'

'I'm afraid Fran and I rather jumped to the conclusion that it was a meeting of – er – minds,' said Libby. 'That's what it looked like from up there.'

'Up where? Oh, the car park! You couldn't see my face, though, could you!' Philip laughed. 'Well, that's a relief. Will you warn me if he plans to come down here again?'

'Believe me, we don't want him to,' said Ben. 'He's gone off with all our archive papers, so unless he brings those back, I can't see us being on visiting terms.'

'I didn't realise you disliked him that much,' said Libby, looking at Ben in surprise.

'I didn't at first, although I think I was always wary, for some reason. But you quite liked him, didn't you?'

'Well, quite, and Bel did, didn't she?' Noticing Philip looking curious, she said, 'Bel's my daughter Belinda. She was down here, too. Everyone had come down to see *Twelfth Night*.'

'I still can't see why Richard was so interested in Nathan Vine and his father, though,' said Philip, 'or why he didn't just talk to you.'

'Well, none of us knew much about any of it at first,' said Ben. 'It was the whole affair of the fake letter that started bringing it to light. First we were approached to put the National Shakespeare tour on here because of the letter, then the letter was withdrawn, then Duncan Lucas disappeared and Gilbert came down saying they mustn't use the letter, then Lucas's body was found. And in between, we found out about Titus Watt and the fact that Russell Wilde had gone off with the archive documents.'

'And presumably gave them to Nathan?' said Philip.

'Looks like it,' said Libby. 'But at some point got them back, as Richard has them all now.'

'Nathan submitted the fake letter to the V&A and withdrew it when they said it was a forgery, and we don't know where it went next, because Duncan Lucas turns up with it. So how did he get it?' said Ben.

'It was the same letter, wasn't it?' asked Philip.

'Oh, yes. Gilbert worked on it first time round,' said Libby.

'You think Richard knows something about it?'

Ben and Libby looked at each other. 'I think he wants to find out,' said Libby. 'We – and the police – want to know where the fake letter came from in the first place. Was it in with the archive documents when Ben's dad passed them over, or was it conceived after that because of the findings in the documents. And who did it?'

'Or caused it to be done,' said Ben. 'So do you think Richard thought you might know?'

'I suppose he might have done. But why? And why be so secretive about it? And the whole thing about approaching me as if we were gay – again, why?'

'Perhaps he actually thought you were,' said Libby. 'After all, you're very neat and tidy and well-groomed, and in some people's eyes that automatically makes you gay. I truly thought that sort of attitude had died out, and to be honest I would have thought Richard was too young to subscribe to it.'

'Maybe, and he thought that was the way to get round me?' said Philip. 'Quite funny, if looked at in the right light.' He looked round as Tim at the bar rang the bell to signal the start of the quiz. 'I must go and join my team. Are you on your own?'

'Yes, this time we are, unless Peter comes in to join us,' said Ben. 'Good luck!'

Peter did arrive a few minutes later and Libby had great difficulty restraining herself from launching into an explanation of everything that had been going on over the past few days. She was able to tell him during the interval while Ben went to replenish their drinks.

'So Cousin Richard's definitely on the suspect list,' said Peter. 'Well, after behaviour like that, I'm not surprised. Sounds like a bit of a dinosaur.'

'Doesn't he?' Libby nodded. 'If we're right, of course. It's all speculation.'

'When isn't it, with you?' Peter grinned.

Chapter Thirty-one

'What do you think about Gideon Law?' Libby asked, as they walked home. 'I still can't fit him into the puzzle.'

'Look, I said, Ian and his minions will be looking into all that. I'm sure by now they've found a link between him and Lucas.' Ben tucked his arm through Libby's. 'Not really our worry. Richard and the archive stuff is, however. I want that stuff back.'

'I wish we knew exactly what they found in Farm Cottage,' said Libby.

'Again, is it our worry?'

'Well, it's linked with Richard's dad and the archive material, so I would have thought yes, it is.'

'I'm going to email him and ask for it all back. After all, it was only loaned to Nathan Vine via Russell. It should really have gone straight back to Dad.'

'Hmm,' said Libby. 'I wish we could get to the bottom of it.'

Ben gave her a sideways look. 'Don't go trying, please Lib. And the thing that puzzles me most is this strange approach to Philip. What *was* he thinking of?'

'Oh, goodness knows,' said Libby. 'Perhaps he's batty.'

The following morning Ben was interviewing applicants for positions at the brewery, along with the owner of the brewery they had visited last autumn when Ben had got the idea, so Libby was on her own.

'I think,' she said on the phone to Fran, 'I'll stroll up and see if the police have taken the tape down at Farm Cottage. Then I might be able to get in and see what was going on.'

'Oh, do be careful, Lib. You haven't got a clue as to what they found, and anyway, don't you think it was probably in that security shed? Which would be locked.'

'Well, I'll just wander up and have a look,' said Libby. 'And I'll pop in on Una at the same time. She was pleased to see me last time.'

Sure enough, the police tape had been removed. 'And Fran's right,' Libby said out loud. 'We've no idea what they found.'

But when she got closer, she saw that security measures around the shed had been increased. There were more padlocks and an extra steel shutter at the front, so whatever was in there was worth protecting.

She was just turning to retrace her steps towards Una's cottage when her phone rang. She fished it out of her basket and saw Tristan's name on the screen, to her surprise.

'Tristan! What can I do for you?'

'Well,' there was a familiar hesitancy in Tristan's voice. 'It's a bit awkward actually.'

Libby sighed. 'Go on.'

'I didn't know quite what to do.'

'About what?' Libby prompted after a minute.

'Well,' said Tristan again, 'I found these messages, you see. Well -' this was getting irritating - 'not exactly messages. Notes.'

'Yes?' said Libby, after another pause. 'From whom? To whom?'

'From Gilbert Harrison to Gideon Law.'

'What?' Libby stood stock still in the middle of the lane. 'But they didn't know each other.'

'It looked as though they were replies to something Gideon had sent to him. And they mentioned – er – Duncan Lucas.' Tristan sounded as if he might start to cry.

Libby felt as if she'd been hit by a cannonball.

'What do they say?' she managed eventually.

'Actually the first one says he, Harrison, doesn't know Lucas. But the second one says he can explain. That's all there is. They're on paper, not emails, so there'll be no copies anywhere.'

'Go straight to the police, Tristan,' said Libby, pulling herself together. 'Have you got a number for a contact in London?'

'No, just a number for someone in Kent. DC Kent, was it? No...'

'Trent,' said Libby. 'She works with DCI Connell. Yes, phone her. And I'll leave a message on Connell's personal phone, too. This is really important, Tristan.'

'Oh, right.' Tristan still sounded uncertain.

'And keep those notes safe. Where did you find them?'

'In a drawer in a desk that Gideon used to use. He worked a lot from home, so he didn't need a permanent office desk.'

'He can't have been too worried about them being seen, then,' said Libby thoughtfully. 'Where are they now?'

'In front of me.'

'Well, put them away! Have you got a briefcase? A safe?'

'I can lock my desk drawer.'

'Not good enough,' said Libby. 'No briefcase?'

'Well, my satchel...'

'Does it lock?'

'No.'

'OK. Fold them inside your wallet or card case or whatever in the inside pocket of your jacket. *Not* the back pocket of your trousers. Now. Do it now. I'm going to ring off.'

She paused, took a deep breath and found Ian's private number. She left a succinct message and began to walk on down Steeple Lane when she was aware of footsteps behind her.

'Hello, Libby! We mustn't keep meeting like this!'

She swung round and came face to face with a manically grinning Richard.

'No,' she agreed cautiously, 'we mustn't. What are you doing here? I thought you'd gone home – again.'

'I thought I'd like to see where Dad was working.' Richard looked round at the fields and fidgeted.

'Working? I thought he and Nathan were just doing a bit of research?' Libby began to move down the lane again and Richard followed.

'Research, yes. And he lived here, too. In Lendle Lane. He had a room.'

'So I believe.' Libby flicked another look at him. 'Have you seen Philip again?'

Richard stopped walking. 'Philip? No. Why?'

'Well after I saw you in Nethergate you met him, so I just wondered.'

Richard's face shuttered. 'No.'

Libby could have sworn he went faintly pink. She resumed walking. 'Were you going to call in on Ben? Only he's rather busy this morning, interviewing.'

'Oh.'

'But of course, if you were going to bring back the archive documents he'd be pleased to see you.'

'Bring back – the documents?' Now Richard looked aghast.

'Well, yes. They weren't your dad's after all, they were loaned to Nathan. They should have come back to Greg – Ben's dad.'

'Oh,' said Richard again.

Libby ploughed on. 'You see, when you brought them

261

down last week for us to look at, we thought you were bringing them back, especially as Michael and Andrew took them away to go into. But then you took them back.'

'It didn't occur to me,' said Richard. Libby wondered whether he'd seen the draft letter.

They came to the end of Steeple Lane.

'Where are you parked?' asked Libby.

'Lendle Lane,' said Richard. 'I discovered I can cut through behind the church.'

'Yes,' said Libby, watching him thoughtfully. 'Well, no doubt I'll see you when you bring the documents back. Or will you send them? Save you the journey?'

'Oh – I – er – I...' Richard looked trapped.

'Well,' said Libby, 'never mind. Ben said he was going to ring you, anyway. Safe journey.'

She watched him make his way across the high street and into Maltby Close, then made a dive for The Pink Geranium.

Unfortunately, it was busy, it being Saturday, but Donna, the occasional waitress and general factotum, saw that she was big with news and sent her through to the back yard. Harry appeared a moment later, wiping his hands on a towel.

'What's up, petal?'

Libby told him, words pouring out in a rush.

'Whoa – slow down!' He pushed her into one of the little white wrought iron chairs. 'Now, start again.'

As she spoke, Harry fished under his apron and brought out his phone.

'There,' he said, 'I've sent Pete a text. He'll be here in a minute. Now, have you sent Ian that message?'

'Yes.'

'Right. Now leave him another one. Richard was obviously poking round Farm Cottage when you were up there, wasn't he?'

262

'Well, I assume so – he just appeared behind me.'
Libby took a breath. 'I think I was a bit scared.'

'Probably. So go on. Send another message.'

Libby texted: "And Richard was poking around Farm Cottage this morning."

'Do you suppose,' she said to Harry, 'that he heard me sending the first message?'

'What, Richard? Does it matter if he did? It wasn't about him, was it? And he didn't have any connection with the V&A people or Duncan Lucas.'

'That's true,' said Libby, just as Peter strolled into the yard.

'Best bring a bottle, my love,' he said to Harry. 'Now, my dear old trout, what's the matter?'

Harry sent Donna out with a bottle of their favourite red wine and returned to his cheffing duties. Libby brought Peter up to speed on both Tristan's phone call and Richard's sudden appearance.

'So what does it all mean?' she asked when she'd finished. 'I knew there was more to this than met the eye, but it's totally confused, now. Shame it didn't just stay at a simple forged letter.'

'Have they found it yet?'

'No one's told me if they have.'

Libby's phone trilled.

'Ben,' she mouthed to Peter. 'Hi – I'm in Hal's back yard with Pete. No – I'm fine, just had an eventful morning. Yes, I'll tell you later. How's it going?'

'Well, how is it going?' asked Peter when she ended the call.

'All right, apparently, but there've been several beer fanatics who don't really know what they're talking about. Good job he's got that other brewery owner with him.' She took a healthy sip of wine. 'Where were we up to?'

'Up to the moment where you were about to suggest you called Fran, I think,' said Peter with a grin.

So she did.

There was such a long silence when she'd finished she thought she'd been cut off.

'Fran?'

'Sorry. Libby, I think you need to get in touch with Gilbert.'

'*Gilbert*? Why?'

'Because Gideon Law was in touch about Duncan Lucas.'

'I don't think you're making sense,' said Libby.

'No? I think Gilbert may be in danger.'

'Well, not from Lucas or Gideon Law. They're both dead.'

'No. I'll think about it.' She switched off.

Libby's phone rang again.

'What have you been up to now?'

'Nothing – honestly! I was on my way to see Una in Steeple Lane,' Libby crossed her fingers, 'and Tristan rang me. I told you what he said when I left the message. So then I was just going across to Una's and I heard someone behind me. It was Richard and he was coming from Farm Cottage.'

'And you hadn't been?'

'Well,' said Libby, going rather pink, 'I did pop up and have look to see if the tape was still there. And no, I didn't go in. Anyway, he was really odd. And Ben and I met Philip – you know the barrister – at the pub quiz last night, and he said Richard was really odd when they met in Nethergate on Tuesday. Was it Tuesday?'

She heard Ian sigh.

'London are sending someone to pick up the two notes from Tristan Scott – yes, he did call DC Trent – and I think we'd better have someone try and pick up Cousin

Richard.'

'What about Gilbert? Fran thinks he's in danger.'

'Does she?'

'Yes. I've just spoken to her.'

'All right. Where did Richard say he was going?'

'He didn't. He said he was parked in Lendle Lane and was going to cut through behind the church. He didn't say if he was going home. In fact I don't know where he's been since Tuesday.'

'I would think not home,' said Ian. 'Right. Leave it with me, and thank you.'

Libby relayed the news to Peter and stood up. 'I'd better go home.'

'No more wine?'

'No, I'll be drunk. And I do not want to fall asleep this afternoon. I need to think.'

When she got home, she called Fran to tell her what Ian had said.

'I'm just wondering,' said Fran, 'why Gilbert is in danger in London if Richard is still down there?'

'Gilbert's in danger from *Richard*?' gasped Libby. 'How? Why?'

'I don't know!' said Fran irritably. 'You know I don't. Perhaps Ian will find out. Is he coming over?'

'I've no idea. He said he was going to get someone to pick up Richard, but that's more about his odd behaviour than anything else.'

'Did you want to come down here for the night? Get away from it all?' suggested Fran.

'We've got another one-nighter at the theatre,' said Libby. 'We didn't have to do last night's, but we're on duty tonight, me behind the bar and Ben hand-holding back stage. He's going straight over there when he's finished interviewing. He'll pop home for something to eat later.'

'What an exciting life you lead,' said Fran. 'See you soon, then.'

Libby made herself a scratch lunch and wandered aimlessly around the garden afterwards, not knowing what to do with herself. She felt she should be doing something, but what, she didn't know. Then the landline rang.

'Libby, it's Richard.'

Libby's solar plexus went into spasm. 'Oh, hello,' she managed.

'Look.' His voice sounded strained. 'Can I come over? I'm still in the village.'

'Ben's still not here,' she said and mentally kicked herself.

'No, no, that's all right. I'll not keep you long. I'll be about ten minutes.'

Libby immediately rang Ben, Peter and Ian, leaving messages for Ian and Ben but making contact with Peter.

'I just feel I need someone else here,' she said.

'White knight number three coming right over,' said Peter.

'Who's number two?'

'Hal, of course.'

To Libby's annoyance, Richard arrived first, looking rather pale, as strained as he had sounded and rather ruffled.

'How can I help you?' Libby said, not sitting down and not suggesting he did either.

'Well.' Richard looked at the floor and cleared his throat. 'I just wondered if there were – um – well, if there were any ...' he trailed off and looked at Sidney, who was staring from the sofa.

There was a sharp knock on the door, and Peter called out: 'Is anybody home?'

As Libby hadn't latched it after Richard, Peter opened

the door and stepped inside, smiling pleasantly at the visitor.

'Well, Richard. Back again?' he said.

'Yes. I – er – I, well -' he stopped. 'I just wanted to know if there were any other papers left behind?'

'You mean of those Nathan had borrowed? That the historians were examining?' said Libby. 'That you took back?'

'Er – yes.'

'Not that I know of,' said Libby. 'Shall I put the kettle on?'

'No, no – don't bother, thank you.' Richard turned to go.

'Richard, wait a moment.' Libby laid a hand on his arm. 'What did you want more papers for? They've all been examined by experts, and you said you had no idea about them.'

Richard stared at her like a rabbit caught in headlights, then lashed out. Luckily, Peter caught his hand as he did so and swept his arm neatly up behind his back.

'You never forget your training,' he said lightly. 'You all right, Lib?'

'Yes, thank you, number three,' she said, slightly shakily, and held her phone to her ear. 'Police, please. Yes, I've just been attacked and it's part of an ongoing enquiry...'

Richard did struggle, but Peter proved more than a match for him, and a patrol car wasn't long in screeching to a halt in Allhallow's Lane.

'Yes, madam,' said one officer, after they'd removed Richard to the back of the patrol car. 'We were advised on the way here, to take the offender into custody, and to tell you that DCI Connell would be in touch with you shortly.'

He took short statements from Peter and Libby, tipped

his hat and left.

'Aren't our policemen wonderful?' said Peter, squeezing Libby's shoulders. 'Now let's have that tea, petal.'

Shortly afterwards, Ben, Fran and Harry all arrived and had to be told the story.

'But we don't know any more, yet,' said Libby, 'because DCI Connell hasn't been in touch. And we're out this evening, so we'll just have to wait.'

Chapter Thirty-two

When Libby and Ben returned from the theatre that night there was a message on the answerphone from Ian.

'Didn't try your mobile as I looked up the theatre diary and guessed you might be there. Believe it or not, I've been invited to lunch at the Manor tomorrow, so I'll tell you then. Very entertaining.'

'I don't think murder is all that entertaining,' Libby said to Ben. 'But I'll give him the benefit of the doubt.'

'I'm still wondering what the hell it was all about,' said Ben. 'Surely Richard can't be the murderer? He didn't know Lucas or Law.'

'And I want to know why he wanted to know about more papers,' said Libby. 'Although – wait! What about the draft letter? Did Michael give that to Ian? That would have been missing, wouldn't it?'

'Yes,' said Ben frowning. 'But that would mean he knew about it, which would also mean he had been through all the documents before he brought them here.'

'And if he was looking for it, that would explain why he took them away again,' said Libby. 'Oh, how frustrating not to know!'

'Ian will tell us,' said Ben. 'Now, nightcap before bed?'

Fran rang in the morning to say Hetty had invited them up for lunch, and they were leaving Sophie in charge of the shop, open as always on summer Sundays.

'She said it looked like it was going to be one of those explaining lunches.'

Libby laughed. 'I think it might be, and thank

goodness for that.'

And indeed, it was.

Ian tried to make them wait until after lunch for explanations, but Libby was far too impatient.

'After all,' she said, 'I nearly got attacked yesterday!'

'I don't see what that's got to do with it,' said Ben, and Libby scowled.

'Well, all right, but it's complicated,' said Ian. 'Yes, please, I will have wine. I'm staying here tonight.'

When they had all settled round the kitchen table and Hetty had carved her platter of roast beef, Ian began.

'We got some of this from Gilbert and some from Richard,' he said. 'Richard tried denying everything at first, until we confronted him with Gilbert's testimony, then he collapsed like a pricked balloon and told us everything he knew.

'Apparently, in the beginning, we assume Russell and Nathan worked the forgery themselves. The new shed, although most of it had been stripped, had been their workshop. We found traces of that still there.'

'Golly! How?' said Libby.

'Forensics, I expect,' said Fran.

'Forensics, yes. Nathan submitted the fake to Gilbert, who as you know, spotted it and gave it back to Nathan.'

'Why didn't Russell submit it?' asked Ben.

'According to what Nathan said later, because it would have been easier to track back if it was one of the Wilde family,' said Ian. 'Anyway, after that, Nathan and Russell either lost touch or had a row, because when Nathan was ill, he got in touch with Gilbert and gave him the fake, saying he would know what to do with it, and Nathan didn't want anything to do with it.'

'So Gilbert - ' began Libby.

'Let Ian tell it,' said Fran.

'Anyway, Gilbert knew Duncan Lucas, who turned out

to be a dodgy arts and antiques dealer - '

'So -' Libby began.

'Libby!' said three voices.

'Anyway, Gilbert approached Lucas and they cooked up the whole nephew scheme together, agreeing, if they could bump the price up, to share any proceeds. Then Lucas spotted the opportunity with National Shakespeare, which, as you know, would have increased interest enormously. However, Gideon Law naturally knew about this, and was keeping a close eye on the whole proceedings. Then, as we know, Michael Allen expressed his doubts about the letter and Duncan withdrew it.

'From what we can piece together, Law got in touch with Gilbert asking about the connection with Lucas.'

'Tristan's notes,' said Fran.

'By this time Richard, who, of course had taken note of the tour and the letter, had gone through the old documents, despite having said he didn't, and found the draft Michael found. He then guessed what had happened, and determined to get it himself.'

'But why?' asked Guy. 'It had been proved to be a fake by then.'

'But at that particular time that hadn't been revealed to the public,' said Ian. 'So Richard, who's a lot more devious than he looks, tracked Lucas down and arranged to meet him.'

'In the hotel in Canterbury?' asked Ben.

Ian nodded. 'And wanted the letter, which Lucas refused to give up. Richard said there was talk of selling to an underground collector. But a struggle ensued, and Lucas was killed. Richard was very careful about forensics and leaving nothing of himself behind, and, of course, we didn't know he existed.'

'And Law?'

'Gilbert, apparently, let it out in an exchange with him,

271

when Law and he exchanged those notes. Lucas had told him, Gilbert, that Richard had been in touch, so Gilbert was in effect trying to pass the buck. So Law, in his turn tracked down Richard, arranged to meet him because he guessed what had happened, and we assume, was going to try a little blackmail.'

'So he met him at the huts.'

'He did. They both thought it was out of the way enough. And that was that.'

'Blimey!' said Libby. 'And all those red herrings everywhere, when it was really quite straightforward.'

'I do *not* call that straightforward,' said Guy. 'I shall probably need it explained to me at least twice more.'

'And I,' said Harry, bursting through the door followed by Peter, 'having wangled time off on a Sunday lunchtime, shall need it explained to me *now*, right from the beginning.'

Everybody groaned.

Author's Note

Dr John Dee was a real figure, but Titus Watt wasn't. There is speculation that Shakespeare was a spy, and although the 1597 tour by The Lord Chamberlain's Men was real, there was, sadly, no stop at Steeple Martin.

Also in the Libby Sarjeant series

Murder in Steeple Martin

Murder at the Laurels

Murder in Midwinter

Murder by the Sea

Murder in Bloom

Murder in the Green

Murder Imperfect

Murder to Music

Murder at the Manor

Murder by Magic

Murder in the Monastery

Murder in the Dark

Murder in a Different Place

Murder Out of Tune

Murder in the Blood

Murder Dancing

Murder on the Run

Murder by the Barrel

Proudly published by Accent Press

www.accentpress.co.uk